UNPAID DUES

A MUNCH MANCINI CRIME NOVEL

BARBARA SERANELLA

SCRIBNER

NEW YORK LONDON TORONTO SYDNEY SINGAPORE

SCRIBNER
1230 Avenue of the Americas
New York, NY 10020

SCRIBNER and design are trademarks of Macmillan Library Reference USA, Inc., used under license by Simon & Schuster, the publisher of this work.

For information about special discounts for bulk purchases, please contact Simon & Schuster Special Sales: 1-800-456-6798 or business@simonandschuster.com

Designed by Colin Joh
Text set in Palatino

Manufactured in the United States of America

1   3   5   7   9   10   8   6   4   2

Library of Congress Cataloging-in-Publication Data
Seranella, Barbara.
Unpaid dues: a Munch Mancini crime novel/Barbara Seranella.
p. cm.
1. Mancini, Munch (Fictitious character)—Fiction. 2. Women detectives—California—Los Angeles—Fiction. 3. Los Angeles (Calif.)—Fiction.
4. Automobile mechanics—Fiction. 5. Recovering addicts—Fiction. I. Title.
PS3569.E66U585   2003
813'.54—dc21
2002042939

ISBN 0-7432-4500-8

For Stephen King
and his wonderful book *On Writing*

You gotta love a man capable of delivering
so many hours of pleasure

UNPAID
DUES

I'd rather not go down in history at all.
I'm going down because of history.
　　　—Sara Jane Olson aka Kathleen Soliah*

*Former Symbionese Liberation Army fugitive, wanted for conspiring to blow up police cars in the seventies. Taken from a December 2001 interview in the *Los Angeles Times*. Ms. Olson is currently serving a twenty-five to life jail sentence after twenty-four years on the lam.

Chapter 1

The sixty-two-year-old groundskeeper of the exclusive Riviera Country Club spotted the bodies at first light. The corpses huddled against each other at the bottom of the concrete storm channel just before it disappeared downstream beneath the golf course. Wide enough to drive through, the storm channel had offered many surprises in the past—hubcaps, beach chairs, the broken shafts of misbehaving seven-irons—but never anything so horrific. Hector Granados had been hoping for treasure this Monday morning, especially after the heavy winter rain the previous weekend. Golf games had been canceled and the typically barren storm drain that ran beneath the course had turned into a raging torrent. This amount of water, he knew, was capable of carrying and then depositing a vast range of large, sometimes valuable refuse.

At first he thought it was a bundle of clothing, then he saw the hands. The larger body, the female, clutched a baby to her bosom. He looked for a long time, and the baby never moved. Its little hand reached out stiffly from beneath a blanket. The slow-moving current carried a branch. It tangled with the woman's hair, causing her head to pull back. The gaping wound in her throat opened into a grotesque and silent scream. Her eyelids were purple and protruded from her face like two medallions of raw liver, and a small stream of foamy pink bubbles trickled from her lifeless mouth.

"Oh my God," he said first in English, then several more times in his native Spanish. He used his two-way radio to contact the clubhouse. "The police," he told Pat, the starter. "We need the police."

"What's wrong?" Pat asked.

"It's terrible," he sobbed. *"Dios mío."*

"What?"

"Bodies, two of them," Hector said, his breath short as if he had been running. "In the canal. Ay, *pobrecito bebé.*"

"Oh, shit," Pat said, "I just let the first foursome tee off ten minutes ago."

Mace St. John, the newly promoted homicide detective-three of LAPD's West Los Angeles Division, arrived to supervise the investigation. The groundskeeper opened the maintenance yard gate at the end of Longworth Drive and allowed the police to set up a command post on the blacktop next to the country club's tennis courts. The other cops on the scene, including St. John's partner, Tony "the Tiger" Cassiletti, busied themselves studying the surrounding houses and their yards, glancing only briefly below.

"C'mon, ladies," St. John said, feeling angry, wanting a live target to harangue. A lot of the officers with families had problems dealing with dead children. Hey, he didn't love it either, but the poor little kid was already dead and someone needed to figure out the who, how, and why of it.

The bodies were slumped against the south vertical wall of the large cement trough. At first glance they appeared to be embracing, but that tender impression was shattered when, after a moment's concentration, St. John made out the rope binding them together. It didn't seem likely that they had been dropped the twenty feet from the bank above. The woman's red shirt was scooted up her back, and her shoulder-length brown hair pointed downstream. They must have been dragged. Another ten yards and they would have been lost forever under the golf course.

Getting them out of there was going to be a trick. The storm channel was bordered by double rows of chain-link fence. There were narrow dirt easement roads in between the eight-foot chain-link fences, running parallel to the channel until it reached the perimeter of the country club. The entrances to those roads were off Allenford, across the street from Paul Revere Junior High School. The gates to the easements were padlocked, and signs posted by the Metropolitan Water District warned off trespassers. But St. John could see by the cigarette butts crushed into the dirt that the warning signs were regularly ignored, probably by students out sneaking a smoke. He was instantly grateful that kids hadn't been the ones to make this discovery. It was a difficult enough sight for even the most seasoned cop.

St. John stared at the dark mouth of the tunnel and the rocky, muddy embankment above it. Climbing down from above was out of the question. There were already piles of loose shale and scrub brush on the storm drain's concrete floor—small-scale replicas of the Pacific Palisades' landslides that had recently narrowed the width of Pacific Coast Highway. All those hopeful idiots who'd built on the cliffs were now paying dearly for their ocean views.

St. John dragged a milk crate over to the fence and climbed atop it. White out-of-bounds markers stuck into sturdy kikuaya grass on the crest of the embankment defined the golf course's border. A low layer of fog hovered over the fairways. The scene reminded him of mornings in Vietnam when the steam rose off the rice paddies.

His radio crackled to life. He lifted the Handie-Talkie from his belt and pushed the transmit button. "Go ahead."

"MWD is on the way."

St. John had had dispatch call the Metropolitan Water District flood maintenance people to bring a key and charts of the system. He studied the chain-link fence again before responding. The poles were anchored in cement at ten-foot intervals. There were no recent tire tracks on the easement. The backyards of the houses on either side of the easement fences were heavily shrubbed. Storm water, he decided, had carried the bodies to this resting place from farther upstream.

"We're gonna need a fire truck with a detachable twenty-foot ladder, winch, litter, and bolt cutters."

St. John called over one of the uniformed patrol officers who had been guarding the scene.

"Where does this feed from?" He looked at the cop's name tag and added, "Henderson."

Henderson pointed as he explained that the system originated at Sullivan Dam to the northwest, and Mandeville Canyon due north. Natural tributaries and storm drains came together above Sunset Boulevard. Here the large concrete storm drain tunneled under Sunset and then ran open alongside the school, following the curves of the boulevard. It also went under Allenford. On the other side of the golf course, the channel reemerged in Santa Monica Canyon and ultimately ran into the ocean.

"We're going to need to look upstream," St. John said.

Henderson nodded and seemed ready to get started immediately. "No," St. John said, "I need you here." He got back on the radio and ordered a chopper to fly the fence line.

The fire engine arrived within ten minutes of the yellow MWD truck. St. John told the water district truck's driver what he needed. Minutes later, the gate was unlocked, and the eighteen-wheeled hook-and-ladder rolled noisily down the dirt easement. Schoolkids gawked as their buses turned into the school's driveway. St. John posted patrolmen at the gate to keep onlookers back. He sent Henderson to stand on the golf course.

"Should we call in divers?" Cassiletti asked.

"There's like an inch of water," St. John said as he snapped photographs with the Polaroid camera he always brought to crime scenes. "I think we can handle it."

Cassiletti cast a nervous eye downward. "That can change in an instant."

"We'll work fast."

To the dismay of the guy from MWD, St. John borrowed a pair of bolt cutters from one of the firemen and snipped the fence away from the pole twenty yards upstream from the bodies. He then asked the fireman to lower a ladder into the channel and was the first to climb down. The storm channel's floor had its own weather system, colder and damper than topside.

St. John understood Cassiletti's concern. It was February 16, 1985, still officially the rainy season, which stretched from October to April. Five feet up from the concrete floor, a crust of lighter wood and floatable garbage marked the height the storm water had reached in the last few days. But today the sky was clear, in fact it was a brilliant blue. The small grove of eucalyptus trees above them had put out small white tendriled blooms in response to the soaking of their roots. One of the houses nearby had a fire going, and the air carried the smell of wood smoke.

Up close, the bodies looked reasonably fresh, especially the child's, whose perfect little fingers were frozen in a reaching gesture. One small plump foot was bare. St. John looked closer and almost laughed out loud in his relief. The child wasn't a child at all, but a doll. No wonder it had yet to show the darkening signs of decomposition. He examined the real corpse, trying to get a fix on her age. She was either a teenager or a small woman. Her hands were ringless and withered from immersion. The face was unrecognizable, rendered a pulpy ruin from repeated blows and death's decay.

He walked past the body and shined his flashlight into the opening of the cement sleeve that ran beneath the golf course, built, he was told by the MWD guy, thirteen years ago in 1972 at a cost of $1.7 million. The tab was happily picked up by the golf course, relieved not to have an ugly cement trough bordered by chain-link fence running through the barranca of the first and seventh fairways.

St. John walked in increasingly smaller semicircles that brought him closer to the body, working with his eyes focused just ahead of his feet, pausing every now and then to squat and study the odd bit of flotsam that might possibly matter later. At last he arrived back at the corpse. The distinct, oddly sweet scent of decay rose to his nostrils. Seeping blood formed a halo on the wet cement around her head. The severity and abundance of the facial wounds meant that the dead woman's attacker probably knew her. The slit throat was very personal.

Had the rains continued, the corpse would have been swept into the tunnel and never discovered. St. John examined the cinder block that had been used to weigh down the body. It was the two-cell variety—the sort of thing college kids used to build shelves for their stereos. Not much in the way of a clue, but every lead must be followed, no matter how unpromising.

He hunkered down next to the body to wait for the Scientific Investigation Division. There was not much more to be done, but the victim had the rest of eternity to be alone and forgotten. He'd stay with her until the criminalists came.

The crime scene photographer arrived and took pictures, beginning with over-alls of the scene, then close-ups of the dead female. The doll's face was buried in the woman's chest, nestled between her breasts. The two had been bound together with white cord, the ends of the rope fastened to the cinder block by odd, looping knots.

Firemen, at St. John's direction, built a dam of sandbags upstream. Kids from the junior high school drifted over to the fence at Allenford, trying to get a peek at what was going on. St. John sent a man to the administration office to find out if any student was absent. He particularly wanted to know about brown-haired girls.

Frank Shue from the coroner's office appeared at the top of the bank. As usual he wore wrinkled, ill-fitting trousers, and his striped, long-sleeved dress shirt was half untucked. "What you got?" he called down.

"Body dump," St. John answered, his voice echoing against

the steep walls. The worst. Smart killers who dump the bodies simultaneously eliminated the victim, the crime scene, and most, if not all, of the trails leading back to the murder.

"Oh, jeez," Shue said, eyeing the ladder and rubbing an open hand across his mouth.

"I'd like to transport the body as is." St. John heard the crack in his own voice and cleared his throat.

"You got it," Shue said. He returned five minutes later with a four-by-ten-foot opaque sheet of plastic and a roll of twine. He joined St. John, wading through the muck in a pair of weathered high-top tennis shoes. The men put on latex gloves and laid the plastic on the paved floor of the storm channel.

St. John used a sharp pocketknife to sever the rope where it threaded through the cinder block, thus preserving the noose-like knots. He grunted slightly as he climbed halfway up the ladder and handed the wet block to Cassiletti. The second, younger detective took the evidence in one of his big hands and lifted it easily, as if it were made of Styrofoam.

"You should be down here," St. John said.

Cassiletti said, "Oh, I'm sorry," in that high, nervous voice of his and set down the cinder block on a sheet of white butcher paper he'd spread on the ground. St. John sighed as the big man climbed almost daintily down the side of the bank, taking his time as if worried that he might break a nail.

Shue secured paper bags over the woman's hands to preserve possible evidence under her fingernails, and then searched her pockets. He found no identification.

Overhead, a helicopter beat back ocean breezes. St. John caught himself listening for distant mortar fire.

"Let's get her out of here," he said, collecting his breath and feeling the ever-present weight in his chest, a reminder of the heart attack he'd suffered four months ago at the age of forty-two. His hand strayed for a moment to his pocket as he assured himself that he had his nitroglycerin tablets. It was a gesture he repeated at least twenty times a day.

The body flopped a bit as Cassiletti and Shue rolled it onto the plastic. The woman was now on her back, her bagged hand fallen to her side. Rigor mortis had come and gone, there would be no point in taking liver temperature readings to determine loss of live body temperature. She had been dead for over twenty-four hours, probably closer to thirty. St. John placed the woman's bag-encased hand over the doll's body, then Shue folded the tarp around the cadaver, burrito-like, and bound the macabre package with lengths of rope at the corpse's waist, ankles, and neck.

"Good thing she wasn't in the water that long," Shue said, "or you'd want to be real careful about tugging on any limbs."

St. John was also grateful the body hadn't been in salt water, where crabs and shrimp would nibble off the smaller extremities.

"See if you can plump up those fingers and get me some prints," he said, blinking into the sun. Her own mother wouldn't recognize the woman's face, not with that much damage.

At St. John's signal, the fire engine's boom swung over the canal, lowering a litter attached to a heavy steel winch hook. The shrouded body was loaded onto the litter, lifted over the embankment, and then laid on a gurney for transportation to the coroner's office.

The detectives and the coroner met up top for a brief huddle. Shue said he'd let St. John know as soon as he had any information on the deceased's identity.

St. John removed his latex gloves, clamped a hand on Cassiletti's big shoulder, leaving an imprint of the white powder from the gloves, and pointed at the cinder block. "Find out everything you can about this. I want to know where it's made, sold, and used. And I want to know it today."

Cassiletti, ever anxious to please, said, "I'll become the world's leading authority."

Leaving the scene, St. John drove the tree-lined, curving canyon roads north of Sunset Boulevard. Large convex mirrors warned of oncoming traffic. Many beautiful homes were nestled in the rustic hillsides, some were under construction—signs of Reagan prosperity—many had stables. He drove slowly, attempting to trace the route of the storm drains, but after Sunset Boulevard the channels weren't visible from the street. Riviera Ranch Road ended at a house that reminded him of the entrance to Disneyland's Frontierland, complete with a two-story outer wall made of logs and a wrought iron chandelier-sized porch light.

Back on Sunset Boulevard, where the channel split, he parked his car in a space between a wooden guardrail studded with orange reflectors and a six-foot-high redwood fence. The easement road here was no wider than a footpath but easily accessible. The chopper pilot had noticed a disturbance in the silt lining the bottom of the channel just before it turned under Sunset Boulevard.

The gate to the wooden fence was open, so St. John peeked inside. He saw six horse stalls, all occupied. A bay mare in the first stall stuck her head over her railing to greet him. He took a moment to stroke her soft muzzle and look into one of her big brown eyes.

"See anybody suspicious lately?"

She twitched her ears and snorted softly. Too bad he didn't have a carrot.

Beyond the mare's swishing tail, St. John noticed that someone had stacked several bales of hay on the narrow easement next to the fence flanking the canal. A strange place for hay. He pushed the top bale aside. The chain link had been cut. The severed ends of steel were still shiny, showing no hint of oxidation. He saw the bend marks where a triangular flap of chain link had been bent outward and then straight again. Using his car radio, he requested a Scientific Investigation Division unit. He told them what he wanted and how badly he wanted it.

Jane Doe 85-00248 was transported to the Los Angeles coroner's office downtown, where workers unwrapped the shroud and carefully delivered the plastic doll from the dead woman's unresisting arms. She was photographed again, X-rayed, weighed, washed, fingerprinted, and prepared for autopsy. Samplings of vegetation, fibers, and soil clinging to the body were also collected and cataloged; pubic hair was combed; debris under the fingernails was scraped into sterile white envelopes labeled with Jane's case number. The life-size baby doll was put in a plain cardboard box, face up.

Results from the fingerprints came in within an hour due to the lucky break that the decedent had a police record. Her name was Jane Ferrar. She had been arrested for prostitution, petty theft, and DUI. Most of her offenses were in neighboring Venice Beach, but one charge was listed in West Los Angeles—St. John's division.

He returned to the station and pulled the hard copy of her arrest report. He had to hunt a bit in the station's archives to find it. The arrest date was ten years earlier, on June 10, 1975. The charge was driving under the influence. He brought the folder back to his desk and opened it. A black-and-white mug shot was paper-clipped to the 5.10 form.

"Oh God." His chest constricted. He picked up his telephone, but couldn't remember the number; digits kept transposing in his head. Still not breathing, he flipped through his Rolodex and stopped at M.

M for Mancini, for Munch, for mechanic, for mother of an eight-year-old daughter.

He punched in the telephone number of the Texaco station where she worked, her photograph gripped between his thumb and index finger. The telephone rang in his ear. Munch looked disheveled in the mug shot. Her light brown hair uncombed, a rebellious sneer on her face, not yet the smiling, sober young woman he'd come to know and—

"Bel Air Texaco," a man's voice answered.

St. John fought to calm his thoughts, trying not to superimpose Munch's face on the battered corpse. "Lou?"

"Yeah."

"It's Mace St. John."

"How's it going? Just a sec." Lou put down the phone and called out, "Munch, line one."

St. John exhaled, and by the time Munch picked up, his heart rate was almost back to normal.

"I need to talk to you," he said.

"Sure, what's up?"

"Not on the phone."

"This can't be good," she said.

"It could be worse. Trust me."

Chapter 2

$$\Longrightarrow$$

Munch held an air gun in her hand, poised to tighten the lug nuts on the wheel she'd just hung, when the silver Seville pulled into the Texaco station with smoke pouring out from the wheel wells.

"Overheat," Lou said, pushing back his sleeves over his wiry arms.

She paused and followed her boss's gaze. "Even worse," she said as the molten tar smell reached her. "Hear that?" she asked, referring to the knocking of the overworked and now probably ruined pistons.

So many people didn't understand that when the red temperature "idiot" light came on it didn't mean "keep driving to the nearest repair facility." It meant "urgent trouble now." The best action would be to pull over, shut off the engine, call a tow truck, and not drive until the car died, thereby turning a twenty-dollar thermostat job into an eight-hundred-dollar cracked block. Better to suffer the price and inconvenience of a tow.

The customer, a man of about sixty, jumped out of the car. His name came to her instantly, as did the last repair she had done on his car. Mr. Hale, rear brakes, and that was a month ago. And brakes, she was as quick to realize, had nothing to do with the cooling system. The engine continued to rattle and ping.

"Shut it off," she yelled.

Mr. Hale flapped his hands once and then did as he was told. The tortured engine gave a last gasping death rattle and then went quiet. Lou was there instantly and pulled the hood release. Munch stood at the front of the car with a rag wrapped around her hand to protect it from the steam. She had already released the second latch when she saw the circle of paint bubbling on the hood.

"We've got a fire here," she said. Mace St. John's sedan pulled into a spot right in front of the office. She waved to him but then her attention was diverted back to the Seville as flames leaped up to greet the influx of oxygen from the now-open hood. The paint job and the engine were history.

The shop's other two mechanics drew closer. Carlos, a known prankster, grabbed a bucket that Stephano had been using to prime a fuel pump. The fluid in it sloshed as he passed it to Lou with a barely contained smirk. Lou grabbed it from his hands and threw it on the flames before Munch had a chance to stop him or warn him that the bucket was full of gasoline. The engine fire roared to a new height with a bang and a flash. Everybody stepped back, shielding their faces from the heat. A moment of stunned silence followed as they all looked at each other.

"There goes the carburetor," Munch deadpanned.

Lou readily agreed, sneaking a brief glare at Carlos.

She grabbed a fire extinguisher from the wall and doused the flames.

"Is this a bad time?" St. John asked, waving away the smoke in front of his face.

"Oh no. Business as usual." Munch grabbed the bucket and threw it to the back of the shop. An open container of gasoline was a violation of air quality regulations and punishable by a huge fine. Rightly so. Gasoline was dangerous, but how else were they expected to prime a fuel pump?

Lou walked over to the soda machine. Munch saw his hands shake a little as he dropped quarters into the coin slot. Mr. Hale collapsed on one of the plastic chairs in front of the office, his right palm pressed tight to the top of his head, his mouth opened wide. Lou handed him a Coca-Cola. Carlos staggered over to the bathrooms before he doubled over, gripping his sides, shoulders heaving silently. She couldn't help but crack a smile as she turned to St. John.

"And how's your day so far?"

St. John didn't return her smile. In fact, he looked grim. The bags under his eyes were a little more pronounced than usual, his lips pursed. He clutched the manila folder under his arm as if it held government secrets. He tilted his head toward Lou's office, turned his back to her, and went inside. Munch, her dread mounting, followed him. She knew Asia was okay. She'd called her daughter's school as soon as she hung up with St. John and made Sister Francis personally go to Asia's third-grade classroom, see the eight-year-old with her own two eyes, and then report back. Asia was fine.

"Is it Caroline?" Munch asked St. John's back. Not that that would make any sense. If something bad had happened to the detective's wife, Munch's former probation officer and Asia's godmother, St. John would be with her, not here. Munch knew full well where his priorities lay. She was high on his list, but would always come second to his wife, probably third overall, right after Asia and tied with his dogs.

"No," St. John said as he entered the office, "it's not Caroline. Close the door. I need to ask you about something."

He opened the file folder and pulled out a familiar-looking document. It was an arrest report. She spotted her picture clipped to the top and winced. There she was, attitude and all, her mouth set in a fuck-the-world expression, her eyes hard and staring out with what she used to think was a fearsome glare. She sometimes wondered if she had ever fooled anyone besides herself.

"What's this about?" she asked.

"How do you explain this?" He pointed to the name typed on the form. Jane Ferrar, it read, aka New York Jane.

"A mistake?"

"Try again."

"Mace, this is like ten years old."

"It was never fully adjudicated."

"So . . . what? Are you here to bust me?" She wasn't overly worried. Surely this was just a matter of a little clerical cleanup. Their friendship would count for something. He couldn't be this hard up for an arrest.

"Do you know Jane Ferrar?"

Munch felt a thrill of fear in her stomach, but she sighed as if weary and sat down on an unopened case of coolant. St. John took Lou's chair. "Yeah," she said, "I know Jane. I haven't seen her in a few—make that seven—years, maybe longer."

"Do you have an address for her?"

"No. If she isn't in jail and still hanging out in Venice Beach, you might want to look for her on Main Street." Even as Munch spoke, she realized her information was dated. The hookers might have moved to Pacific Avenue, or that little strip on Washington in front of the Jolly Roger. It was, by nature and necessity, a migratory business.

"How did your photograph and fingerprints show up in a file bearing her name?"

Munch looked at the arrest report and pretended she was thinking about it. The charge was drunk driving. It had happened during one of the spells when she was trying to drink herself off drugs. "Cleaning up" by her old definitions. So much of that period was a blur, but it was hard to forget an arrest and the night in jail that invariably accompanied it.

"I got pulled over by the cops. I was drunk. I wasn't carrying any ID, so I gave them Jane's name."

"Why her?"

"I knew her date of birth and I knew she had a driver's license. It would have been, uh, imprudent to give them my own name. We're also about the same size."

"I noticed," he said, sounding pissed off.

She wondered why he was making such a big deal out of one little misdemeanor. Feeling a little on guard, she continued. "If I gave them some made-up name and birth date, it would come back unknown and make the whole situation much more, uh, complicated. This way I knew they'd come up with a licensed driver and just bust me for the DUI."

"But you'd still go to jail," he said.

"Oh, yeah. That was a given. One night and they'd kick me out in the morning with a court date."

"A court date you never kept and a warrant issued in your friend's name."

"She had an alibi, as I remember. She was back home in New York. Her dad was having heart surgery. We all kidded her about her dad getting a valve job." Munch stopped talking, remembering too late St. John's sensitivity on the subject of malfunctioning hearts. "Sorry," she said in a small voice.

St. John waved away her apology with an annoyed expression.

Munch spread her hands in a gesture of repentance. "Look, I'm not saying it was right. I was a jerk. Then. And frankly, I forgot all about it. What do I need to do to clear this up?"

"Was Jane married? Did she have any children?"

"Not that I know of, but really, I don't know anything. I never see those people anymore unless they wander into an AA meeting. You know that. Why all this interest all of a sudden?" She was keeping her voice calm, but she could feel the sweat forming in her palms and armpits.

"Jane Ferrar was murdered."

"Oh," she said. Now it all made sense, his questions, his attitude. "I don't know anything about Jane and any murders."

"Murders?"

Chapter 3

$=\!\!\!=\!\!\!\!>$

Murders," St. John said again. "You said murders."

"I meant murders in the general sense." *God,* Munch thought, *what an incredibly stupid slip. You'd think I had a guilty conscience or something.* She conjured a quick image of Jane, but couldn't picture her with anything but wary fear on her face. Jane always tried so hard to please, and always chose to hang out with the people who cared least about her. "Do you know who killed her? Any suspects?"

She heard the whine of the air gun through the office door, and wished she were still out there tightening lug nuts.

"We just got her identified. That's why I came to you for help."

She clenched and unclenched her fist, working the finger that had been broken by one very bad guy the last time she played cops and robbers. A month had passed since then. The flesh wound on her arm had required twelve stitches. She was told the scar would fade with time. The orthopedic surgeon said Munch would most likely have trouble with her damaged knuckle, that she would almost certainly lose flexibility. When the splint was removed, Munch could barely crook her finger.

She had woken up all through that night, bending and unbending the finger until the pliability was completely restored. Dr. Yuen had been amazed; she'd even called in the receptionist to witness the miracle. What the doctor didn't know was that beating long odds was one of Munch's special talents.

"I'm sorry," she told St. John. "I wish I could help you, but I had nothing in common with Jane and her crowd besides drugs. The last time I heard from Jane was right after I got sober. She wanted to get together. I asked her what for and she said we could go shopping." She gave St. John a wry look. "Not my idea of a good time either. I told her that I couldn't associate with her—that the only thing we ever did together was get loaded and that since I wasn't doing that anymore I had no reason to hang out with her. She got kind of bitchy with me." Munch affected a lofty tone of voice. "She said, 'I didn't know you were nothing but a bag chaser.'" Bag chaser—meaning any typical drug addict who only cared about drugs.

"I said, 'I don't know how you could have gotten any other impression.'" Munch laughed at her own punch line.

St. John smiled.

Munch liked to think he knew and appreciated how much those small acts of defiance cost her, how, each time she stood up for her new way of life and let another piece of the old life fall away, she had to face the lurking monster within. The monster whispered that she was a chump, a turncoat, a sellout. She didn't argue. You didn't beat the monster by arguing. The only way out was through surrender. That's when the miracles happened.

Most of the time, in day-to-day life, work, caring for Asia, cleaning, cooking, whatever, memories of the old days didn't intrude. Especially lately, with the mess her love life was in, she was properly distracted from the risk of relapse. That would sound odd to a lot of people—normal people, that is. They might expect that a recovering addict who was having problems would be the most shaky, when actually, the opposite was true. In her experience, the good times were the most dangerous. That's when people in recovery might be tempted to think they didn't need a Higher Power, that they were handling their own destiny, that maybe an occasional pill or drink would be as easily handled.

The monster was a sneaky bastard.

As long as she kept up her connections to AA, she felt safe. Not 100 percent content or at one with the universe, but at least firmly trudging the road to happy destiny.

"So you don't know if she had a kid?" St. John asked again.

"It's entirely possible. She and Thor wanted one, though I don't know what kind of parents they thought they'd be. Thor had some big idea about having a son—you know, to carry on his name and all that bullshit."

"And who's Thor?"

"He used to be Jane's old man, but I'm pretty sure they split up. He's probably in prison or living under some freeway bridge if he's still alive."

"You got a last name for this guy?"

Munch thought a minute and then shook her head. "Sorry. He was always just Thor to me. He might have used Jane's last name."

"I think I'm noticing a trend here."

"Hey," Munch said, "it was war out there."

She watched him leave and fought the urge to make a phone

call. Cops looked for things like that—who you called right after they left.

St. John searched CLETS, the California Law Enforcement Telecommunications System, for any information on Jane Ferrar, updating her status as deceased, the victim of a homicide. He also cross-referenced her by name through the station's new and not yet reliable CAD system, the Computer Automated Dispatch. He came up blank, which didn't surprise him. If there was any recent activity on Jane Ferrar, chances were that information would be at the Pacific Division station that handled Venice Beach.

Even though the LAPD was beginning to emerge from the dark ages, none of the eighteen geographic divisions' computer systems were linked by a network, nor were they even compatible. When St. John needed files from any other division, he had to drive there.

After stating his intentions to Cassiletti, who was sitting at a table in the roll call room with the cinder block in front of him, St. John grabbed his keys. His Buick had over a hundred thousand miles on the odometer and needed a couple minutes of warm-up before the lifters quieted down and the oil cleared out of the combustion chambers. Or so Munch had explained.

He set the heater to low and headed off. The radio was tuned to an FM station and an old Steppenwolf song played softly beneath the static of his police radio. The song had come out when he was twenty and wearing the uniform of the U.S. Army. In the early days of his tour in Vietnam, he'd felt like some kind of god, just out of high school and put in charge of million-dollar equipment. And the hookers, they were everywhere—young, beautifully exotic, cheap even by a cocky young American's standards.

He'd never felt so alive, especially as his belief in his immortality wavered. Every morning was a victory. Every taste, smell, and sound was savored—the moist morning air, men laughing, stale cookies baked and sent from elementary-school kids stateside. This was, of course, before the children were taught to be ashamed of the war. Before all of them were. That came later.

While he was in-country, while the cause was still righteous, the world around him blazed with intensity. Coming home had been a letdown. Colors seemed duller, everyday concerns seemed unreal and unimportant.

He drove away his first wife, Nan, with his stock dismissal to any and all of her complaints: "Is anyone shooting at you?" How could any problem be a big deal if no one was shooting at you?

He grasped entirely the seduction of urban warfare.

Now he wondered who that weathered old fart was who stared back at him from his bathroom mirror each morning. Time has passed, he told himself. The war is over. As Munch would say, move the fuck on.

The Pacific station on Culver Boulevard rewarded him with a plethora of information. In addition to Jane Ferrar's criminal record he found an instance where officers had responded to a disturbance at the Star Motel on Rose Avenue in Venice Beach.

He went to the files and pulled the original copy of the incident report. Management had phoned police when a coffee table burst through the front window. The officers responded and discovered a domestic dispute between Jane Ferrar and a man who identified himself as Mac Ferrar. Mac Ferrar was described by officers as a tall, red-blond, bearded white male. Jane convinced the officers that the fight was over and that it had all been her fault. The beat cops admonished her to pay for the window before she checked out.

Those cops would be sued for that same shit now. Sued and sent for "sensitivity training."

St. John ran the name Mac Ferrar but found nothing. No criminal history, no California driver's license, *nada*. He wasn't surprised. The name Mac Ferrar was no more real than the baby in Jane Ferrar's arms.

Cassiletti measured the dimensions of the cinder block and wrote down his findings on a legal pad. He also drew a sketch of the block, noting the tongue-and-groove joints on either end along with their widths and depths, and the two-inch-wide furrows at the tops and bottoms of the long-facing sides. The block was a light salmon color and weighed thirty-two pounds. Feeling he'd exhausted his observational skills, he grabbed the thing by the web between the two holes and carried it to his car.

His first stop was the Builder's Emporium on Bundy. He held the block in his left hand and away from his side so as not to snag his dark slacks. Building materials were in the outdoor yard next to garden supplies. The bitter scent of insecticides and fertilizer assaulted him as he walked down the narrow aisles.

"Can I help you?" asked a clerk wearing a green apron.

"I need some information. What do you know about cinder blocks?"

"Aisle two."

"I need one exactly like this one," Cassiletti said, holding up his evidence.

"Hmm, I don't know. Ours are darker, but you could always paint it. I'll show you what we have."

Cassiletti followed the clerk past flats of brightly colored petunias and stopped at a pallet loaded ten high with dark gray cinder blocks. These differed from his in more ways than color.

They had wider tongue-and-groove joints and no inset cuts on the face. Cassiletti pointed this out to the clerk.

"Chisels are in aisle eight," the guy said, looking past Cassiletti for a less-demanding customer.

Stamped in black on the base of the pallet were the words *Enco Block.* Cassiletti noted the name. "Is this Enco Block local?"

"I don't know, man," the clerk said, starting to look seriously put upon.

Cassiletti pulled out his badge holder, relishing the moment when this guy's attitude would change. He held his shield close to the guy's face and watched the clerk's posture straighten, the color drain from his cheeks.

"This is police business. Can you get me the information I want or do I need to see the store manager?"

"No, no. I can help you. Follow me."

Cassiletti pocketed his badge and smiled secretly at the guy's back as they made their way to the rear of the store and through a door marked EMPLOYEES ONLY. A quick search through one of the file cabinets in the accounting office produced an invoice with the Enco Block address and phone number. It was in Sun Valley, an industrial section of the San Fernando Valley.

Cassiletti thanked the man, took his block, and left.

It took forty minutes on three different freeways to get to Enco Block, which turned out to be a large operation near the railroad tracks. The company logo was painted in red on a tall silo and was visible from a quarter mile away. He followed a line of pickup trucks driven by beefy, sunburned contractors wearing short-sleeved T-shirts and turned-backward baseball caps to a driveway you would have had to know was there to find. Cassiletti felt more out of place than usual as he parked in front of a windowless building and followed the signs to a door labeled

OFFICE. He introduced himself to the secretary, whose nameplate identified her as Terri Ordell. She listened to his request, inspected his badge, smiled coyly, and then pushed a button on her telephone.

"Mr. Kulek?"

A man's voice said, "Yeah?"

"You have a police detective out here to see you. He has some questions about cinder blocks."

Seconds later a robust balding man emerged from the inner office. "You the cop?" he asked in a booming voice—one no doubt trained to carry over the sound of a cement mixer.

Cassiletti handed the man one of his new business cards. He'd had them printed himself at his own expense, paying extra for the embossed image of his detective shield complete with his badge number. The city provided only generic blue-and-white cards that had blank lines for the officers to fill in their names, ranks, and phone numbers.

"Oh, shit," Kulek said. "What's happened?"

"I need some information," Cassiletti said, "about this cinder block."

"Like what?"

"Anything you can tell me."

Kulek studied the block for only a second. "A, it's not a cinder block. It's concrete. Cinder block is made from cinder. It's a couple pounds lighter per block and you'd see the darker particles, especially in a split-face block like this one. And B, it's not one of ours. Our eight-eight-sixteens have a thicker web between the cells and we don't do a Malibu cut."

"Eight-eight-sixteen?"

"Yeah, those are the dimensions in inches."

"Actually, it's a bit smaller than that."

"I'm talking with mortar," Kulek said. His tone seemed to suggest that this was information any man should know.

Cassiletti felt a momentary fluster. St. John probably would have picked up the eight-eight-sixteen thing immediately.

"What's a Malibu cut?" Cassiletti asked, pressing on.

"This inset on the face," Kulek explained.

"What's it for?"

"Architectural design. Same as the color. We make our stuff for the do-it-yourself stores like Builder's Emporium and National Lumber. We use the darker concrete that comes from Mexico, and we don't add pigment." The phone on the secretary's desk rang. Kulek looked at it and then back at Cassiletti. "Anything else?"

"A list of your competitors?"

"Terri," Kulek said, answering the phone himself, "give the man what he wants."

Chapter 4

⟾

Munch and Asia ate a quick dinner that night and then headed over the hill to the San Fernando Valley. Munch was speaking at an AA meeting held at a church on White Oak. A lot of AA members brought their kids to this meeting and the church provided a playroom for them while the meeting was in progress. Munch's sponsor, Ruby, was all for sheltering the children from the confessions and observations of recovering addicts and alcoholics. Her own son, Eddy, followed her to meetings when he was young and Ruby once confided to Munch that she thought that early exposure had hurt his chances of taking to the program when he needed it.

Munch was just as happy not to subject Asia to the cigarette smoke and cursing. She had quit the former already, and was working on giving up the latter. This was also Munch's AA birthday week. Time to blow out eight candles on top of birthday cakes at the several meetings all over Los Angeles where she had gotten sober. It might take two weeks.

The meeting didn't begin until eight-thirty. Munch got to Ruby's house at a quarter to eight. Ruby lived in Sherman Oaks, south of Ventura Boulevard. Eddy, her three-hundred-pound alcoholic son, had a room fixed up in the garage. Ruby's deaf mother lived with them too. The mother refused to use a hearing aid, but kept a long, orange plastic transmission funnel beside her armchair for when something on the television interested her.

Asia joined the old woman in the living room, which left Ruby and Munch alone together at the kitchen table. Ruby had changed out of her Denny's uniform and was wearing black pedal pushers and a thick cable-knit sweater.

"The water's still hot," Ruby said, nodding toward the tea-kettle. "Want a cup?"

"I'll make it," Munch said, selecting a tea bag and pouring in sugar.

Ruby eyed her from the kitchen table. "What's up?"

Munch cast a quick glance into the living room to make sure Asia was out of earshot. "I got a visit from Mace St. John today."

"And?"

"This woman I used to run around with was murdered."

"Was she still using?"

"She was the last time I saw her, so, yeah, probably."

Ruby clicked her tongue and lowered her eyes in sadness. She had a deep well of compassion for losers, the alcoholics and addicts who couldn't get to the program in time.

"Yeah, well, anyway," Munch broke in after giving Ruby her moment of silence, "this friend was involved in something pretty terrible about ten years ago. Something I knew about."

"Do you think it has something to do with why she was murdered?"

"I kind of doubt it. Everybody involved was pretty lowlife. Those things have a way of working themselves out or else everybody involved tends to forget about it."

"So you didn't mention this to Detective St. John?"

"I really didn't see the point."

"Do you want to tell me about it?"

"They'd probably all be dead by now anyway," Munch said. "They were all heavy dopers and career criminals."

"Like you?"

"Even worse. And this happened ten years ago." In a world far removed from the one she inhabited now. So far removed that sometimes she had trouble believing she had been that other person who used and abused herself and everyone around her. It was the drugs that had produced the creature she had been, and when they were eliminated, a different woman was born— a person who didn't steal or cheat or hurt other people. Knowing that, she was able to forgive herself and move on. Most of the time.

"Thor is probably dead or in prison by now," she said, hoping it was the former. "Sleaze John is dead. Now New York Jane is dead. That just leaves one other friend who's way out of the picture anyway. Why should I stir up the whole mess?"

"Are you afraid of charges being brought against you?"

"I didn't do anything."

"Isn't that part of the problem?"

"You mean I should have snitched them out?"

Ruby stirred her tea. The sound of canned laughter intruded from the living room. Munch heard Ruby's aged mother mumble something unintelligible and Asia laughed. Asia found the old lady's dementia highly amusing, but not in a mean way—more like a what-a-silly way.

"What would you want Asia to do?" Ruby asked.

"You mean if she was hanging out with dope fiends and knew they'd just killed a bunch of other dope fiends? I'd want her to put as much distance as she could between herself and them and then come and put fresh flowers on my grave because I would be dead before I'd let her fu— Ah, mess up her life that way."

"You think you would have control over how she chose to live?"

Munch sneaked an unintended look at the door leading to the garage, where Eddy was either slumbering off a binge or preparing to do it all over again. "Maybe not, but I wouldn't make it easy for her."

Ruby reacted as if she'd been slapped. "I can't turn my back on the boy, not while Mama is still alive."

"Who do you think will die first?"

"That's up to God."

Munch let the age-old cop-out go unchallenged. Ruby had a real blind spot when it came to Eddy. She seemed to have forgotten the rule that you were supposed to "carry the message, not the addict" when it came to her own blood.

Ruby's sobriety stretched back to the year Munch was born. She was a great sponsor. Capable of such gems as "Honey, you're going to meet people in AA you wouldn't have gotten drunk with," when Munch complained about somebody she didn't like at an AA meeting. Ruby told her to run as fast as she could in the opposite direction when Munch confessed that a guy she loved in her first year of sobriety went back on the needle. Ruby was great at the giving advice part, but if she didn't get a handle on the guilt she carried about her son's early years, she was going to enable him to his grave.

Munch looked at the clock over the stove. It was time to leave for the meeting if they were to get there in time to help make the coffee. She rinsed out her mug and put it in the drain board by the sink. "Like I said, it's best to let sleeping dogs lie."

"Sleeping dogs have a way of waking up sometimes and crapping all over your living room."

The following morning, as Munch unfolded the *Los Angeles Times* on her breakfast table, a news item on the front page of the Metro section jumped out at her: BODY OF WOMAN CLUTCHING DOLL FOUND IN STORM DRAIN.

Munch's body flushed with heat and she felt a dropping sensation in her stomach.

The photograph showed the police gathered in what looked like a parking lot, except for the basketball hoops. The caption identified the location as the maintenance yard for the Riviera Country Club. Munch knew the area; she had customers who lived around there. It was only about five miles from the gas station. A mere blink for Angelenos.

WOMAN CLUTCHING DOLL.

Was this why St. John had asked if Jane had a kid? And was that kid still out there somewhere? Alone and scared?

Munch called to Asia to get ready. It was earlier than they usually left the house, but Munch had a reason. Asia climbed into the passenger seat, pulling her Pee Wee Herman lunch box onto her lap.

Munch turned right on Pico instead of left. They passed blocks of shabby, thirty-year-old apartment buildings that needed paint and landscaping. It wasn't going to happen; this was rent-control land. The landlords were locked into late seventies rental rates, which left them no budget for painters and gardeners, whose fees had kept up with the cost of living.

"Why are we going this way?" Asia asked.

"I thought we'd take the scenic route." She turned right again on Ocean Avenue, passing the entrance to the Santa Monica Pier.

"Where's Joseph and Mary?" Asia asked as they drove along Palisades Park.

"Oh, honey, they took all that down a month ago." Asia was referring to the series of life-size dioramas of the Nativity that the churches of Santa Monica erected every year. All that was left now were dead spots of grass where the consecutive scenes depicting the events of Christ's birth had stood, encased in anti-vandal mesh. She had taken Asia to see the Three Wise Men bearing gifts, the pregnant Mary aboard her burro, and finally the Baby Jesus in his crib.

Asia looked hard anyway. She was the kind of kid who savored her holidays and was all for the concept of a birthday week. Just last month she had announced that she wanted eight different husbands so she could have eight different weddings.

It's been done, Munch assured her.

They turned right on San Vicente Boulevard. Large branches dangled broken from the massive coral trees filling the median. The orange-flowered limbs were no contest for the strong winds of last week's storms. The heavy flow of commuters kept pace with a steady stream of joggers dressed in two-hundred-dollar tennis shoes and slit-seam shorts. The runners breathed deep the morning exhaust fumes as they toned their bodies. Munch said a small prayer of gratitude for her job at the garage, which kept her fit.

She turned left on Allenford Avenue behind a big yellow school bus. Asia sat up to study the teenagers filing into Paul Revere. Munch cruised slowly, straining to see the cordoned police area. She didn't know what she was looking for. She just felt the need to be here. Someone had stuck a bouquet of flowers in the fence.

Allenford dead-ended on Sunset Boulevard. Munch turned right and drove alongside the sprawl of bungalow classrooms, noticing that the storm drain also followed the contour of the school. She had plenty of time to study it while she and three other cars waited for the light at Mandeville Canyon. A utility truck with A-1 FENCE painted on the door was parked in the dirt driveway on her left. She watched two men strap a new sheet of chain link between two poles.

"Aww," Asia said. "Horsies."

"Uh-huh," Munch said absently, "pretty horses." What really had her attention was the yellow flutter of more crime scene tape. The light changed and a motorcycle cop parked at the curb motioned for her to move on.

She dropped Asia off at school and then pulled over and opened her *Thomas Guide* map. She traced her finger between the two hot spots of police activity and realized that that was where the storm drain went under Sunset. Last Saturday night, Valentine's Day, it had poured rain, really matching her mood as a matter of fact. The evening's torrent had been more than enough to wash a body into the open.

The real question was: With all the places in Los Angeles to dump a dead woman—a woman she knew—why did the killer have to choose a spot within a couple miles of her job?

Ruby was right, as usual, about sleeping dogs.

Chapter 5

$=$

That night Munch opened her front door to find a six-foot-tall black man on her porch staring back at her. That was her first impression. His blackness, his size. She hated that she did that. He was dressed in a Pendleton-lined Levi's coat, jeans, and lace-up work boots. A second later she noticed the duffel bag at his feet and that he was young, despite the sparse goatee. Her next thought was that he was some inner-city kid bused into the neighborhood to sell something, but usually they chose really dark-skinned kids for the door-to-door stuff and this kid was obviously a half-breed.

He said, "Munch?"

Her mouth dropped open, then she blinked and said, "Boogie?" He wasn't some stranger. It was her little Boogieman. Her old running partner Deb's son all grown up and wearing his hair cropped short instead of in the big Afro Deb used to spend hours picking with a wide-toothed comb.

37

"What are you doing here?" she asked, too surprised to do anything but stare.

His face went still, and whatever expression had been forming—joy, hope, relief—dissolved into impassiveness.

"Never mind," she said quickly. "You just blew me away for a second. I mean, look at you, you're a man." She swung the door wide open and pulled him into a hug. He was so tall that her face was level with his chest. Would Asia one day be taller than she? It was hard to imagine. "Come in, come in," she said after releasing him. "How did you get here? How long have you been in town? I can't believe how much you've grown."

He made a half-grin, came inside, and deposited his duffel bag next to the couch.

Munch reached up to run a hand over his short hair. She realized part of what she was feeling was relief. Relief that he had made it to this age and hadn't been terribly damaged in some irrevocable way. That was the burden of parenting, even the shared parenting of your friends' kids, the never-ending worry. There were always the ones who didn't make it. She thought again of Jane and the doll found wrapped in her arms, then pushed the awful image aside and smiled at Boogie, grinned actually, like some kind of idiot. He hadn't seen her in seven years and all she could do was gape at him as if he had arrived by teleport.

"The last time I saw you, you were this high." She put her hand just below her chest. "Come on, there's someone I want you to meet." She led him into the kitchen, where Asia was finishing her macaroni and cheese.

Asia looked up, wide-eyed and curious.

"Asia, this is Boogie. I've known him since he was a couple months old, but I haven't seen him in"—she looked at Boogie, her hand cocked in question as she calculated—"seven, almost eight years."

"That's about right," Boogie said. He sounded as if he was forcing his voice into its lowest octave. "And I go by Nathan now."

Munch had a quick memory of how wet and cold it had been in Oregon that October seven years ago, and her eight months off the antifreeze. Boogie running through Deb's little cabin to fetch his mama her pipe. Deb and their other friend Roxanne, smoking bright green Oregon homegrown, drinking cheap wine, and snorting speed at the kitchen table as the logging trucks barreled down the highway outside.

Munch had flown up there to find Sleaze John's killer and Asia—his orphaned baby. Back in the day Sleaze John aka John Garillo had been many things to Munch. Lover, coconspirator, friend. He had been shot to death within hours of visiting Munch at her work. He had stopped by to tell Munch about his baby and the death of that baby's birth mother, Karen. And, of course, being Sleaze, he had come in need of a small "favor."

Munch came close to losing everything in the week that followed: her newfound sobriety, the baby she hoped to save, her freedom, even her life. With all that at stake she should never have been tempted to get loaded with her old friends, but old habits die hard and the good ones are the easiest to break. Dope had a funny way of screwing up an addict's memory even before he or she used any. Ruby said that's why alkies and druggies needed meetings, because everybody together didn't forget the same things at the same time.

The trip to the great Northwest that long-ago autumn ended happily enough. Munch stayed sober, Asia became her daughter, and the extra bonus was that a longtime friend and using partner, Roxanne, found the program and moved to Sacramento. Deb, being Deb, found a new ol' man as the old one was carted off to prison. As Ruby would say, *That Old Boy upstairs works in mysterious ways.*

"Nathan," she repeated. "I like that. This is my daughter, Asia." She didn't qualify the nature of their parent/child relationship. Asia knew she was adopted, but it didn't need to be mentioned every time either one of them turned around.

Nathan shook Asia's hand and said, "Hey, Asia."

"Actually, you two have met," Munch said. She turned to Nathan. "Remember when I came up to Oregon for your seventh birthday? Asia was just a baby and I had about eight months of sobriety."

Nathan stared at Asia for a second and then said, "You're Sleaze John's kid?"

Asia nodded and looked skyward. "He's dead. So's my other mother. She took too many drugs."

"I remember," he said.

"So you're fourteen now?" Munch asked, wondering what else his memories held.

"Yeah," he admitted somewhat grudgingly, "but I've got ID that says I'm eighteen."

She could see he passed for that easily. Fourteen was a long time ago, but she couldn't remember any of the boys she knew in her adolescence who weren't puny little geeks. Maybe if she had gone to high school, she would know different.

"Where's your mom?" Asia asked.

"Amsterdam."

Deb had called Munch last month from overseas wanting what she termed "a small favor." Her current boyfriend, Aaron, was a parolee fugitive, and had taken Deb with him to Amsterdam. Apparently there was no extradition treaty between the two countries. Deb wanted to send some letters to friends stateside and she didn't want them postmarked abroad. She was hoping to mail Munch a package to divvy up and forward. Munch told her no and chewed her out for even asking. Deb's voice had sounded hurt after that, and it was all Munch could do to not take her words back.

"Don't you go to school?" Asia asked. "I'm in third grade."

"Nah," he said, "I'm through with all that. I've been working since last summer. What's high school going to do for me?"

"Asia wants to be a vet," Munch said.

"Or maybe an astronaut, like Sally Ride, I haven't decided."

"Either way, she wants to go to college," Munch said.

"That's cool." Nathan looked around him, his expression neither approving nor disapproving, just taking it all in.

"Have you eaten?" Munch asked. "Are you hungry?"

"Sure." He sat down at the table and waited for her to serve him. She wondered if that was the adolescent in him or the man. Deb did backflips for the men in her life, always trying to prove what a stand-up, perfect ol' lady she was.

Observe, ladies and gentlemen. She cooks, she cleans, she gives head, and always looks cute doing it in her tight jeans and heels, bangles on her arms, rings on every finger, long brown hair down to her ass.

Deb also had a way of putting on her Southern accent and saying, "Oh, g'wan," as she laughed at some guy's stupid jokes. Munch had spent years watching her charm the leather off the bikers they had both known. Yet how many times had one of those same bikers turned to Munch and asked, "What's your friend doing with a nigger kid?"

41

Once, tired of the question, Munch had told a guy that Deb had picked him up on her travels to Zimbabwe. Damned if the idiot hadn't believed her.

Without looking up, Nathan cleaned half the plate Munch set before him. Asia sat opposite him, utterly fascinated. Munch wondered how long it had been since his last meal.

Asia looked at the duffel bag by the couch. "Are you going to stay with us?"

"For a couple days, if that's all right," he said.

Munch didn't hesitate. "Of course it's all right. You're still my little Boogieman."

"Your ace boon coon?" Nathan asked, a funny half-smile turning up his dusky lips while his brows met in a frown. It was the sort of expression people make when someone they care about hurts their feelings.

Munch winced, recalling the little jingle she used to recite to him. *"You're my ace boon coon, my pride and joy, an ugly mother-fucker, but you're still my boy."* What kind of a jerk uses that kind of language with a little kid?

"Nathan—"

"Yeah?"

"I, uh . . . I'm . . . You want to clean up, maybe take a nice bath?"

"Sure," he said, standing up, not bothering to take his plate to the sink.

She fetched him clean towels. He met her in the hallway. She was aware of his height again. The small boy she used to know was almost a man. Fourteen going on twenty-five. It seemed like yesterday when she had held his little hand as they crossed the street.

"I'm doing a load of laundry if you have any dirties."

"Thanks," he said, smiling shyly. "They're in my bag."

Munch felt another urge to hug him, but they were alone in the doorway of the bathroom, and she was suddenly gripped with a shy attack of her own. Seven years is a long time in a kid's life. She wanted to reestablish a connection, but recognized that she would have to tread slowly. She contented herself with giving his arm a motherly pat.

The phone rang, and Asia jumped up to answer it. A moment later she was spelling her name loudly to the caller; then she rolled her big brown eyes saying, "It's Rico," and tried to hand the phone to Munch.

Rico. Munch took her time with the plate she was washing and then carefully wiped her hands dry.

Asia wiggled the receiver in the air, bulged her eyes, and pressed her little lips together in frustration.

"I'll be there in a minute," Munch said.

Asia liked the idea that her mom had a cop as a boyfriend. Munch suspected it made for good show-and-tell. What Asia didn't know was that Munch and Rico had agreed to keep their romance quiet until his current girlfriend, Kathy, transferred to her new job in Boston. Rico didn't want Kathy to know he'd found someone else. He wanted her to leave town believing that he just wasn't ready for a serious relationship instead of knowing the more hurtful truth.

Munch had agreed to the terms. The alternative would have been never to see him again and that, as far as her heart was concerned, was unthinkable, or at least it had been in January. But now she had to ask herself what she was doing pining away for a guy who had spent Valentine's Day with his soon-to-be-ex-girlfriend, who was supposed to be moving away? Soon-to-be-ex-girlfriend. Not a term that exactly rolled off the tongue. What had she bought into? It wasn't a great concept to begin with, and it was feeling shakier all the time.

Munch took a deep breath and accepted the phone from Asia. "What's up?" she asked him, trying not to sound as if she cared.

"I was thinking about you," he said.

"What were you thinking?"

"I want to see you."

"Are you sure you can squeeze me into your schedule?" Munch looked over at Asia. Asia had a glass of milk to her lips, but wasn't taking a drink. Munch picked up the phone and moved into the hallway.

"Don't be like that," he said.

Munch looked at her watch even though he couldn't see her and said, "Gee, is it March yet?"

"I'm sorry we couldn't get together the other night," he said. "I just need you to be patient a little longer."

"I know."

"I can be over there in twenty minutes."

"Not tonight," she said, fighting the part of her that wanted him above anything else. The mother inside at war with the lover. "I have company."

"What kind of company?"

"His name is Nathan. He's the son of a friend of mine."

"Oh, a kid."

"Not so much anymore. He's in town looking for work." As she said the words she figured they were probably true. She also wondered why she felt the need to promote Nathan's virtue to Rico. She never felt she had to explain herself before. "He needs a place to stay for a few days."

"How old is this kid?" Rico asked.

"Um, almost eighteen."

"So, he's a man."

"Just about."

"How did he find you? Where has he been living? Doesn't he have any other relatives?"

"Look, I didn't give the kid the third degree. He's tired, he was hungry. I'm not going to turn him out into the streets."

"I don't like this," he said.

She didn't say anything.

"Munch?"

"I'm still here."

"I'm just saying that if this kid is on his own, then he shouldn't be mooching off you."

"I sort of owe it to the boy. I've known him since he was a baby. And don't forget," she added, "if it wasn't for my generous nature I would have told you to take a hike a long time ago."

"You still can."

She sighed. "I know. A month isn't forever, but it sure feels like it sometimes."

"For me too," he said, his voice soft.

Yeah, she thought, *but you made the schedule.* "Look," she said, spotting Nathan's duffel bag lying unzipped by the couch, "I've gotta go. This kid has a ton of laundry."

"I'll call you tomorrow."

"Good." She hesitated, bit her lip, looked down at the carpet at her feet without seeing it. "Miss you."

She took the phone back into the kitchen, told Asia to go brush her teeth and wash her face, and then started sorting through Nathan's clothes, astounded at the mountain of soiled laundry that the kid had managed to jam into his bag. She got a load of his jeans and flannel shirts started, and then went into her daughter's room to put her to bed.

Asia fought sleep as long as she could, hoping for another glimpse of their houseguest.

"He'll still be here in the morning," Munch assured her before kissing her good night and tucking in the blankets. When she closed Asia's door, she heard the shower shut off.

Nathan emerged from the bathroom with a towel wrapped around his waist. His arms were muscled and tattooed, his chest hairless.

"Do you have pajamas?" she asked.

"I usually just sleep in my underwear," he said.

"Not here you won't." She went to her room and returned a moment later with a set of men's pajamas. "You can use these."

"Whose are they?"

"Um, leftovers." She felt herself blush.

When she heard him come out from the bathroom the second time, she joined him in the living room.

"Remember this?" she asked, handing him a framed photograph she'd taken off her bedroom wall. They were sitting together on the couch, which she'd made into a bed with sheets, blankets, and an extra pillow from her own bed.

He took the picture into his big hand, a hand roughened by calluses, Munch noticed.

The picture was a poignant black-and-white photograph Nathan had taken with an ancient Kodak camera when he was only six years old. It showed a group of black kids in front of the mural on Windward Avenue in Venice Beach eating sunflower seeds. Four were seated, the one in the middle was standing. Only one of the kids was halfway smiling, and he appeared to be the youngest. The others' expressions were in turn suspicious, wary, and concerned, as if they already knew what the world had in store for them.

"You kept this?" Nathan asked, a big unexpected smile breaking over his face.

He really was a beautiful kid, she thought. He had Deb's dimples.

"I love this picture," she told him. "You really captured something here. Are you still interested in photography?"

"Yeah," he said. "I had a job last year, working at a film lab. It didn't pay much, but I got to use the darkroom."

"Are you looking for work now?"

"I already talked to some guy. I'm starting tomorrow."

"Oh, so you're planning to stay?"

"My mom gave me a list of people I can call."

Munch could only imagine who that group entailed. Boogie—that is, Nathan—did right coming to her first.

"Remember New York Jane?" she said.

Nathan scrunched his face in concentration. "Barely."

"You took pictures at her wedding?"

"What about her?"

"Nothing. I mean, she died, but if you don't remember her . . ."

Nathan shrugged. "Sorry."

"Yeah, well, never mind. Get a good night's sleep."

She waited while he climbed under the covers, hovered for an awkward moment, and then kissed him on the cheek. His forehead was pebbled with acne. Poor thing. Fourteen was an awkward age. He belonged in school.

"Good night."

"Thanks," he said.

Munch included Nathan in her prayers that night. The kid was due a break, but she didn't know where it would come from. Like her, he had no family to fall back on, not that Deb hadn't started out well. Boogie's first few years of life had been good.

47

Deb was entirely focused on him then. She dressed her little man so cute, spent hours on his hair, really doted on him.

Munch lived with Deb for a while back then. She'd been the same age as Nathan was now, and Deb a worldly sixteen. Munch saw Boogie take his first steps at only nine months old, her name was his first word. She had sworn then to protect him, a promise forgotten when drugs and alcohol shoved anyone and anything aside.

Deb and Nathan moved to the "country" in 1976, the year before Munch got sober. Deb's motives were good. She wanted the clean air and the small-town atmosphere. Unfortunately, she brought her alcoholism and love of the fast life with her, finding another group of bigoted, mangy outlaw bikers to hang with. Munch knew the scene only too well.

"Quick, kill it before it gets big," was a common joke directed at Boogie. It always drew rough, drunken laughter.

Munch asked Deb once what Boogie made of the word nigger. Deb thought a minute and then said, "Asshole." As if that was okay, that the kid wasn't getting scarred because he was oblivious to the word's racial connotations.

It would have been different if he'd grown up somewhere else or been able to spend some time with his daddy's people. All Deb had ever said about his daddy was that he was a musician named Walter. And a few times, when it had been just the two of them talking, Deb would say how fine Walter had been and how good in the sack. Munch might then admit that, if Walter looked like Billy Dee Williams, she wouldn't kick him out of bed either. *But to have a kid with the guy? What were you thinking?* Their mutual friend Roxanne's theory was that having a half-breed kid was Deb's way of thumbing her nose at her parents.

They'd all been stupid. Stupid and too young to be making

any judgments, especially about having kids they couldn't take care of, much less appreciate.

"Forgive me," Munch whispered now, before she dropped off to sleep, "and thank you for my life." She remembered the other thing then, the murders. What would God have her do? She'd call Roxanne tomorrow. If anyone checked her phone records she could always say that Nathan's arrival prompted the call.

Chapter 6

⸺

Thor, 1974

Walking out into the alley, Thor heads for his Ford pickup truck. New York Jane is with him. So is Munch. It's twilight in Venice Beach.

It usually is.

The three of them form a loose pack, hanging together like abandoned dogs gone feral.

The trio are on their way to the liquor store to buy another six-pack for Thor and wine for the women. He has on combat boots, adding another inch to his six feet. He also wears jeans and a camouflage jacket over his long-sleeved thermal. His keys dangle from a hook on his belt loop. There's a hunting knife strapped to his right thigh, barely legal at a smidgen under six inches long and technically not concealed.

His hair and beard are long, like the guys in ZZ Top, but Thor doesn't sing, play an instrument, or work. No one gives him shit about how he fills his days, least of all his woman. They share everything, and

Thor's all for that. He brings his muscle to the mix, his attitude, his utter disregard for everyone else in the world. Fuck 'em all but seven, he says, six pallbearers and a motorcycle cop.

As they get close to Thor's truck, they see movement in the cab. Some young hippie-type with long black hair has broken in and is rifling through the glove compartment. Thor doesn't shout; he doesn't even break stride. He hands his keys to Jane and pulls back his own long hair with a rubber band. The women hang back, unsure of what will happen next. Thor sticks his head into the open door of his truck.

"You need any help, bro?"

The dark-haired guy jumps a little at the sound of Thor's voice, but quickly recovers. Thor is calm, relaxed, his smile friendly.

"No thanks, bro," the hippie says. "I'm doing all right."

"Because I was thinking," Thor says, reaching for the sawed-off baseball bat—his "nigger-be-good stick"—that he keeps behind the bench seat, "that you might want this."

The hippie knows he's in trouble now, but he has no idea how much. He looks at the women, then back at Thor. Thor's mouth contorts into a frown before he brings the bat down on the guy's knee, then across the guy's arm when the would-be thief holds it up to ward off the attack. Something goes crack. The hippie doesn't even scream, there isn't time before Thor drags him into the street. Thor doesn't want blood on his upholstery, so he waits until the guy is on the ground before he whops him across the nose. It makes a smooshing sound, a wet thud.

Munch winces.

"Let him go," Jane says. "That's enough."

Munch thinks so too, but she says nothing. What's the point? Thor would ignore her. He's clearly oblivious to the world as he drags the barely conscious hippie by his hair over to a cement curb and positions the guy's face against the edge.

"No," Jane says.

"You know this motherfucker?" Thor asks, pointing an accusing finger at her.

Munch knows Jane has fucked up. It can happen that quick with these guys. One minute you're their friend, the next they're your worst nightmare.

"No," Jane says, her eyes lowered. She'd bow like a geisha if that would help. She'd crawl on her belly.

"Then what the fuck do you care?" Thor's eyes blaze with excitement. He brings his boot down on the back of the thief's head. "Eat that, fuckhead."

The guy doesn't move. Blood runs down the gutter. Munch is afraid the guy is dead. She takes the keys to the truck from Jane. "Let's split."

Thor bends down, turns the guy's pockets out, and finds some folding money. This pisses Thor off.

"What's he robbing me for?" he asks, genuinely indignant. He stands and kicks the unconscious man again.

Munch starts the truck and pulls into the street. She thinks that if Thor were driving he might run the guy over. Her mouth is dry. She feels cold and something else, something she hasn't felt in a long time: conscience. She's seen plenty of fights before, sees them every week, but usually someone's drunk. Thor wasn't even high this time and his cold-blooded side scares her more than anything else. She decides to cut both him and Jane loose, to find other people to hang with, but like many other resolutions she makes while using, she keeps this one too late.

The damage will be done, and it will haunt her into her next life.

The coroner's office was in downtown L.A., so St. John went alone. Wednesday was the earliest Sugarman could schedule the autopsy of Jane Ferrar. Cassiletti had an appointment with a brickyard in Ontario.

St. John entered the coroner's office through the side entrance, the one the meat wagons used for deliveries and pickups. There was an empty steel gurney by the door, and a coiled green garden hose with a still-dripping nozzle. The smell of wet concrete vied with petroleum and alcohol fumes.

Dr. Sugarman was in his office and on the phone. "I'm sorry for your loss," he was saying. St. John wondered how many times a day the pathologist uttered that line.

St. John remained standing in the doorway; Sugarman looked up at the clock as he hung up the phone. It was eight in the morning.

"You're here for the Jane Ferrar post?"

"Yeah," St. John said.

"Haven't seen you for a while," Sugarman said. "How are you feeling?"

St. John rubbed his chest, slightly left of center, out of reflex. "I'm all right."

"Good. Good to hear it."

Carrying his own camera, St. John followed Sugarman through navy-blue doors into the powder-blue tiled chamber of the autopsy suite. The neon bug-zapper buzzed as insects were drawn to a purple death. Sugarman's assistant opened the door to the cooler and wheeled out a body covered with an opaque plastic blanket. Even that was tinted a pale blue in the reflected light.

Sugarman and St. John donned surgical gowns and gloves. In the old days, medical examiners never wore gloves. The gloves inhibited dexterity and sensitivity and were a hassle to put on. It struck St. John that the same arguments could be used against condoms.

"We should buy stock in the company that makes latex," St. John said.

"This AIDS epidemic is going to get worse before it gets better," Sugarman said, checking the body's toe tag. "Mark my words."

St. John grabbed a face mask from the box by the door and pulled it on over his nose and mouth. The only sound above the hum of the refrigeration was the buzz of the bug zapper. The ME swept the plastic tarp off the body with a practiced flourish, and what remained of Jane Ferrar lay spread out naked on the cold steel table.

Sugarman verbally documented every injury into the microphone hanging suspended over the table. Most notable was the throat wound, cut all the way through to the spine. There were also numerous facial lacerations, two other long shallow slashes on her torso, and a large shallow dent in the back of her skull, which they were attributing to either the initial drop into the storm drain or her head bashing against the wall as the current carried her body downstream. The bruising on her upper arms appeared to have been made by fingers. The ID techs took picture after picture. St. John took a few of his own.

Naked and supine, the body revealed another abnormality that became clear to the investigators. Jane Ferrar's right leg was considerably smaller than the left. Sugarman found a two-inch discrepancy in length, and when St. John reexamined the woman's shoes, he noticed that the right shoe was a size four and the left shoe was a size seven.

"Polio?" St. John asked.

"Most likely. The poliomyelitis virus usually attacks the spinal column and brain stem of children and causes this lack of development."

X-rays revealed that both of her forearms had been broken within the last few years.

St. John envisioned her in a defensive pose. In his imagination she was on her knees, begging for mercy that never came.

X-rays also revealed a years-old fracture of her right eye socket. The inside of her thigh was peppered with both fresh and ancient needlemarks. A tattoo on the back of her left shoulder read PROPERTY OF THOR.

Sugarman spent many minutes on the neck wound before drawing St. John's attention to the color and texture. "She was dead before her throat was cut. I'm seeing seepage around the wound, but the veins would have flared open more if the heart had still been pumping."

"So it was the head trauma?" St. John asked.

Sugarman nodded as he parted the hair above the right ear to show St. John a star-shaped wound; then he spoke into his microphone. "The victim has a three-inch stellate scalp laceration with several branches running laterally and distally to the right ear. The skin is split rather than sliced, which indicates blunt force trauma."

St. John leaned in for a closer look at the gray mushroom of brain matter poking out from the hole in her skull.

Sugarman moved on to the pelvis, swabbing the woman's orifices, and checking for signs of sexual assault. "I'm seeing no signs of vaginal trauma and no traces of semen. And judging from the pelvic structure, this woman never gave birth."

Jane Ferrar's arms lay flat at her side. The buttons from the doll's dress had left impressions in the soft flesh of her lower arms where she'd clutched the plastic baby to her chest. St. John looked again at the slashes on her abdomen. There was a deliberateness about the two lines that came together just above the navel. The letter V, standing for what? Victim? Victory? Vengeance?

"What do you make of this, Doc?"

Sugarman peered at the cuts with a magnifying glass. "Non-serrated blade, I'd say."

St. John took another photograph. Had the killer signed his work?

Sugarman made the Y cut, commented on the cirrhosis of the liver as he removed and weighed it. An hour later, as the pathologist was sewing the body back together, St. John told him that he was leaving.

"I'll call you when I get back the tox results," Sugarman said.

"Yeah. Let me know." He needed to get back to the station, contact Missing Persons, and see if anyone had been close enough to Jane Ferrar to notice her absence. He also wanted to put out feelers for an asshole named Thor aka Mac Ferrar.

Jane, 1974

She is not Thor's first choice. Jane has eyes. She sees the way he watches Munch, how he puffs out his great chest, even makes an effort to brush his hair when he thinks he might be seeing her. But Munch isn't interested and Jane is.

Lately, Jane wonders why she and Thor bother to think of themselves as a couple. They are not faithful to each other, though her sexual encounters are usually business while his are more matters of control, conquest, and opportunity. She fears him and that fear is one of the few emotions that touches her. He says he wants a kid from her, a boy. She makes her tricks use condoms, especially the ones who don't have red hair. He pretends she only screws white men, and she knows it's best to let him believe what he wants.

Thor broke her nose when he was in one of his moods; afterward he brought her flowers and a new pair of sunglasses to hide the black eyes. She was back on the street within days, and he was extra sweet to her for almost a week. She even explained to all their friends that she had asked for it, been mouthy at the wrong time, and really hadn't left Thor much of a choice. Munch just snorts when she hears Jane's version.

"He's an asshole," she says. "I don't care how big his dick is."

Sometimes days will pass and Jane doesn't see him—her supposed old man—but she keeps track of him through their network of bartenders and connections.

Once, after not hearing from him in days, Munch said that Jane needed to have a little fun and that she had earned a girls' night out— the other girls being Deb, Roxanne, and Crazy Ellen. Munch and them took her barhopping over to a dive on Lincoln, and there was Thor with some floozy, some little blonde bitch sitting on his lap. Jane had to hide in the bathroom until he left. He would have broken her nose again if he found her out on the town without him.

Her dad asked her once what she was doing with these guys, these men who treated her like shit. He didn't understand and Jane couldn't explain that she liked being with the baddest of the bad, a man feared by all. She was envied every time she walked in a bar with him, could feel the respect trickle down to her. He was her pirate, her Jesse James. She would do anything for him, whatever the cost.

One day Thor'd wake up and notice what he had, and they'd all just see.

Chapter 7

==

N athan was gone when Munch and Asia woke up. He'd left his clothes and made a halfhearted effort to straighten the blankets on the couch. The towel he used the night before was still damp and crumpled in a corner of the bathroom floor. Munch picked it up and hung it over the shower stall. She was going to need to set some ground rules.

She went outside and retrieved the morning paper. The story was on page three of the metro section with the headline BODY OF WOMAN FOUND IN STORM CHANNEL IDENTIFIED. The one-paragraph article went on to remind the reader that a Caucasian woman had been discovered dead in the storm drain near the Riviera Country Club. The woman was identified as Jane Ferrar; the apparent cause of death pending autopsy and toxicology reports was bludgeoning.

Munch sat down heavily. Jane had spent her life getting beat up by one man after another. She had been pretty when Munch first met her. She had one of those heart-shaped faces with high cheekbones, cat eyes, and a narrow jaw, but every few months, some new trauma would chip away at those looks. The straight nose was broken and healed slightly crooked. One of her front teeth was knocked out and the replacement tooth was too white. It wasn't all Thor, the son of a bitch, although he'd done his share.

Munch checked the time and then reached for the phone.

Five hundred miles away, her old friend Roxanne answered with a sleepy hello.

"Good morning," Munch said. "I'm going to ruin your day."

"What's up?"

Munch told her about Jane being murdered and the visit from Mace St. John.

"What did you tell the cop?" Roxanne asked, sounding fully awake now.

"Pretty much the truth, that I hadn't seen Jane in a long time, and that as far as I knew she didn't have a kid although Thor wanted one."

"You mentioned Thor?"

"Yeah, well, the two names went together."

"Yeah, but still."

"I know." Munch looked at the newspaper article and how much it didn't say. "I also talked to my sponsor about it. I told her about Jane and Thor and Sleaze John being involved in something heavy ten years ago."

"Just them?"

"I told her that there was one other person who was way out of the life now."

"Can you trust her?"

"Sure, she's my sponsor. It's like talking to a priest or something."

"Not exactly," Roxanne said. "You shouldn't have said anything. Now there's one more person to worry about."

"She'll be cool."

"I hope so."

"By the way," Munch said, "speaking of lost causes, have you heard from Deb?"

"Oh yeah. She's back in Amsterdam."

"I knew about that."

"You'll never guess who arrived on my doorstep last month."

"Calling himself Nathan?"

Roxanne laughed. "So you're on his list too?"

"It appears so."

"Yeah, I put him up for three weeks. I even found him a job with an outfit that unloads freight from train cars. They were paying eighteen bucks an hour. He went through the whole training program and then split."

"Well, you can't expect the kid to be a model citizen with the upbringing we gave him."

"That's what I told myself when the phone bill came with about a hundred bucks' worth of long-distance calls."

Munch clicked her tongue. Mother and son were cut from the same cloth all right. "Send it here. He said he has a job lined up. He's got to learn to be responsible for his debts."

"No, it's okay."

"I'm serious. We won't be doing him any favors letting him slide on his obligations."

"All right, I'll do it today."

"And, Roxanne . . . ? If anyone were to ask why I called?"

"You don't need to tell me. It was about the boy." Roxanne paused. "You know, Thor's probably in prison."

"You think?"

"That's where he belongs," Roxanne said.

"There but for the grace of God . . ."

"I hear you."

"Do you know his last name?"

"Something Irish, I think."

"What? Like McButthead?"

"Yeah, that could have been it. I remember writing it out when we went to visit him at Chino that time, but it was so long ago."

"And we were probably stoned." The three of them—Jane, Munch, and Roxanne—had gone to visit Thor. Jane and Munch carried heroin wrapped in balloons in their mouths and passed them to Thor with tongue kisses while the guards looked on. "Were we just too stupid to get caught?"

"I guess."

Munch said her good-byes and could only hope that their combined good fortune held. After getting sober, Roxanne had settled in Northern California, gone back to school, and learned how to program computers. Munch was proud of her.

Neither she nor Roxanne needed a bite in the ass from the past.

Munch, 1974

This is their year, 1974. Seventy-four is a magic number, the cubic-inch displacement of a V-twin Harley engine. It is also the year that Munch turns eighteen and has to be more careful. Her arrests will count more; she is an adult. Not that she hasn't already racked up a string of adult charges in a variety of names, but she's always had her juvenile standing to fall back on.

She and Sleaze John are running together fairly regularly. Sleaze John doesn't have a Harley, but he has an El Camino with a big block 454 and that thing hauls ass. A truck with an open bed and plenty of horsepower comes in handy when someone's bike breaks down, a keg needs transporting, or if some valuable goods happen to fall off a truck.

Sleaze John makes hustling fun. He can con dope fiends out of their dope and money and leave them shaking their heads and laughing. She should know.

Part of his charm is his originality; then there is the charisma thing and how goddam pretty he is to look at.

There is always a price for picking the pretty ones.

In some ways she is no better than New York Jane, how she lets the guy walk all over her for the sake of his company. As much as Munch is capable, she loves Sleaze. Even when he's with other women.

She finds him one morning sitting on a door stoop in Venice Beach. He is as quiet as she's ever seen him, really dejected, and all out of play. She is up early that morning; he hasn't yet been to sleep. She stands in front of him, not saying a word. When he finally looks up, she offers him her hand and leads him back to her place.

It takes a few days to get that mojo of his up and working again. She even buys him a black silk shirt with some of her trick money. She would buy him a motorcycle if she had the means. The shirt looks dynamite on him with his dark hair and brown eyes.

"You almost look good enough to keep," she tells him.

"We should get married," he says. Then he laughs, and she quickly laughs back twice as hard.

"Can't you just see me with a husband? Who needs that shit?"

"Jane and Thor are getting married," he tells her.

"Get out."

"I shit you not."

"What's the point?"

John shrugs. "Maybe they wanted an excuse for a party."

Jane, as it turns out, really takes the whole wedding thing seriously. She buys herself a long lacy white dress at a thrift shop on Windward

Avenue, and gets all fussy and stressed out the morning of the big day, even buys film for Boogie's camera so he can take pictures. The ceremony takes place at the beach near the pavilion at the end of Venice Boulevard so the guys can keep an eye on their motorcycles. Thor wears a new black T-shirt for the occasion and is drunk by nine in the morning. Jane does her hair up with baby's breath and walks barefoot through the sand. Flower George donates a bouquet of daisies and acts as minister.

That right there should have said it all. Flower George is the biggest degenerate of all time.

Munch smokes a joint the night before the ceremony, then sits down and writes a story about the event for Easy Rider *magazine. She prints it in pencil on lined notebook paper, finishes it in one draft, and mails it off. It gets published in the April issue; the magazine pays her one hundred and twenty-five dollars—a small fortune—and she's the talk of the clubhouse for a week.*

Her dream is to save up the impossible sum of two thousand dollars and buy her own Harley, a Panhead with a white tank. She'll call it Prince Charming and ride off into the sunset.

The reality is that all the money goes for dope for her and Sleaze. It's gone within a few days.

In the fictionalized version of the wedding that she wrote for Easy Rider, *she made out like Jane and Thor were getting married for tax reasons. She left that part kind of vague, not really understanding how that whole income tax deal worked, only that married people paid less. Some of the guys she knows in the Satan's Pride Motorcycle Club have straight jobs, but they don't talk about them much. One guy drives a school bus, another works for Pacific Gas and Electric.*

The closest Munch ever had to a real job was the month she spent at a wholesale bakery, wrapping big chocolate chip cookies in cellophane and sealing the seams with white paper labels. The job didn't last long.

She only took it to satisfy her probation officer who said she needed to show some legitimate source of income. Her boss, the lady who owned the bakery, fired her for nodding off after her breaks.

"No hard feelings," the lady said. "It's just that you're a junkie."

Munch said she understood completely.

Her magazine story also had a happy ending. The married couple partied all night, the bikers did their own version of kissing the bride, and the bridesmaids made off with the groom. The real story would not have made good copy, especially the part where the bride had to hide all night in Munch's closet and throw away her ruined, bloody white dress the next day.

Midmorning, St. John met up with Cassiletti in the hallway outside the detectives' bullpen on the second floor of the West Los Angeles police station.

"What you got for me?" St. John asked.

Cassiletti was holding a white paper bag and a cardboard tray of coffee. "One decaf, black," he said, "and a low-fat bran muffin."

St. John spotted flakes of pastry on the younger man's jacket and felt a sudden intense resentment toward his partner, followed by an acute attack of self-pity at his own morning regime of egg-white omelets and dry toast; his smokeless, liquor-free evenings; his dick put into a coma by blood pressure medication. It was true what they said, that youth was wasted on the young. He was thinking like an old man and he wasn't even that old.

"Anything on that cinder block?"

Cassiletti handed the muffin and decaf to St. John, looked for a place to set the empty coffee tray, and then settled for sticking it under his arm while he rummaged through his pocket for his notebook.

St. John relieved Cassiletti of his coffee cup, freeing the big guy to flip back the cover of his notebook.

"Is that real cream?" St. John asked.

Cassiletti took the cup back and cleared his throat. "I have a few more block manufacturing companies to check out. It's not a cinder block, by the way, it's a concrete block."

"That's all you found out?"

"No, no. There's more. It's not the kind you buy at one of those warehouse building-supply stores. It's more the kind contractors use."

"There's a lot of building going on up there," St. John said.

"Right. Yes, sir. I could run down building permits, but I think it would be quicker to find the supplier and then request a client list." Cassiletti checked his notes. "The engraving on the face of the block is called a Malibu cut," he said with a knowing look.

St. John wondered if he expected praise for that little nugget. "All right, stay on that. You're, uh, doing good."

Cassiletti took another long swig of his creamy, caffeinated coffee.

St. John spoke while the man still had the cup to his lips. "I watched them cut Jane Ferrar this morning. Sugarman did a full bone survey." Meaning a complete set of X-rays of every bone in the woman's body.

Cassiletti, perhaps sensing it was his turn to say something, spit a little coffee back into his cup. "And?"

"Many signs of long-term abuse." St. John explained that the post had shown that Jane Ferrar had never given birth.

Cassiletti looked thoughtful. "Maybe the doll was her way of going back to childhood, to a safer time for herself."

St. John wanted to ask if they were all going to hold hands now and sing "Kumbaya," but said instead, "Good thinking."

"Yeah?"

"Yeah, and I'm not just saying that."

Cassiletti's smile froze on his face.

Oh, good Christ, St. John thought. *His feelings are hurt. Again.* "I'm going to run out and see Munch, see if she can give me any more on this Thor guy. You keep going with the block thing. I think you're really on to something, I mean that." He made his mouth smile and patted the big man's shoulder.

Cassiletti's voice was flat as he said, "Yeah, I'll get right on it."

St. John didn't know who he wanted to kick harder, Cassiletti for being such a pussy, or himself for being such a bonehead. Caroline was right, he needed to learn to give a compliment and then shut up.

Chapter 8

I'm honored," Munch said when Mace St. John told her he was coming by for a second visit. What she really felt was dryness in her mouth and an urge to feel wind in her face.

By 9 A.M., the customers were backed up three-deep. Munch ran from car to car with her clipboard. Each work order had to be completely filled out with the customer's name, address, work and home phone numbers, then she had to record the make, year, model of the vehicle, license plate, VIN number, and mileage. All that before she even got to the problem. She had boxes to check for routine maintenance such as tune-ups or oil changes—that saved a little time. If the car was there for a certain problem, she wrote brief descriptions of the customer's complaint—AC not cold, overheating, hard start in the morning—made a guesstimate at cost, had the customer sign, and then gave him or her the yellow copy. In a small box in the upper right corner, she would write in the mechanic's initials. This came in handy later if there was a problem with the work. It also ensured that the correct technician got credit for his or her labor when Lou did the books.

She and Carlos and Stephano all had their own customers, although Munch's job as service manager gave her the power to assign the work as she pleased. She did her best to keep everyone happy, finding that she got much more production out of the guys if their noses stayed in joint. Some jobs were gravy, others were shit, and she did what she could to distribute them equally.

Stan from the pharmacy across the street came in complaining of a noise emanating from his Datsun. From past experience, Munch knew chances were good that something was about to fall off. He was the kind of guy who waited until he had to steer the car into a curb to stop it before he got his brakes repaired.

"I'll check it out when I get a free rack," she told him.

She took down his information and promised to call him when she knew more. Then Mrs. Hartley brought in her Mercedes, complaining of a horrible racket under the car. Munch went on a test drive with her, and on the third time around the block Mrs. Hartley finally said, "There, you hear that? It just did it."

"I'll make a safety check," Munch told her. "You're going to have to leave it."

"Fine," Mrs. Hartley said. "I can't drive it like this."

"Do you need a ride?"

"No," she said, "Rosita followed me down here."

Munch looked to where Mrs. Hartley's maid waited in her Ford Pinto with a patient look on her face. They exchanged a smile of solidarity.

Munch parked the Mercedes on the lot and walked back to the service desk to arrange the day's work. With three mechanics and only two lube bays, there was the usual shortage of available hoists.

Stephano had an old Jaguar on the rack. He had been working on it all week with not much progress as far as Munch could see.

"Now what?" she asked, coming to stand beneath the car. Stephano turned at the sound of her voice and opened his mouth— a sure sign that bullshit was about to emerge.

"It's still not shifting right," Stephano said, managing a strut in the short distance between his toolbox and the car. He would be handsome, she often thought, if he wasn't such a snake oil salesman.

The Jag's owner was a twenty-something office worker who had inherited the car, and she really couldn't afford the maintenance. Stephano had no heart where money was concerned and had already racked up a bill of four hundred dollars. He claimed to have done a "major" tune-up and had a long line of patter for the customer about synchronizing her carburetors and calibrating her dwell.

As far as Munch could tell, all he'd really done was change the spark plugs and perform a basic transmission service, which really only amounted to changing the fluid and filter. It was needed maintenance, but it wasn't solving the problems that the car came in for. If Stephano put half the energy he used coming up with excuses into trying to fix the car, they'd all be better off.

The Jag's undercarriage was a mess. Everything leaked, the transmission, the power steering, the crankcase, the radiator. Someone needed to put the car out of its misery before Stephano drove its owner into bankruptcy.

"Did you check the modulator?" she asked.

"I don't know if these have one," he answered.

She wanted to say, *You're supposed to be the expert,* but she knew he'd just get all huffy and treat her to a string of technical terms that meant nothing. All the talk in the world wasn't going to convince an engine to run better.

"What's this?" she asked, pointing to what might be a vacuum pod sticking out of the transmission. Stephano looked, but said nothing.

"Put it down, and start it up," she said. "I want to check something."

Stephano did as she asked, not letting his male chauvinism stand in the way of free help.

She put the car back up in the air with the engine running. The idle was rough, and slightly higher than it should be. The part she suspected of being the transmission's vacuum modulator valve had a small pipe nipple. The tubing was slightly cleaner than the other metal around it, suggesting that at one time it had been covered. Munch grabbed a drop light and searched until she found a dangling, sixteenth-inch, neoprene hose. Heat and age had hardened the rubber, causing it to split. She put her finger to the end of it and felt vacuum. She snipped it down to where the rubber was still soft enough to be pliable, pulled it gently to create enough slack so that it would reach the nipple on the valve, and then stuck it back on the exposed tip. The engine idle immediately slowed down and smoothed out.

"Try it now," she said, "and let me know. You've got a water pump on an Alpha Romeo coming in."

"Thanks," he said, puffing his chest into her face. "Anything I can do for you, just ask."

"I'll keep that in mind."

A guy Munch didn't recognize pulled up in a BMW 320 and got out.

"Can I help you?" she asked.

"I spoke to Carlos," he said.

She gave him a quick appraisal. Up-and-coming white-collar professional, thirtyish. Probably rented a condo on Montana, leased the Beamer, and drank wine spritzers with his pasta. Total Yup. Big show, but tight with the dough.

She left him and moved on to the next customer, smiling when she saw it was Mrs. Obie. Everybody loved Mrs. Obie. She was a widowed, retired schoolteacher, had an older house up in the hills, and was the original owner of an absolutely cherry, metallic green 1966 Pontiac Bonneville. If anything ever went wrong, she got it fixed, no questions asked, paid any price requested, and did all the recommended maintenance. Even Stephano went easy on her.

"Hi, Mrs. Obie," Munch said. "What can we do for you today?"

"Brakes. You said I'd be due in five thousand miles. It's only been three, but I need an oil change, so we might as well take care of both now."

"Do you need a ride home?"

"Yes, dear, if it's not too much trouble."

"Not at all," she said, looking around for Pancho, the shop's gofer. She noticed that the guy with the Beamer was still standing by his car and looking impatient. Carlos was under the hood of a Honda that was parked in front of the office. "Pancho," she said, peeling two sheets of carpet protectors off the pad under the service desk and handing them to him, "I need you to take this lady home. Okay?"

"Sure t'ing, baby," he said in his Jamaican lilt, flashing her a smile that showed off the gold edging on one of his front teeth.

"What did you need?" she asked the guy in the Beamer again.

"I got my tire fixed here last Saturday," he said, "and it's still losing air."

"No problem," Munch said, thinking no wonder she didn't recognize the guy. She didn't work Saturdays. Carlos had a new baby on the way, and took all the hours he could get. "Sometimes a plug leaks, or you might've had more than one nail."

"All I know is that I still have the problem, and now I'm missing work."

"And Carlos knows you're here?"

"I called an hour ago."

"Oh," Munch said, seeing the mix-up, "but you haven't spoken to him in person yet?"

"I've already been waiting"—the guy looked at his Cartier tank watch—"over fifteen minutes."

Obviously the thing didn't keep accurate time. "Carlos," Munch yelled, "you talked to this guy about his tire?"

Carlos looked up, then at the guy. "Oh yes," he said, in his thick, nasal El Salvadorean accent. "I be right there. Jus' one minute."

The Yuppie shifted feet, tapping a shiny loafer on the cold concrete. He clearly was not accustomed to waiting.

Carlos wiped his hands and went to the back of the shop to fetch the floor jack. The expression on Mr. Yuppo's face grew more exasperated by the second.

"Do I have to sit here and take this from him?" he asked. Saying *him* as if Carlos were some piece of scum.

Munch's face went hot. "He's going to help you right now."

"He's ignoring me. I don't see why I'm expected to take this kind of shit."

"How much did you pay for the tire repair?" Munch asked.

"Eight dollars," the guy said petulantly, as if this was another point in the case building against Carlos.

Eight whole frigging dollars, wow.

Munch went to the cash register and pushed the return key. The drawer slid open and she pulled out a five and three ones. She motioned for Carlos to wait, walked back to the guy, and thrust the cash into his manicured hands. "Here's your money back, now get the fuck out of here."

Carlos looked embarrassed. The guy in the Beamer looked like he was going to burst a facial vein. "I want the manager."

"You're looking at her."

"Then the owner."

"Be my guest," she said. "He's in the office. Here, I'll show you so you don't get lost."

The guy followed her into the office. Lou looked up from his desk, his weathered face expectant.

"I want to register a complaint." The guy explained his version of the event, ending with, "And then she said, 'Get the fuck out of here.' I mean, can you believe the mouth on this woman?"

Lou pursed his lips thoughtfully. "Is that what you object to? Her language?"

The guy looked confused and then said, "It's her whole attitude."

Munch opened her mouth to speak, but Lou beat her to it. "Maybe," he said, "you'd be happier taking your business elsewhere."

The guy stormed out of the office and burned rubber as he left the shop.

"Can't win 'em all," Munch said.

Lou shook his head. "I mean, what an idiot. For all he knew I could be in love with you."

She didn't want to look at Lou's face, afraid of what she might find. Her life was already too complicated. She was trying to find a graceful exit line when Lou glanced out the window over his desk. "Your cop buddy is here."

"Yeah, I was expecting him."

He proved that he had read her tone correctly when he said, "You want me to tell him you joined the Foreign Legion?"

"Nope, it's too late for that." Ten years too late.

Chapter 9

⟐

Munch had trouble meeting St. John's eyes and
didn't know what to do with her hands. "Let's get
this over with," she said.

"Bad as all that?"

"I'm just not sure what you want from me."

"Tell me about this Thor character." They were standing outside the office. He pulled out his notepad and clicked his pen
open. "Start with the basics. How old is he?"

She did a quick calculation, surprised to realize that he would
have aged. She avoided driving past her old haunts, seized by an
unreasonable certainty that if she turned down certain familiar
streets she would find herself with the old gang and nothing
would have changed. It would all be exactly as she had left it:
Boogie would still be a little kid. Sleaze would still be alive
and flashing his trademark devil-may-care grin. Her few close
women friends would still be capable of laughing without it

sounding forced and harsh. Flower George would still be leering at her with his one good eye. In her mind, Thor was always in his twenties, old enough to be on the lam from a felony warrant back East, young enough to still be crazy dangerous. "Mid-thirties," she said. "God, he could be as old as forty."

St. John raised an eyebrow. "Old as that, huh?"

"I didn't mean forty was old."

"How tall is he?"

"Six feet, maybe six-one, I never measured exactly." She had a quick image of herself holding a wooden ruler next to Thor's erect penis. Ten inches, like the Aerosmith song. They had both been impressed.

"Build?" St. John asked.

"Strong. He was very strong."

"Hair?"

Munch looked over at the open lube bay. If she didn't soon claim the bay, Stephano would tie it up for another hour. "Reddish, like, not a carrot top, lighter. Blondish."

"Beard? Mustache?"

"When I knew him he wore a full beard, covered his neck." She turned so that her feet were pointing toward her toolbox.

"Eyes?" St. John turned the page.

"You mean the color?"

He looked up at her, his pen marking his place. "Yeah, listen, I only have the rest of my life here. You think you could step it up? You know what I want."

"You want to find him, see if he had anything to do with Jane's death."

"That's right."

"I really don't—"

"Why would you want to protect any of these assholes?"

"It's not that."

"What then? Are you worried this is going to come back to you? You want to be an anonymous source?"

She looked past his shoulder, feeling the increasing gap between them. She didn't want to be a source at all. Anonymity wasn't the issue. She knew how this worked. They could start pulling on some of those threads from the past, and the next thing she knew, her whole life could unravel.

"I have another question I'd like answered," he said. "The autopsy showed that Jane never gave birth. Why would Jane Ferrar be clutching a doll?" He paused.

"I don't know." She remembered how Jane sometimes sucked her thumb, and tried not to picture her dead.

"I'd really like to find out where she spent her last days."

"And who killed her," Munch added.

"Yeah, especially that. We haven't been able to get any kind of line on Jane's whereabouts prior to her murder. She didn't have a current driver's license, hadn't applied for any government aid, didn't have any utility bills or a listed phone number. Her last known public activity was an arrest five years ago for shoplifting."

"What was she stealing?"

St. John flipped backward in his notebook. "A stuffed animal, an Easter bunny."

Munch said to herself the most dangerous phrase in the English language—the short version of the Serenity Prayer: *Fuck it.* She looked St. John full in the face. "Thor had brown eyes. Ten years ago he drove a Ford pickup. Sixty-two or sixty-three. Brown, stick shift, six cylinder." He also owned a big black boat of a Chrysler New Yorker, but that car was long gone, so she didn't mention it.

"He had some felony beef in Pennsylvania, I don't know what it was, but knowing Thor, it was for hurting someone. He's one of the scariest guys I've ever known. Unpredictable, violent, and smarter than you would think. His last name might have been Mc-something. He did a short stretch at Chino about twelve years ago. I'm sure he's been back since. If not there, then some other joint."

"How about identifying marks?"

"Oh yeah," Munch said, "he had a few of those." She told him almost everything she could think of. Almost. "I'll call you if I remember something else."

"Will you?"

She rearranged the work orders on the service desk. "Yeah, sure, why not?"

"I don't know."

That's right, she thought, *cops didn't call it snitching, they called it "doing the right thing."* As if the choice was always that clear.

St. John wanted a cigarette. Badly. He knew Munch was being evasive if not outright deceptive, and he hated that he knew that. Too many years on the job had given him a suspicious nature. He wished he could turn it off sometimes. He couldn't. His innocence was just another thing in a long line of casualties his profession caused.

He returned to the police station with a heavy heart and pulled old Field Identification cards. Munch had described Thor's skin art in good detail. It was the usual sidewalk commando, bad-ass biker, wannabe shit—a dagger dripping with drops of red blood, crossed pistons, a flaming skull with Viking horns.

He took a box of Polaroids and settled downstairs in one of the old holding cells that had been converted to a storage room. In addition to the station's collection of memorable skin art, he had amassed his own private album over the years. His favorite was one some gangbanger brain surgeon had done on his belly. It was a life-size replica of a pistol. When the guy was wearing pants and an open shirt, it looked like he had a weapon stuck in his waistband. Real brilliant. St. John also had a picture of "Flower George" Mancini's foot, taken at the time of his death. There was a dotted line leading to the man's big toe and the instruction: HANG IT HERE, MOTHERFUCKER. Very nice.

St. John spent an hour sorting through stacks of long-haired, sneering assholes that all started to look alike. He found numerous misspellings—*Devil's Disiples, Don't Tred on Me*—but no Viking horns. Fuck this, he thought, rubbing his burning eyes. He went back upstairs, grabbed his book of assorted business cards, his telephone, and started dialing.

Whenever he met cops from another city, he collected their business cards. He sorted them according to geography and kept them in leather-bound organizers with plastic insert pages. The most worn book in his collection covered the Westside. Santa Monica, Beverly Hills, and Culver City were all incorporated cities that had their own police stations. Venice Beach and the worst parts of Culver City were in the Pacific station's jurisdiction. St. John had worked the Pacific station beat for more years than he cared to count. Rico Chacón was a detective there now, but St. John didn't want to call him.

He had heard some disturbing rumors about Chacón and his loyalties, rumors he thought he'd rather ignore. St. John treaded carefully, not sure if he wanted to find shit on the guy or not. Every cop he knew, including himself, was a little dirty, had nightmares about being in jail, caught for some minor indiscretion—a cut corner—and prosecuted to the full extent of the law.

Chacón was in the fight game, a business notorious for its criminal underpinnings. A little of that shit was bound to rub off from time to time. Best to leave it alone unless the rumors got heavier.

And then there was Chacón's thing with Munch. St. John had introduced them and his wife, Caroline, kept him updated on the status of their interrupted courtship. St. John didn't like it at all. His wife reminded him that he wasn't the guy's conscience or his rival.

Besides, Chacón had only been in L.A. for a few months, so he wouldn't have some asshole from the seventies filed in his memory bank.

He called Sergeant Flutie over at Pacific and asked to speak to someone from a street team, or one of the C.R.A.S.H anti-gang units, someone on the job for at least ten years.

"You should talk to Nunn," Flutie said.

"I thought he was retiring."

"This coming Friday, but he's working like he still means it. You coming now?"

"I'll be there in fifteen."

Detective Bob Nunn was a good choice, thirty long, hard years on the force, twenty-one of those years in Venice Beach. His memory for names and dates was legendary. The job was going to lose one dedicated detective.

St. John parked his Buick in the lot on Culver Boulevard. He signed in at the front desk and was buzzed through to the detectives' bullpen.

"You coming to the party on Saturday?" Nunn asked.

"I'm bringing the toe tags."

Nunn smiled good-naturedly. "What you need?"

"I'm looking for a guy." St. John gave Nunn everything he had on Thor. "First cop that can bring me a last name and hopefully an address, I'll buy a steak dinner."

"Sizzler?"

"Pacific Dining Car."

"You must want this guy bad. Let me think a minute." Nunn lit a cigarette and sucked it like he was drowning. St. John stood where he could get the full benefit of the secondhand smoke. It smelled wonderful.

A poster of the Rocky Mountains on the wall showed a beautiful twelve-point buck in silhouette before snowcapped peaks. He'd heard Nunn was moving to Colorado when his thirty was up. After a lifetime of busting murderers and other bad guys, he was going to spend his declining days shooting Bambis. Go figure.

"I had an aggravated assault case that sounds like your guy. The victim was a woman named Christine Hill." Nunn tapped out his cigarette and lit a fresh one. "I've never seen a face rearranged like that on a living victim. Her assailant was a creep named Cyrill McCarthy aka Thor."

St. John's pulse quickened. Was it really going to be this easy?

Nunn stood and opened the top drawer of a ponderous gunmetal-gray filing cabinet. The sides bore dents at kicking level. He pulled out a file folder. "The date of the offense was March 3, 1981." Four years ago. "I've got a case number for you too."

St. John wrote as Nunn dictated.

"The case fell apart at trial. Christine Hill bugged out. Wouldn't testify. It's all in the DA's packet. Let me know if you get anything else on this guy. McCarthy all but skated and it still fucks with me, you know?"

St. John nodded. Nunn didn't need to be reminded that he had an appointment with a deer and a thirty-ought-six.

"Go see the DA. He's got the file."

"You know where McCarthy is now?"

"He was in Chino for the holidays, but you'll have to check with them."

"Bobby, I owe you."

"Yeah, I won't forget. Pacific Dining Car."

St. John left the Pacific station and drove over to the West L.A. courthouse. An Assistant District Attorney named Josh Greenberg took him to find the court documents relating to the case number Nunn had given him. They were in a cardboard legal file box in storage. The file on McCarthy was an inch thick and covered with dust. Someone had made an annotation on the cover: a dot inside a circle with a small "3" in the upper right. DA code for *Asshole to the Third Power*.

St. John sat on a bench in the hallway to read the various court transcripts, affidavits, and investigators' reports.

After Christine Hill bugged out, the only witness willing to testify against Cyrill McCarthy was a woman named Stacy Lansford. She was painted by the public defender as one of McCarthy's disgruntled exes. This was a vast understatement according to the investigator's note. Stacy Lansford was discredited by the public defender when it was revealed that all her knowledge about the crime in question was second- and thirdhand, thereby ruled as hearsay.

Another blow to the prosecution's case came from the judge, the honorable David Helmer. Judge Helmer noticed a mistake in the prosecutor's court filing—the date of one of McCarthy's prior offenses showed the wrong year. Judge Helmer, for whatever reasons of his own (cops and prosecutors had a theory about the dye in the robes), refused to let the DA amend the date.

The result was a deal where McCarthy was allowed to plead guilty, and the judge ignored his earlier convictions. McCarthy was sentenced to only three years and was out in less than two.

After the sentencing phase, Stacy Lansford had written a letter to the court. It was in the DA's file and addressed to the judge.

"Your Honor, sir, please do not take what I have to say as a lack of respect, but you have made a terrible mistake. I met Cyrill McCarthy when I was in high school; he was older than me and seemed very experienced in the world. I was unhappy at home, so I jumped at the chance to escape. We married when I was sixteen. I didn't realize until he had taken me away from my family and friends what a terrible mistake I had made."

She then went on to recount two years of terror during which McCarthy had made her play Russian roulette, beaten her so severely that she had to have her spleen removed, and had even gone so far as to kidnap her once from her parents' home when she tried to seek refuge.

St. John checked the dates. McCarthy's relationship with Stacy Lansford had happened after Munch severed contact with the guy. He kept reading.

"When I first met Mr. McCarthy he told me his previous girlfriend had set the upholstery in his car on fire. Later, the story changed. He told me he burned the seats himself because the fabric had soaked up too much blood. I thought he was just trying to scare me at first, but after I got to know him better, I believed he was capable of anything."

St. John flipped back to the beginning of the file. The case that was ruled to be ignored was from eleven years ago, initiated after a confidential informant reported that the Satan's Pride was stockpiling grenades at a house in Inglewood. Warrants were served. The police raided the premises at three-thirty in the morning. There had been two occupants in the house, Cyrill McCarthy and a severely battered woman. The woman was nude, handcuffed to a portable potty chair, and, as tox reports would later prove, under the influence of the barbiturate Seconal. The skin across the cheekbone of the woman's left eye was broken open, and blood matching her type was discovered on the toe of Cyrill McCarthy's steel-toed boot.

The police searched the premises. They found several knives circa World War II, Nazi paraphernalia, small amounts of narcotics, including the amphetamines known on the street as "bennies," a half-ounce of marijuana, and three red capsules later identified as Seconal. No grenades were found.

The officers serving the warrant had taken both McCarthy and the woman into custody. The woman refused to answer the officers' questions and didn't want to press charges. When the detectives discovered that she was only seventeen, they no longer needed her help to arrest McCarthy for statutory rape. He was convicted of corrupting the morals of a minor and sentenced to eighteen months at the California Institution for Men in Chino, California. He was out in ten.

The juvenile in the case was identified as Jane Ferrar.

Bingo.

St. John returned to the copy of Stacy Lansford's handwritten letter.

"After the baby was born, I feared for both our lives. Thor was so disappointed that Katie was a girl and had even accused me of cheating on him, as if his sperm would only produce a male child. Katie even had red hair, just like his."

St. John sat straight in his chair. The reference to "Thor" was highlighted in yellow. The investigator had made a notation in pencil in the margin. *Moniker?*

"Thor told me he had killed three colored guys who had some drugs he wanted (he called them "niggers" of course). It was probably sometime in 1974 or 75. He said the one guy crawled the length of the hallway with his throat cut. The noise this guy made sounded like a broken accordion and Thor said it was so funny, he wouldn't mind hearing it again.

"There is no doubt in my mind that he was guilty of this crime and many more. I just wish I had some way to prove it."

The last page in the file was the report of a psychologist who interviewed Cyrill McCarthy:

It seems to him that his appointed task in life relative to members of the opposite sex is to extract as much pleasure from them as he possibly can, while at the same time inflicting as much pain and anguish as possible.

He shows no remorse or inclination to alter his perverse and dangerous sexual behavior. It is quite likely to continue.

Chapter 10

$\Longrightarrow$

Late that afternoon, Munch went to use the bathroom, but when she pulled on the door to get out it was stuck.

"Shit!" she screamed to the ceiling.

Carlos's voice came in through the transom. "Whas the matter?"

"The frigging door is stuck again."

"You need some help?" This time it was Lou's voice.

"We gotta fix this door," she said.

"Beat on the upper right corner," Carlos said.

She hit it with the palm of her hand.

"No. Higher," Lou said.

"I can't reach any higher."

"Maybe if you took off your shoe."

She slid off her tennis shoe and whacked at the door.

"Is that the hardest you can hit it?" Lou said. His voice

sounded strangled. She realized why. The door opened inward. At their direction, she had jammed it farther shut.

"You guys."

They laughed. Energized by her embarrassment, she yanked the door open. There were tears in Lou's eyes.

"I'm not forgetting this," she said. She returned to her jobs in progress with a laugh in her throat.

Asia's school bus let her off at the gas station at four-fifteen. Asia spent the hour before they went home doing her homework in Lou's office. That evening, Munch heard the front door open, followed by the sounds of Nathan's and Asia's voices. She couldn't make out the conversation but was pleased that the two of them were establishing a relationship of their own.

Nathan came in the kitchen. His jeans were dirty and he looked exhausted.

"So how'd it go?"

He opened the refrigerator and stood there staring at the shelves. Asia hovered beside him.

"You said you were going to call some guy. Some construction gig?"

"Yeah, yeah. I got it." He pulled out the carton of milk and unfolded the spout.

Munch grabbed a glass out of the cabinet over the sink and handed it to him. He poured himself a glass of milk. Asia took the carton from him and put it back into the refrigerator.

"That's great. Good for you." She looked at the plaster dust clinging to his face and hair. "Why don't you clean up? Dinner will be ready in about fifteen minutes."

"Good, I'm hungry."

"Asia, have you done your homework?"

"Yes," she said, staring after Nathan.

"Anything exciting happen at school today?"

"Not really."

"Who did you eat lunch with?"

"Uh, Brittany and Alyssa."

"What did you talk about?"

"Brittany's sister is having a baby, so Brittany is going to be an aunt."

"How old is the sister?"

"Eighteen."

Munch wondered if the girl was married and if the birth father was sticking around.

"Hey," Asia said, brightening at the memory, "I almost forgot. We learned a new song today."

"You did?" Munch tried to sound enthusiastic.

Asia burst into a robust rendition of "John Henry." Munch had no idea there were so many refrains as her daughter belted out verse after off-key verse, complete with pantomime about the hardworking steel-driving man. Nathan came back in the room and joined in. Asia was flabbergasted.

"How do you know the words?" she asked. "I just learned that song."

"It's been around awhile," Munch said, hiding a smile. "But I know how you feel." When she first got sober, learning to live in the straight world had felt like a continual game of catch-up. She was three years sober before she first heard about health insurance. She still remembered her pleased surprise that such a good idea already existed.

She handed Nathan forks, napkins, and three place mats. He stared at them as if they were pieces of a Rubik's cube.

"You're supposed to set the table," Asia said.

"I'm not sure how," Nathan said.

"Oh, I'll show you," Asia said with a sigh that sounded forty years old.

Nathan winked at Munch before following Asia to the table and watching her fold the napkins, then set the forks on top of them.

Munch stirred the spaghetti sauce and checked the pasta by pressing a noodle against the side of the pot with a wooden spoon. It cut easily, so she turned off the burner and sent Asia to wash her hands, leaving her and Nathan alone in the kitchen.

"She looks like him," he said.

The observation surprised her. "You remember Sleaze?" She drained the pasta and added it to the sauce.

"Yeah, he was an asshole."

"Sleaze was a lot of things, and watch the language."

"Sorry."

She took down three plates and filled them with spaghetti. "Wasn't he always nice to you?"

Nathan didn't answer and Munch knew why. His mother had probably told him that Sleaze was a snitch and that's why he was killed. There was a whole lot more to that story.

"You know, not everything is black and white," she said. "In fact, hardly anything is. A person can do stuff, stuff that's wrong, stuff that maybe hurts someone, and not be a completely bad person. Sometimes people get caught up in things and get in over their heads. You get one side of the story, but not the whole story."

He just stared at her. She couldn't read him. He wasn't exactly hostile, but he didn't look like he was accepting her wisdom either.

"I'm only saying 'judge not lest ye be judged.' " A rote saying.

She tried again. "Do you think you would ever see yourself in a situation where you might need to call the cops? Maybe to protect yourself or someone you love?"

"I could have called the cops on you a few times."

"And that would have been all right. Getting busted saved me. It drove me to a place where I needed to get straight or go to jail. If dope were legal, like in England, I'd still be strung out. I wouldn't have my work, or Asia, or this home. So maybe if you had called the cops way back when, I would have gotten sober that much sooner." *Maybe your mom would have too,* she thought.

"I don't know," he said. "I was raised that you don't rat. Ever."

"I was too. 'Snitches end up in ditches.' Right?"

He looked at her with surprise, the way Asia did when she learned something new in school and then found out her mother already knew. Kids. They all thought they'd invented the wheel.

"It's all bullsh— Uh, baloney, Nathan. Stupid rhymes that cons run by each other to perpetuate their loser lifestyles."

"Would you drop a dime?"

She didn't tell him that she already had. "Depends on the situation and who was getting hurt. You get to be my age and you learn never to say never."

He smiled, and she felt a ray of hope.

"And another thing, my boy. You're welcome to stay here, but I'm not your maid. I expect you to help with the other chores around here. You can start by doing the dinner dishes."

Nathan began to protest, but then stopped himself. Perhaps he sensed the thin ice.

"And don't even think of doing a crappy job so I don't ask you again. I'm hip to that trick."

He grinned as he picked up two of the steaming plates of pasta and took them to the table. "I don't mind helping. I can even baby-sit sometime if you want."

"I just might take you up on that, but don't call it that in front of Asia."

"No, I hear you. She's a cool little kid."

"Thanks. I think so too." She watched him move awkwardly around the small table. He'd shed his work boots, but he was still tall and gangly. His face was unguarded for a moment as he aligned the dinner plates. She had a quick vision of him as a four-year-old in stocking feet. "How are you going to get to work?"

"Bus, I guess, until I get some wheels."

"Do you have a driver's license?"

"Yeah. I even got a passport. My mom's going to send me a ticket when she gets settled."

Munch hid her reaction to the boy's slim hope. "I've got this little Honda Civic at work. I've been fixing it up. It runs okay, paint's not bad considering. Can you drive a stick?"

"Yeah, my mom's truck was a stick. Three on the tree."

"Well, are you interested?"

"What are you asking?"

"I'll sell you the Honda for what I have in it, but you have to get insurance and put it in your name." The name that was on his driver's license anyway.

"For real?" he asked, that big smile of his threatening to break out.

"This is L.A. You need a ride."

"I get paid Friday."

"All right, come to my work and we'll go to the DMV together." She went to her desk and found the business card of her insurance company. His having fraudulent identification was not something she cared about. It wasn't his fault that he was on his own and forced to take care of himself so young. She'd had her own set of ID when she was fourteen and was driving. The important thing was taking responsibility, and having insurance was part of that package. "These people have the lowest rates around. I use them for my limo business and my personal cars."

"Yeah, I saw the limo in the back. What's the deal with that?"

"Barely worth the effort, I'm sorry to say. I have the one car and an ad in the Yellow Pages. I do weddings, some airport runs. Most of the time it just sits around costing me money, but come spring, especially May, I make some good bucks."

"What happens in May?"

"High school proms. See what all you're missing?"

"When did you want me to baby-sit?" he asked.

"How about Friday night?"

"Sure."

"You're all right, kid. Now go find madam and tell her dinner is served."

After dinner, Munch pulled down a box from the upper shelf in her bedroom closet. She kept precious few artifacts of her old life. Most had been lost to fire and moves and unplanned incarcerations. Deb had always been the one who was into pictures and keepsakes. She had compiled three albums devoted to Nathan's milestone events by the time he was four. Over the years, she also had collected and saved photographs of most of the old gang. When Munch adopted Asia, Deb had sent pictures of Sleaze John. Asia kept them in her own little keepsake box in her room.

Munch's mementos fit in a shoe box: a courtesy card from the Satan's Pride, a tooled leather belt made by a former boyfriend, and a few old pictures. She unrolled the belt and studied its imperfect craftsmanship. The tooling was a craft he'd probably learned in some youth rehabilitation facility; '76 was stamped above the rivets holding the belt buckle and next to that were two lightning bolts signifying Aryan Brotherhood. Then came the words WE EAT SLEEP RIDE BREATHE DREAM LIVE AND LOVE MOTOR-CYCLES, H.D. (for Harley-Davidson), more lightning bolts. A large *Venice* in between two Harley wings. Beneath *Venice* smaller letters that read IS NOT MARINA DEL REY. And finally, a nicely rendered marijuana leaf.

Thank God, she thought for not the first time, that she had never gone in for tattoos.

She put the belt back in the box and then opened an envelope of pictures. There they were: the pictures of Thor and Jane's wedding. He looked drunk, sneering at the camera. Whoever had taken the picture—Boogie, probably—had held the camera crookedly, so that Thor and Jane stood at an angle. Jane, in her white dress, smiled brightly, happily oblivious to what was coming.

Chapter 11

$$\Longrightarrow$$

Cassiletti sipped his morning coffee and stared at the braided rope before him. The whole cinder-block thing was on hold for the moment. The killer had either been experienced at concealing his crimes or dumb lucky to dump the body in water. Moving water at that, one of the biggest enemies in an investigation that depended on trace evidence such as fibers and fluids.

St. John was working the victim angle, but Cassiletti believed the answers lay in the killer's methodology. He dreamed of coming up with the significant something that would give them the killer. St. John would grin, shake his head, and say something like, "That Cassiletti, he's something. Son of a bitch." He'd use a tone of gruff admiration. "Fucking Cassiletti, huh? Tony the goddam Tiger."

Cassiletti would shrug modestly, play down St. John's praises of him in the bullpen—no, better yet—a bar, a cop bar full of men angling to buy him a drink and pat his back. This would be the day of the trial, when the defense attorney attempts to break him and fails. Cassiletti looks the jury in the eyes as he explains himself and his thought process. The jury deliberates less than an hour before returning a verdict of guilty.

When the newspapers take his picture, he doesn't smile. He has an intelligent expression on his face, maybe does something with his hands to show how he's pieced together the clues to re-create the crime.

He takes off his coat so that his weapon and badge show. It looks impressive, his big black thirty-eight in the tan holster and next to that, his gold shield. He wears his gray slacks that day and a black belt, the Italian one.

A dispatcher from downstairs walked by. Cassiletti shook himself back to reality.

Both he and St. John believed they were looking for a strong man as their offender. A man perhaps comfortable around horses, good with his hands.

The rope the killer used was white, or had been when it was new and clean. It appeared to be made of nylon. The ends had been sealed by some heat source that left them blackened. When it extended, the rope would have been six feet long. Cassiletti could only estimate this, as the knot that had been fastened by whoever tied the cement block to the body was still intact.

The core of the rope was braided. He went over to the crime lab and checked other samples of rope. Many were braided on the outside, fewer had a center core, and he could find no samples of rope that were a braid encased in a braid.

The knot, the block, the rope, the doll. They were all going to mean something. He could feel it.

* * *

St. John put Cyrill McCarthy's scriptors out over the network of police agencies with a "wanted for questioning" stipulation. He'd been released from Chino a month earlier, on January sixteenth. His parole officer was on vacation and wouldn't be back until the following Monday.

St. John also ran Stacy Lansford's name through every system in the Department of Justice's database—CLETS, NCIC, DMV, voter registration, even the phone book—and had come up with zip. She had existed once, but the paper trail had died four years earlier. He had struck out similarly with Jane Ferrar. Christine Hill died from breast cancer in 1983. Poor kid.

Cassiletti knocked on the glass of his cubicle. "Want to take a ride?"

St. John threw down his pencil. "Yeah, might as well." He followed his younger partner out to the parking lot. "Where are we going?"

"The scene of the crime," Cassiletti said, making his voice melodramatic. "One of them anyway."

He held up an evidence bag that St. John saw contained a length of rope.

"I want to follow some leads." Cassiletti laughed that high silly laugh of his that was so incongruent with his large build, and St. John half smiled as he fastened his seat belt.

"Let's take Sepulveda," St. John said. "I want to stop at Munch's Texaco station. Would you mind?"

Cassiletti stared out his side window, the slightest hint of disapproval in his tone. "No."

When they arrived at the gas station, Lou was on a ladder at the gas pumps, replacing one of the fluorescent bulbs in the canopy.

They pulled up beside him, and St. John rolled down his window. "Munch here?"

"She's on a test drive. Be about fifteen minutes. Want to wait?"

"No, we were in the neighborhood. Tell her we stopped by."

Cassiletti nodded to Lou, and for just a moment St. John saw a look pass between Cassiletti and Lou that seemed to echo Cassiletti's earlier tone of reproach. St. John felt a split second's guilt, as if he'd been caught with his hand in the cookie jar. He almost said, "We're just friends," but stopped himself.

"What are you waiting for?" he asked, instead.

Cassiletti's foot spasmed on the gas pedal, sending the car forward with a lurch.

"Watch it," St. John said.

"Do I yell when you drive?"

"You don't need to."

"I wouldn't do that to you."

"Would you just go already? Christ, you sound like an old woman."

Cassiletti burnt rubber onto Sunset Boulevard, smiling slightly when St. John gripped the handhold over the glove compartment. He drove in silence until they arrived at the site that St. John had identified as the spot where Jane Ferrar's body must have been dumped into the storm drain. Cassiletti parked the Buick on the dirt easement beside the stables where a woman in tight Levi's and a long-sleeved blue shirt was mucking out the stalls. St. John waited so Cassiletti would be the first to approach the woman.

"Excuse me, ma'am," Cassiletti said.

St. John winced. Women under thirty, as this one appeared to be, preferred to be addressed as "miss."

She paused, leaned against her rake, and studied them. Most

of her attention was on Cassiletti, taking in the detective's full height of six-three. She had a friendly smile on her tanned face even though she gave St. John no more than a cursory glance.

"Patricia," she said. "Patricia Kelly."

"I hate to bother you, Miss Kelly," Cassiletti said, "but I was wondering if you could help me."

"Call me Patty." She rested her rake against the corral wall and pulled off her leather work gloves. "And you're?"

Cassiletti handed her a business card and her eyes lit up even more. St. John watched with a pang of nostalgia. Something about the badge parted more knees than the Charleston.

"What do you need?" Patty asked.

Cassiletti was all business as he produced the plastic evidence bag containing the rope that had been used to bind Jane Ferrar. "Is this the type of rope you use around here?"

"May I?" She reached for the bag.

Cassiletti let her take it. She studied the rope for a moment. "Nylon."

"That's right."

"We'd never use it here, not for a lead. I like cotton, much softer on your hands if the horse shies. Nylon burns your hands and when you cut it you have to seal the ends or it unravels."

Cassiletti showed her the melted end. "Seal it like this?"

She looked, leaning in much closer than she needed to, St. John thought. "Exactly," she said, giving her long brown hair a flip and smiling with all her teeth for Cassiletti.

"One more thing," he said.

"Sure."

"Were you here last Saturday?"

"In the morning. I came in and fed the stock."

"How about later?"

"You mean Saturday night?" She looked at him speculatively. "I had a date, a very boring date, and I went home early."

St. John waited for her to add "alone." With Cassiletti, she'd be better served if she hit him over the head and then lassoed him with one of her soft cotton ropes.

"Thank you, Patty," Cassiletti said. "You've been a big help."

"Do you want my number?" she asked. "In case you have any more questions?"

"That would be great. Thank you very much." Cassiletti wrote down her full name and phone number, checked his watch, and made a notation of the time. All business.

Patty touched his hand. "And that's 'Miss.' "

Cassiletti nodded without looking up. His ears darkened and he cleared his throat.

Fuck, St. John thought, *this is truly painful to watch.*

When they walked back to the car, St. John held his hands out for the keys. Cassiletti relinquished them without protest.

St. John swung a U when there was a break in traffic. "You going to call her?"

"About what?"

"Have I taught you nothing?"

Cassiletti let out one of his trademark giggles and rolled his eyes. "Oh," he said.

"Yeah," St. John said. "Oh." He looked across the seat. "What *did* you do last Saturday night?"

"I cooked dinner for my dad."

"What about your mom?"

"What about her?"

"I don't know, you never talk about her."

"She was a model from England. And very beautiful."

That would explain Cassiletti's hazel eyes and long lashes. St.

John had met the father, a hefty but short Italian. His son's looks hadn't come from him. "Is she still alive?"

"Probably." Cassiletti stared out his window.

"You don't know? When's the last time you saw her?"

"I was eight when my dad kicked her out."

"And he kept custody of you?" St. John didn't mean to pry, but this was too surprising not to demand an explanation.

Cassiletti looked at him, then at his knees as he smoothed his impeccable slacks. "My dad kicked her out because he came back from a business trip and the makeup she put on me rubbed off on his hand."

"She put makeup on you?"

"To cover up the bruises. My dad put it together, realized the other things weren't accidents."

"The other things?"

"The burns, the chipped teeth." Cassiletti shrugged as if to say: "History."

St. John drove in silence. *Well, no wonder then,* he thought. His dad used to say: "Everybody has a story." Digger St. John was right about that.

Munch was not surprised to see St. John's Buick swinging out from the spot where she'd witnessed the new fence being installed. She didn't honk or wave and neither St. John nor Cassiletti had seen her. She was driving a customer's big white Ford Bronco, which had a whine in the rear end.

A cowgirl was leading a large gray horse out of one of the stables. Munch pulled in beside her and put a big smile on her face. "Hi, did I miss them?"

"You mean those cops?"

"Yeah." Munch shifted the truck into park and rested her

elbow on the windowsill. "They ask you if you saw anything the other night?"

"You mean Saturday?" The woman walked the horse over. "I wasn't here. I told them that. They were asking me about some rope."

"What kind of rope?"

"Just regular nylon, might have been clothesline, I guess. Not the kind we use here." The horse nudged her arm. "So you know those guys?"

"Yeah, they're friends of mine."

"Do you know if he's married? I didn't see a ring."

"Which one?"

"The cute one. The big guy."

"Oh, him." Munch had to smile at the relief she felt, as if it made any difference which cop this woman had taken an interest in. "No, he's available, but he's shy around women. Why do you think the rope was clothesline?"

"Because it was white, I guess. Why?"

"They're investigating the murder of a friend of mine."

"The woman in the storm drain?" The horse put his head into her back and pushed. She stumbled a few steps forward, then pushed back and stroked the horse's face, admonishing him to be patient.

"That's the one."

"I'm sorry."

"Yeah, me too." Munch fished Thor's photograph out of her pocket. "You ever see this guy before?"

"No."

"How about without the beard?"

"That would be hard to say. Maybe. Who is he?"

"Nobody important."

"Somebody who looked like that would really stand out around here."

"Yeah, he always stood out."

Chapter 12

=⟩

When Munch got home that night, she found that a thick letter with a Sacramento postmark had arrived. Roxanne's telephone bill. Many long-distance phone numbers were circled. There were at least thirty to Oregon, another ten to Los Angeles, and three to Amsterdam.

Munch wondered what time it was in Amsterdam as she put the call through. With Deborah, the boundaries between night and day didn't matter. The last time Munch had spent time with Deb, it had been "wine-thirty" pretty much all day.

"Yeah," a sleepy voice answered.

"What are you doing?" Munch asked without bothering to identify herself.

"I was sleeping. How the hell are you?"

"Good. Are the tulips blooming?"

"Oh, yeah, it's fucking beautiful." A half a world away, Deb yawned loudly. "What's up?"

"Your son's staying with me. I thought you might like to know."

"Is he there right now?"

"No, he's still at work. He got himself a job doing construction."

"That's the man I raised."

Oh, shut up, Munch wanted to tell her. *How dare you take credit for his survival skills?* "He sure did grow up nice."

"Yeah, I'm real proud of that boy. He had some rough spots, but he got through 'em."

"You ever hear from his father?"

"I thought you knew. Walter died."

"He did? No, I didn't know. Bummer. How?"

"Yeah, it was really sad. Just when he was going to get to know his son."

Munch was quiet. In the years she had known Deb and Boogie, from when he was six months old until he was a cute little boy of seven, his father had made no attempt that she knew of to spend time with his son—not that Munch was especially tuned in to that kind of thing then.

"I've been going through all this bullshit with Social Security to get Boogie survivor's benefits," Deb said. "But it's a big hassle because, you know, we weren't married and I didn't put Walter's name on the birth certificate."

"Why not?"

"It wasn't anyone's business. I tried to change it, but that was a whole other hassle and I had the wrong year for Walter's birthday."

"Sounds like real work," Munch said, but Deb missed the irony.

"Tell me about it. That man worked three jobs at a time when he was trying to get his band together. Shit, the government took half his paycheck."

"Not half."

"Damn near."

Munch chuckled, remembering her own shock at her first legitimate paycheck and how much deductions had cut into it. It wasn't easy to be young and single and following all the rules.

"I'm only trying to get what's coming to my son. They're being real assholes about it. I already gave them copies of Walter's death certificate and tax returns."

"How'd you get those?"

"Walter's mama sent them to me."

"What else do you need?"

"They want more paperwork that documents Walter was the father. I showed them a few cards Walter sent when I was first pregnant, and he wrote a song about it. But that wasn't enough. Now they want me to get all these affidavits from people who knew us then to swear that Walter was the daddy."

"How many do you have?"

"I'm still working on it, you know, trying to track people down. It's not easy."

"Especially from bum-fuck Amsterdam," Munch muttered.

"What?"

"How about Thor? Heard from him lately?"

"Jane's Thor?"

"Yeah, only he's not Jane's anymore. She's been killed. Beaten to death and dumped in a storm channel."

"Damn."

"That's what I thought too."

"Shit, I haven't heard from Jane in a long time. She called me a few years ago. She was holed up in some women's shelter in

Santa Monica. I told her to come on up to the country, but she thought word might get back to Thor somehow and he'd get her."

"He'd go all the way to Oregon?"

"She seemed to think so. I never heard a woman so scared."

"It appears she had good reason."

"Yeah, and don't you go looking for him. You're doing good. You don't want to mess that up."

It was like having an anorexic tell you to clean your plate. Deb seemed to have forgotten that their relationship had shifted. Munch was the one leading the straight life with a real job. She knew very well what was at stake.

"What was the name of the place where Jane holed up?"

"Gimme Shelter, something like that," Deb said, yawning loudly again. "Or Helter Skelter."

"The Helter Skelter Shelter?" Munch asked, laughing. "I don't think so."

"Hell, I don't know." Deb laughed herself into a coughing jag.

"All right, thanks."

"Say, Munch?"

Across transatlantic lines, Munch heard a match strike and Deb inhale.

"Yeah?"

"Take good care of my boy."

"I'll do whatever I can."

After Munch hung up with Deb, she went to her purse and pulled out her wallet. She wrote Roxanne a check for a hundred dollars and stuck it in an envelope, wondering if she was being a hypocrite after all her talk about tough love and teaching the boy accountability for his actions.

She called her sponsor next, dialing Ruby's number from memory.

"Aren't you involved with some abused-women shelters?"

"Why?"

"Is there one on the Westside that sounds like Gimme Shelter?"

"There's a facility in Santa Monica called Shelter from the Storm."

"That must be it." Munch wrote down the name.

"What's this about?"

"Remember my friend Jane, the one I told you got murdered?"

"Yes."

"I think she maybe stayed at Shelter from the Storm for a while. I need to get in there, ask a few questions, see what I can find out."

"The location is a closely guarded secret. Those women are running for their lives."

Munch heard the front door open and Nathan's voice in the living room.

"I won't tell anyone," Munch said into the phone, then added, "I'm helping Mace St. John."

"I'm glad."

"So can we do it?"

"Let me call ahead."

Munch left Nathan and Asia eating pizza and watching television. Ruby met her at a Mexican restaurant on Pico, near the college. Munch offered to drive to the shelter. The truth was, she hated going anywhere in someone else's car. Ruby directed her to a large warehouse-type building near the college.

The sign on the door read SACKEE'S SEED. There was a driveway that led to a large roll-up door that was closed. Ruby rang the bell.

"Can I help you?" a woman's voice scratched through the intercom.

"It's Ruby." The door buzzed.

The outer office had a tall counter desk. The woman seated behind it had a phone at her disposal. A television monitor connected to what had obviously been a concealed camera pointed at the outside entrance. After Munch and Ruby entered, the door behind them closed with a heavy thunk.

Ruby escorted Munch through another door that opened onto a large compound of two-story buildings. Munch could see children playing in a gymnasium as she and Ruby walked through a rose garden full of meandering paths, birdbaths, and sculptures.

A few women sat on the benches, wrapped in thick coats to ward off the evening chill, their faces and spirits in varying states of repair.

"The kids aren't allowed in this garden," Ruby said, speaking in low tones. "Sometimes the moms need a break."

Ruby took her through what she explained was the schoolhouse. Several children were doing their homework, concentrating over maps of California, painstakingly labeling mountain ranges and bodies of water. Munch reached out to stroke the head of a little boy who looked Asia's age, but he shied away from her touch.

"Those are the living quarters," Ruby explained, pointing to what looked like motel rooms. "They're double suites connected by bathrooms. We had to install industrial fixtures to keep up with the wear and tear of traffic."

"Where is everybody?"

"Let's try the cafeteria." They walked to another building with steaming vents and a large Dumpster parked outside. Ruby pushed the doors open and they were greeted by the clatter of banging pots and running water. Six women were cleaning up after the evening meal. They stopped and stared at Ruby and Munch; then someone said, "They're okay," and work resumed.

Munch pulled the picture of Jane out of her pocket and showed it around. The first few women she approached glanced at it quickly, shook their heads no, and turned their backs to her. Finally one woman asked in a suspicious tone, "Who's this?"

"Friend of mine. I was hoping someone here remembered her."

"I know her," a skittish little bleached blonde said. Her head twitched as she spoke, as if she were fighting the urge to flinch. "She's good people."

"You know her from here?"

"Uh-huh. She makes dresses for the kids' dolls. Really fancy ones. I can show you if you want."

"Please."

"Okay. Yeah, sure. This way."

Munch and Ruby followed the woman to one of the housing buildings.

"I'm Tammy, by the way, but if you call here to talk to me, you'll have to ask for Lizzie. That's my code name."

"I'm Munch, this is Ruby."

Tammy made a queer bobbing bow with her head. "Pleased to meet you." She giggled inappropriately, then opened the door to what must have been her room. Toys were scattered across the floor. The bed was unmade. A suitcase sat on the floor, half unpacked.

"She's good at fixing them too." Tammy reached into the suit-case and retrieved a plastic doll in a red velvet dress. The dress was trimmed with white lace, but one of the sleeves was missing. With a sheepish grin Tammy showed them a naked doll whose arm had been torn from the socket.

"Uh-oh," Munch said.

"My son did that. Janie said she'd make it good as new."

Munch couldn't help but raise an eyebrow.

"He's a good boy. He just gets overexcited sometimes."

"How old is he?"

"Seven. And I know what you're thinking. He's old enough to learn to control himself. That's what my husband used to say before he disciplined him."

Munch spoke in her warmest tones. "I wasn't judging your son or you." Although the husband sounded like an asshole.

"Kids are like anyone else," Ruby said. "There's no such thing as too much love. Just you being here tells me you're on the right track."

Tammy looked at her shoes. "Thanks. You didn't have to say that." But it was clear she was pleased.

"When's the last time you saw Jane?" Munch asked.

"A few weeks ago. She's supposed to come around for group, but she missed it. You know where she is?"

"She died. I'm sorry." Munch watched Tammy closely to see how she reacted to the news. Tammy's eyes immediately filled with tears.

"What?"

"She got killed sometime around Valentine's Day."

"Oh no." Tammy sank to the floor and covered her mouth with her hand. "How?"

"She was beaten to death."

"That's how she always expected to go."

"I know. When I knew her, she seemed to be waiting for it. The cops are trying to retrace her last few days. They haven't had much success. Do you know where she lived?"

"I do. I've got it in my book."

Chapter 13

⟹

Friday morning, when St. John and Cassiletti pulled into the Texaco station, Munch was hammering a wheel bearing race into the hub of a Lincoln Town Car. A big-gutted man in an ill-fitting suit sipped coffee from a king-sized freeway mug and looked on.

She was fifteen minutes away from finishing the job, and the driver (she suspected he wasn't the owner) was impatient. She would have insisted he leave the car to have the work done, but the lube bays were conspicuously vacant, and she had no good excuse for why the guy couldn't wait and watch other than that she found his company annoying.

Lou walked out of the office to shake St. John's hand. "Munch, your fan club's here."

She looked up, exasperated, her hands full of thick wheel bearing grease. Couldn't he see that she was working as fast as she could? She still had to pack the new bearings, rehang the hub, brakes, and tires. Then there was the ever-important test drive, and the equally important task of writing and collecting the bill.

"I only have two hands here." A lock of hair that had worked loose from her braid fell over her right eye. She pushed it back with a clean section of sleeve on the top of her right arm. "It's going to be a minute."

"This will only take a second." St. John pulled back his coat to reveal the shield clipped to his belt and said to the big guy hovering over Munch, "Sir, if you wouldn't mind stepping away?"

Munch grinned. "Stay as long as you like."

St. John crouched so that he was eye to eye with her. She caught a whiff of his cologne over the pervasive odors of petroleum and asbestos dust.

"You find out anything?" he asked.

"I talked to a friend," she said, keeping her voice to a conspiratorial whisper so that he was forced to lean in closer. "She said the last she heard from Jane, she was in a shelter for battered women."

"Which one?"

"Some place called Shelter from the Storm. I went there last night and met someone who knew Jane. She gave me Jane's address and phone number. It's in my pocket."

There was an awkward moment while they both looked at her shirt pocket and then at the gooey grease coating Munch's fingers. She had a sudden impulse to point her breast at him and see what he did. Cassiletti would probably faint.

"I'll wait," St. John said.

Munch finished with the messy part of the job, wiped her hands clean, and then fished out the phone number herself.

Another time, she thought, *another place, another life.* Certainly not in a world where a nice lady such as Caroline St. John could get hurt.

"Did you find Thor?" she asked.

"I'm getting closer all the time."

"You might want to think about shooting first."

Before driving over to Jane Ferrar's apartment, St. John wrote and got approval for two search warrants—one to the telephone company for a list of all calls made to and from Jane's number in the last month, and another to search her apartment for any clues to the circumstances of her murder. The search warrant would be necessary if Jane hadn't lived alone. As it was, the building manager unlocked Jane Ferrar's apartment without asking to see anything besides St. John's badge.

The living room, single bedroom, even the kitchen and bathroom of the small apartment in El Segundo were full of dolls. All types. In the living room there were Cabbage Patch Kids, Betsy Wetsys, Chatty Cathys, numerous Barbies and Skippers. Even a few Kens staged in nonthreatening poses—arms down, faces blank. She obviously did her repairwork here. A card table held various doll heads, arms, legs, shoes, and clothes. The bedroom was devoted to less commercial, more collectible brands (as he deduced from the brass nameplates): Madame Alexanders, Ellenbees, Storybook. The dolls were decked out in elaborate costumes and frilly dresses and displayed on shelves, some under domes of glass. The bedroom closet was devoted to miniature wardrobes, divided evenly between winter clothing and summer dresses. There were several framed ribbons on the wall, including a first-place award from the 1983 Orange County Fair for "Best Formal." Next to the medallion and attached blue ribbon was a newspaper clipping showing a smiling Jane. The caption identified her as Marie Dobson. No wonder he had been unable to turn up any trace of her. Jane Ferrar had gone underground, but not far enough.

Perhaps her killer had used her affection for dolls to lure her out of hiding.

In her kitchen trash he found pieces of a greeting card. There was also a blue envelope that seemed to match the card. He slipped on a pair of latex gloves, gathered the torn pieces, and assembled them on her kitchen table. The printed message read: "I think of you often, though the years and miles have divided us." There was an additional handwritten note, unsigned. It read: "I haven't forgotten you."

St. John made a note to obtain Cyrill McCarthy's jail booking records for a sample of his handwriting.

He called Shelter from the Storm when he got back to headquarters. An operator answered. She told him that he needed to speak to an advocate, then took his name, badge number, and supervisor's name. The call was returned to him through dispatch.

"This is Janet Moriarity from Shelter from the Storm," she explained in a pissed-off tone of voice. "I'm returning your call."

Not: *What can I do for you?*

"I'm trying to solve a homicide. I have reason to believe that the murder victim volunteered at your facility and I'm trying to reconstruct the last few days and weeks of her life."

"Was she killed by her batterer?"

"We don't know that yet."

"Look at the statistics. In fact, why don't you check your nine-one-one logs and see how many times your officers were called out to save her?"

Yeah, he thought, *and how about how many times she refused to press charges?* "Her name was Jane Ferrar."

"I can't give you any information," she said.

Her hostility was palpable. He took a calming breath. One of them needed to be composed.

He knew where she was coming from. Women went to shelters because they had been battered, were seeking haven, and understandably had a problem with trust. St. John's team had once lost a witness when they placed her in protective custody at a battered women's shelter under an assumed name and then misplaced the pseudonym. The staff at the shelters felt a deep responsibility to keep their clients safe and their identities confidential. They wouldn't confirm, even to the police, especially not to the police (who were often batterers themselves), if a woman was there or had ever been there. The LAPD had a bad habit of not taking domestic violence seriously and in fact was being sued for it.

St. John remembered working patrol and how he and his fellow officers felt about domestics. If a cop was going to get hurt, chances were it would be during a husband/wife thing. Standard operating procedure was to pull the woman aside and ask what she had done to provoke the guy. Then they told the guy to take a walk and calm down. They treated them both like criminals. Eighteen required hours of "sensitivity training" later, all that had changed.

"Ma'am, we are trying to catch her murderer."

"So you say. Seventy-five percent of the women killed by their abusers are killed as they are leaving them."

"Yes, ma'am," he said as politely as possible. He hadn't called for a lecture, and he was tempted to direct her attention to other statistics. For instance, how many times these women returned to their batterers after leaving them. He'd guess on average a half a dozen per woman. Maybe he'd read that somewhere. And how many of those women got restraining orders and then broke them and made contact with their supposed enemy? His wife, Caroline, had explained the psychology of it all once, or tried to. It still didn't make any sense to him.

"My information is that Jane Ferrar was a substance abuser."

"Drugs and alcohol are against our rules. They're often a big part of the overall problem."

"I'm sure they are," he said. "I'm also looking for another woman who was a victim of the same man."

"When we get these women in a room together to talk about their experience, it's as if they were all married to the same man. The men all use identical isolation tactics, repeated attacks to the women's self-esteem, unpredictable outbursts of anger followed by physical abuse."

He held up a palm, translating the gesture into his tone of voice. "I'm not arguing with you. I'm one of the good guys."

She made no response.

"This woman's name is Stacy Lansford. As I said, she's a previous victim of our prime suspect. I'm very concerned about her. In fact, we're about to file a missing person report." He hoped the ploy would pry some bit of confirmation out of her.

Janet Moriarity didn't sound the least bit fazed by his announcement. The most she would agree to do was post a notice on the various bulletin boards, and *if* Stacy Lansford was around, and *if* she saw the notice, and *if* she chose to respond, he would hear from her. The notices could be delivered to the outreach office in Santa Monica and Janet Moriarity would see to their distribution from there.

St. John wasn't optimistic. Stacy Lansford had been missing in action for four years. The odds were slim that she would still be availing herself of a shelter unless she was still in the horrible back-and-forth phase before breaking free. He composed a flyer asking for information about Stacy Lansford and Jane Ferrar, explaining in candid terms that he was a homicide detective hoping to bring Jane's murderer to justice and that any information about Jane's whereabouts prior to her death would be most helpful to his investigation. He made it clear that Stacy Lansford was not a suspect and that anyone contacting him could do so with complete anonymity. He included his telephone number and a photograph of Jane, made ten copies, and took them to the outreach office in Santa Monica.

Nathan arrived at Munch's work a little after three. Munch didn't see who had dropped him off. She looked up to see him swaggering her way. He stopped to give a car the right of way and then spit on the cement as it passed him out the driveway. She shook her head, remembering how Deb spit all the time and how cool and tough it had seemed when they were teenagers.

"Don't do that," she said now as Nathan got within hailing distance.

"What?"

"It's crude."

"You want me to swallow it?"

"Just don't make such a point of it."

"Whatever." He squinted at the passing traffic.

"Did you get paid?"

He patted his pocket by way of answering.

"Well, let's go check out your new car." Munch grabbed the key off the Peg-Board above the service desk and led Nathan around the side of the shop to where a white Honda Civic was parked. Nathan approached the car reverently, spreading his large hands over the hood as if to assure himself it was real.

"What do you think?"

"Totally rad."

She lifted the hood, pleased he was so happy. "Let me show you a few things. This is the dipstick for the crankcase and here's the brake fluid. Don't rely on the coolant level in the overflow bottle; once a week check the radiator, but always when it's cold." She walked him around to the trunk and showed him where the spare tire and jack were stowed, then explained how to use them.

"I've got lots of spare parts from the old engine if anything goes wrong."

"This is a new engine?" he asked.

"New used. I buy them cheap. I've been doing this for years: buying cars with mechanical problems, fixing them up, and then selling them. A few months ago I bought another Honda I thought just needed a valve job. I had already bought the car and was manually rotating the engine by turning the crankshaft pulley and then I saw something move from where I shouldn't have been able to."

"What was it?"

"The piston moving up and down. There was a big hole in the block I hadn't seen before. Now I'm fucked, uh, screwed, because the engine is history. I started looking in the *Recycler* and I see all these ads for used Japanese engines, I mean, like, cheap. A hundred dollars on average. I found out that in Japan when the cars get thirty thousand miles on them they have to get a new engine. It's their smog law. So anyway, they ship all the good used engines by the tanker over here. Cost me less to swap out the engine than it would have to do a valve job and I wound up with a better product. Of course, you don't know how well the previous owner took care of his car, but for a hundred bucks it's worth the gamble."

Nathan nodded throughout her recital. "Awesome," was his only comment.

She gave him the ownership certificate, which had already been signed off, the registration, a smog certificate, and a bill of sale for one hundred dollars. "You're going to need to pay sales tax when you register it in your name, so I had to put something down. I've only had this car a week, so it's still in the last owner's name. I'll drive over to the DMV with you today if you want. Did you call that guy about insurance?"

"Not yet."

"You're going to have to have liability at least before I can give you the keys."

"I'm going to do it."

"C'mon, you can use the phone in the office."

She pocketed the keys and he followed her around the front of the building. "I talked to your mom last night."

"Oh yeah?"

"I told her you were working. She said she was real proud of you."

Nathan beamed.

It always astonished Munch how a person could be the worst parent in the world and still be loved, how the parent's praise or any little nod of approval would be cherished. And the worse they were, the fewer crumbs it took to make their kids happy. In fact, some of the sweetest-natured kids she knew had junkies for mommies and daddies.

"She told me how much she missed you. You should write her."

"I'll call her tonight."

"That's awfully expensive. I hate to see you burn up all your paycheck on my phone bill."

"No, it's cool," he said. "I've got a credit card number to use."

"That's not going to happen."

"Why not?"

"It's stealing."

"No, here's the thing. It's a big company. They won't even notice."

"Not the point."

"Man," he said, looking exasperated.

"Listen, I'm going to need you to watch Asia tonight. You do that for me and you can make one quick call to your mom. Sound like a plan?"

"Sure. And, uh, Munch? Thanks for everything."

"I'm happy to do it."

They reached the office. Nathan called the insurance company. When Asia's school bus arrived at four-thirty, the three of them drove to the Department of Motor Vehicles after first stopping at the insurance office and picking up Nathan's insurance certificate. The only problem came when the guy wanted to sign Nathan up for a year. They finally came to an agreement whereby Nathan paid for three months now and would pay the balance in May.

One day at a time, Munch thought.

Chapter 14

$$\Longrightarrow$$

That night, Munch gave Rico Chacón's number to Nathan. The two kids were sitting on the couch watching a show called *Family Ties*. Asia let Nathan hold the "cartooner," which had been Munch's and Asia's word for the remote control for as long as either of them could remember. Asia absorbed the show with her jaw dropped open. Nathan seemed equally enthralled.

Munch had scrubbed her hands raw, put on makeup, and sprayed her throat with Charlie perfume. She had on boots, which she wore outside her jeans, and a sheer polka-dot blouse under her bomber jacket.

When she bent down to kiss Asia good-bye, the little girl wrinkled her nose.

"You don't smell like you."

Munch was a little surprised, never thinking of herself as hav-

ing a particular scent. She imagined it was most likely petro-
leum-based.

"You don't like my perfume?" she asked. "Doesn't it smell like
flowers?"

Asia waved her hand in front of her face. "It's kinda strong."

"You're hurting my feelings," Munch said, imitating Asia's
I'm-about-to-cry voice.

Asia pretended to faint into the cushions. "Somebody open a
window."

"I like it," Nathan said, shoving her shoulder playfully.

"Thank you. I'm glad to see someone in this house has some
manners."

Asia coughed by way of answer.

Munch squeezed Asia's toes. "I'll see you all later."

She arrived at Rico's at eight-thirty.

He answered his door barefoot, smelling of warm soap. She
hoped he would kiss her right there, under his porch light, in
front of God and everybody. Instead he pulled her inside and
shut the door. Then the kisses started. They barely spoke for the
first hour.

Several more hours passed, until finally they parted—each
lying spread-eagle on the bed, the bedsheets in a hopeless tangle.
She expected the mirror on the closet to be dulled by their steam.

Munch's clothes lay in a heap on the floor. Traffic on the street
had quieted to the occasional car, the buses having stopped running at midnight. She glanced at the clock on his nightstand,
shocked to see it was after one.

She rolled on her side and snuggled into him.

"Tell me something you're ashamed of," she said. Her hand
rested on his bare chest. His heart sped up a beat, even though
his breathing stopped for a moment.

"Where did that come from?"

"You told me once you'd done things, things you weren't proud of. Tell me one."

He gripped her fingers and squeezed gently. His eyes were on the ceiling. "Okay," he said after a few seconds. "There was this one time, when I was on patrol, I did a traffic stop on this kid. He gave me his license, but I forgot to give it back to him. A week later I see the same kid, and I pull him over again. This time I give him a ticket for driving without a license. About a month goes by, maybe more. I see the same kid, only now the ticket has gone to warrant, so I arrest him."

"That's it?"

"Pretty shitty, don't you think?"

"I guess." She twirled the hair that grew in the cleft of his pecs. There was a glass of now-melted ice on the nightstand. He had brought the cubes in earlier and used them to trace the outlines of her overheated body. She didn't ask him where he'd learned that trick.

She always felt as if she was holding her breath around him. The tension was close to unbearable. There were times she almost envied his ex-wife. At least she knew where she stood with him.

"Now you," he said.

The first thing that came to mind blocked out everything else and of course it was the very thing she couldn't tell him—probably ever. When all was said and done he was an officer of the court and her confession would put him in an impossible position. She didn't want to do that to either of them. Finally she shoved that one memory aside and thought of something to share—an experience of equal value, equal depth, equal candor. "It was a work thing. I've got this nice young rich couple that comes in. She's beautiful; he just got promoted to president of the company."

"What's the company?"

"I don't know, but she has a gray-market Mercedes, and he has a Porsche." She pronounced it as a one-syllable word. It sounded too snooty the other way. Pretentious. "Anyhow, her air conditioning went out. She needed a hose, and it was a dealer item."

"Which means?"

"No after-market manufacturer. You're pretty much stuck going to Mercedes and paying their price. We double whatever our cost is when we rebill. Carlos was doing the work and he told me the cost of the part so I could call the lady and sell the job. Only he gave me the list cost, and I thought he was giving me the wholesale price. So I double it and tell the lady this astronomical amount it's going to take to fix her car.

"Her husband calls me, and I explain that those hoses are expensive, and what are you going to do. He gives me the go-ahead. I knew he would. He wasn't going to let his wife run around without air-conditioning.

"I realized the mistake while I still had time to correct it, but I never did. I keep telling myself that I'll make it up to the lady on another job."

"You can't tell her now," he said. "I don't think Lou would be very happy about giving them a refund."

"The real truth is I don't want them to know I cheated them."

"It was an honest mistake. These things happen everywhere." Case closed, his tone said.

She rolled on her back, feeling alone.

"You cold?" he asked.

Before she could respond, he took her face in both his hands and kissed her deeply. His tongue was insistent, demanding, and she answered him in kind until he was the first to pull away.

"Just checking," he said.

"Still here," she managed to say.

He lifted his head and looked at the clock on his nightstand. "You hungry?"

She giggled. "Starved."

"C'mon," he said, pulling her to her feet.

Rico walked across the living room naked, moonlight reflecting on his damp skin. He seemed as comfortable with his clothes off as on. She slipped on his T-shirt, rich with the scent of his sweat, and followed him to the kitchen.

She knew she'd follow him anywhere. *Resolution number one thousand and eight: Get to know a guy before you screw him. Sex shouldn't be one of your screening devices to see if you like him, especially if he's as good a lover as Rico.* Not that she believed he was this good with anyone else. What they had was personal chemistry like none she'd ever experienced. She saw it in his face too. The way he looked at her with the same mixture of surprise and wonder.

A woman could lose herself easily for that payoff at the end of the day—overlook things she shouldn't. Once, at a women's stag AA meeting, they all started talking about orgasms. A few of the women confessed that they didn't understand what the big deal was, and they were looked upon with sympathy. Munch asked for a show of hands and discovered that a huge majority of those who had had orgasms during sex were still with the man responsible.

Passing the plate-glass window in the living room, she caught a glimpse of her hair. It was teased into twice its usual volume, curled by hours of sawing against first the pillows, then the mattress, the carpet, and finally back up on the bed again. The skin on her back and butt glowed warmly with rug rash. She imagined his knees felt the same.

Rico opened the refrigerator and pulled out a plate of roast chicken.

"I responded to an armed robbery call this one time at a chicken place on El Cajon." He tore off a chunk of white meat and offered it to her. "We got there as one of the guys was running out the back. He pulled out a gun. I pulled out mine and fired. Afterward, I went up to make sure he was dead. I pulled his mask back and saw his face. I wished I'd never done that." He stood there for a minute, lost in the memory.

Then he asked, "You ever have food poisoning?"

She thought a minute. She'd been dope-sick enough times and was told that was close. "Yeah."

"That's what I felt like for two weeks afterward. I still dream about it."

Munch walked over to the sink, ripped two paper towels off the roll on the dispenser, and handed him one. What she really wanted to do was to step right into him, to be absorbed by him.

Rico tore off a drumstick and bit into it.

"Is that another thing you're ashamed of?" she asked.

He looked at her and she watched that change take place, the stony expression that hardened his features when he went into cop mode.

"Not ashamed, no."

"But something you wished had never happened."

"I tell myself the guy was a punk."

"I know, you had to do it." What she really thought was that some people needed killing. He probably would agree with her, but she didn't think he'd be comfortable with her saying it first.

Attitudes like that don't make for good wife material. She realized she had put on her saleswoman hat, but she was selling a product whose qualities she could merely guess at. Her only guide was to ask herself, *What would Caroline St. John say?*

He put the chicken away without asking her if she wanted more. "C'mon, we need some sleep or we'll be dead meat tomorrow."

Head on his pillow, his arms holding her, she closed her eyes reluctantly. The minutes they spent together were precious. She had never been so unleashed in bed, nor had such a hungry, innovative lover. She lived to drain him, to make him spend it all on her so he'd have nothing left for his other girlfriend, that Kathy chick. She hated to waste any part of the night with him on sleep. Now she propped herself up on an elbow so that she was facing him in the dark.

"When Nathan was little, like about four or five, we were all out partying one night."

"Nathan?"

"The kid who's staying with me."

"Oh, right, him." Rico took no pains to hide his disapproval.

"You haven't even met this kid."

"I don't have to and I don't want to."

This attitude of his, his complete confidence that he had a situation sized up and was accurate in his judgment, was at times appealing, but more often frustrating. A lot of cops she knew— well, the two anyway—seemed to have this quality. Mace St. John evaluated people quickly and definitively. He was usually right, which didn't help when she found herself on the other end of the argument, trying to prove that people changed sometimes or deserved a second chance. There was an Italian expression for it: *testa dura.* Hard head.

"So you were all out partying . . ." Rico prompted.

"Yeah. This is his mom, Deborah; Asia's daddy, Sleaze John; and some other guy, I can't even remember now."

"Deborah's date?" Rico asked.

She grinned. "Probably. She's rarely without a, um, date. Anyway, we drove around all night, looking for parties, whatever, and we wound up in some house in Tujunga. We all had to crash on this mattress in the garage. I'll never forget Nathan's little voice saying, 'Mom, I'm hungry.' We didn't have anything, no money, no food, the car was out of gas. We didn't even know where we were. Deborah said, 'Go to sleep, son, and dream about food.'

"The really pathetic part is that we all thought that was hilarious. Everybody but Boogie."

"Who was Boogie?"

"Nathan. That's what we used to call him back then. His daddy was a musician."

"Where's this guy now? Why isn't he taking care of his kid?"

"He's dead."

"How about other family?"

"I feel like I'm his family." Munch realized her tone had grown defensive.

"But you're not. When's his mom coming back?"

"I don't know. She's not somebody to count on. I talked to her on the phone last night. Nathan might be eligible for some Social Security benefits."

"What does that have to do with you?"

"She needs affidavits from people who knew her and Nathan's dad, knew they were together and that he was the daddy."

"You don't have the time to be hunting down ghosts from her past."

"I can ask a few questions." She pulled away from him, annoyed that he thought he knew what she did and did not have time for.

"So you want me to run the father's name through the system?"

"Won't you get in trouble?"

"Let me worry about that."

"I think he got busted once in the early seventies, but it was just for pot."

"If you know when and where he went to trial," Rico said, "the court transcripts would be a matter of public record. They would probably yield all sorts of information. It's all available to you as a private citizen. Actually, you don't need me there."

Yeah, she thought, *but just once I'd like to do something with you in public.* She got out of bed and gathered her clothes.

"Can't you stay?" He reached out a hand to stroke her thigh before she pulled her pants up. "I hate to have you out on the streets this late."

She sat on the edge of the bed and pulled on her boots. "I don't want Asia to wake up with me not there."

"That reminds me," he said, plumping up the pillow behind his head. His features were soft in the dark, making him look young and deceptively vulnerable. "My daughter wants to meet you."

"She does? When? I'd love to."

"I'll set it up and let you know."

He rolled out of bed with a grunt, pulled on a pair of sweat-pants, and walked her out to her car. She kissed him good-bye and drove away happy, thinking how it was a definite move in the right direction to meet his daughter.

She was very aware that she hadn't mentioned Jane's murder or St. John's visits. Partly she held her peace because she sensed tension between the two cops whenever one of their names was mentioned to the other. Why the two most important men in her life seemed to be at odds was a cruel cosmic complication. But then, even Lou didn't get overjoyed at the sight of either Mace or Rico. She wrote it off as misdirected machismo and tried not to get too frustrated at their childishness.

She also didn't want to get into a big question-and-answer session with Rico. The lies by omission she had going on with Mace were bad enough.

She'd like to see Jane's murderer brought to justice, but did that have to mean dredging up the details of events better left forgotten? Maybe she was just being paranoid, but that horrible episode had linked a group of four people in a knot of complicity for nearly a decade, and now the second of two of those people was dead. That still left two little Indians who had a lot to lose.

The program even had a provision in the twelve steps to cover this contingency. Step nine was the amends step, and like all of the others was written as a suggestion only. In step eight, you made a list of all persons you've harmed. In step nine you were urged to make direct amends to such people wherever possible, except when to do so would injure them or others.

A spiritual program with loopholes, you had to love it.

When the twelve steps were written decades ago, the transgressions the founders had had in mind were probably more along the lines of marital infidelity. The confessions of a cheating spouse would only make the spouse who had been cheated on feel worse. Was she wrong in how she applied that step to this situation? If she told all she knew, people would be hurt. There was no statute of limitations for murder.

As she drove away, she absently pawed at her shirt pocket as if searching for a pack of cigarettes. This was especially weird since she'd been quit for years. She assumed she was over them. Maybe she was wrong. Maybe that addiction was just one more wolf snapping at her door, looking to chew her up if she let her guard down.

Chapter 15

$=\!\!\!=\!\!\!/$

Saturday morning was St. John's honey-do day. Caroline had on her yellow rubber gloves and was scrubbing the bathroom. St. John's duty was trash and anything that could be washed clean with the hose. He adjusted the nozzle to its smallest aperture and aimed the stream toward the eaves of the house where cobwebs gathered. The pleasure he derived from directing the water's force had to be a guy thing.

"Hey, master blaster," Caroline called from the doorway.

He kinked the hose. "Yeah, hon."

"I need your big, strong muscles in here."

He smiled and flexed his arm. "Yes, ma'am. A gal in need is what we tough guys are all about."

"Impress me with the sofa. I'm vacuuming."

St. John shut off the hose and followed his wife into the house. They pulled the couch away from the wall together. Caroline bent down to work the pipe attachment in the corner. St. John grabbed her ass. "Not bad for an old married lady."

She pushed his hand away. Her rubber glove on his skin brought up unwanted images of the dead woman, Jane Ferrar. He had not been able to learn any more about her. His queries had not turned up friends or a work history. There were relatives back East, but they hadn't had contact with her for years and were not stepping forth to claim the remains. Jane Ferrar had been a ghost, it seemed, long before she died.

Sensing his mood, Caroline shut off the vacuum. "What's up?"

"Just thinking about something."

The phone rang and Caroline went in the kitchen to answer it.

"Hi, kiddo. The eighteenth? We'll be there."

"Who's that?" he asked.

"Munch," she said, not bothering to cover the mouthpiece.

"Does she want to talk to me?"

Caroline listened for a moment and then shook her head no. St. John went back in the living room and pushed the furniture back against the wall. Caroline was saying, "Uh-huh" and "That sounds nice" and "Just be careful."

St. John wanted to pick up the extension and listen in, but had to content himself with standing near the doorway. When he heard her hang up, he hastened outside.

She came to the back door a moment later looking thoughtful.

"Is she all right?" he asked.

"I hope so. Rico's taking her to meet his daughter."

"On the eighteenth?"

"No, that's Asia's play. Next month. She's getting us tickets."

"Sounds fun." St. John liked kids in theory. Asia's occasional visits, his and Caroline's attendance at the kid's various performances and graduations suited his comfort level. St. John had been an only child and Caroline was the oldest female sibling of a large family. Helping care for the brood most of her young life had cured her of the desire to have her own children. It was not a subject they argued about.

On the way to Nunn's retirement party, St. John told his wife about Cassiletti and what he'd revealed about himself.

"We're lucky," she said, reaching for his hand.

He kissed her fingertips, loving the delicate softness of her. "I think that every day."

"I hope Munch isn't setting herself up for a fall with this Rico."

"She's a big girl."

"Big girls get hurt too."

They didn't speak again until they arrived at the restaurant. He liked that about them, that they could be comfortable with each other's silence, didn't have to intrude or be privy to every single thought.

The party was in a private room at the Billingsly Restaurant on Sawtelle, a favorite haunt for Westside cops.

Art Becker and his wife were in attendance; so were Rico and Kathy. Half the cops there were with different partners than they'd had at the last shindig. Caroline pointed out with arched eyebrows that Rico didn't treat Kathy like some soon-to-be ex, and Kathy in turn seemed rather proprietary, picking lint off of Rico's jacket, and generally giving the evil eye to other young women at the party.

"I'm going to snub them," Caroline announced.

"You do that," St. John said, smiling, knowing that in his wife's case "snubbing them" meant she would not offer to cook them a three-course dinner on the next available Saturday night.

They probably wouldn't notice her version of a cold shoulder.

The men gravitated to the bar, and Caroline joined a group of women. As St. John walked past, he heard one of the women say, "I love my husband, but . . ."

He didn't need to hear the rest. He stopped to pay his respects to Bob Nunn, the guest of honor. Nunn was holding court from a bar stool. He had a highball glass in his hand that he was using like a baton to punctuate his words.

A group of five middle-aged cops that St. John knew by sight if not by name was Nunn's audience.

"In English," he was saying. "In my day, the signs were all in English. My parents didn't come to this country and expect everyone to speak Russian. No, they learned the language. They assimilated."

"Shut up, you fucking Commie," a red-faced narc from Parker Center shot back good-naturedly.

"Hey, am I right? Tell me I'm wrong. Fucking spics are taking over the city. Five more years they'll be running everything."

"Yeah, Bob, that's right." St. John clamped a hand on his shoulder and brought his face in close. "Couldn't do worse, could they?"

"Hey, St. John." Nunn pulled him into a boozy hug and kissed his cheek wetly. "How the hell are you?"

St. John patted his back. "Looking good, babe. Let's get some of that chow."

"Nah, I'm not hungry. Here, have a drink."

"In a minute."

Nunn swung his drink hand across the crowded room. His eyes moistened. "We gave it a good run, didn't we?"

"Sure did, Bob. You done good."

"Not all the time. Couldn't get them all." Another drink appeared on the bar behind him. Nunn grabbed at it but missed. Half the booze spilled. St. John figured that was just as well. Nunn growled in frustration and pulled a bent cigarette from the pack in his pocket. St. John struck a match and held it steady while the drunk detective homed in on the flame.

"I won't miss it," Nunn said, his eyes tearing.

"Sure you won't." St. John blew out the match, patted Nunn's shoulder, and moved on. Against the far wall were long tables covered with food. Art Becker had two plates, and was heaping salad on each, balancing them against his substantial gut.

"Where's the beef?" St. John said.

Becker looked up and smiled, transforming his pockmarked face into a mask of creases that all but obliterated his small eyes. He had to be about the ugliest man that ever walked, and St. John knew that Becker used that mug of his to good advantage when he wanted to intimidate a suspect. Becker went out of his way for victims and their families, even bringing them home on occasion. He also had all kinds of outside hobbies. That's what saved him, kept him balanced.

Salvation was a funny thing.

Eight years ago, St. John had had his first conversation with Munch in a biker bar in Venice Beach. Him playing the cop, her his drunken prey. They had talked about redemption then and Munch had said in a tone completely innocent of irony, *Maybe we can save you too.*

The weird thing was he had understood her and had even felt an odd stirring of hope.

"Ahh," Becker said now, "they got me on all this rabbit food. I haven't trusted a fart for five years."

"Tell me about it," St. John said, eyeing a platter of deviled eggs. He envisioned the thick yellow yolk paste coating his arteries.

With a furtive look to his left, Becker sneaked a chunk of cheese into his mouth. "I understand you're looking at a mope named Cyrill McCarthy, street name 'Thor.' "

"Yeah. I caught a homicide of a woman who used to hang with him," St. John said. "Someone beat her to death and dumped her in a storm drain."

Becker shook his head like he was really pained and sighed. St. John wondered what the guy was still doing in homicide. Too much empathy was a bad thing in their business. A little was absolutely necessary.

"I saw the bulletin. You think Cyrill McCarthy is your guy?"

"His name keeps popping up. You know him?"

"Yeah. I always had a sneaking suspicion that he was involved in a triple homicide in the Oakwood Projects ten years ago. We questioned him, some witnesses put a car like his at the scene, but he never broke."

"Wait a minute," St. John said. "Are you talking about the Ghost Town Three?" The killing of three black men in an apartment building in Venice's black section, a little Watts-by-the-Sea, had been impressively gory, rivaling even the Tate–La Bianca murder scene, but without the fancy zip code. As in the Manson tribe killings, the murder weapons had been knives. St. John remembered looking at the photographs and being amazed at the sheer volume of congealed blood in the bedroom, ponds of human gelatin. He saw the image of a blood trail across a wooden hallway in his mind's eye, but couldn't be sure if he was remembering photos from the murder book or confabulating with the help of Stacy Lansford's letter and her description of a murder victim crawling down a hallway with an open jugular.

"Shit," he said, popping a naked carrot stick into his mouth, "that takes me back. We were up to our eyeballs in gang wars. The All Black Shoreline Crips versus the V-Thirteen Homeboys. I thought the wisdom on that one was that it was a turf dispute. McCarthy is a white guy, a biker. What makes you think he was messing around in Ghost Town?"

"We found scales and bags of cut at the scene. It was probably a dope rip-off."

That made sense, St. John thought. *Even the most color-conscious doper would overlook race when it came to copping a fix.* "How'd he do in a lineup?"

"We never got that far. Our witness became unavailable. The case fell apart, and we got busy with other investigations."

"I've come across something you're going to want to read," St. John said, "another case involving McCarthy where the witness disappeared. He bragged about having a hand in some murders when threatening a woman he was involved with. I'll bring it by Monday and take a look at the Ghost Town Three murder book."

Across the room, Rico Chacón said something to Kathy and she laughed loudly, too loudly, St. John thought. He found Caroline's eyes, and her expression told him that she had noticed as well.

"How's your partner working out?" St. John asked Becker.

"We're not together anymore."

"Is that a good thing?"

Becker grew wary. "Chacón puts in the hours. He's been on the rotation, working cold cases. We still talk. That's why McCarthy's name rang a bell."

"Hey, look, I wouldn't ask, but a friend of mine has been, uh, getting involved with him and I'd hate to see her get hurt."

"The mechanic? What is it, Munch?"

"Yeah, Munch."

"She helped us out on the Summers's double homicide last month. Brave girl."

"Yeah, she's got heart all right."

"What have you heard about Chacón?"

"Something about him accepting gratuities from the wrong kind of people."

Becker's face puckered as if he'd bit into a raw olive. "We got deputy chiefs flying to Vegas with their families for three-thousand-dollar weekends—all expenses paid." He bent his nose sideways with a stubby finger and gave St. John a knowing look. "But a cop gets a few front-row seats at a middleweight bout and people get all shook up."

Becker looked over to where his wife was sitting at one of the booths sipping a soda and shifting her weight. St. John had heard that she had health problems, something degenerative in her nerves and very painful. It was rare to see either of them out socially. She was no beauty either, but they made each other happy as far as he could see. They had been high school sweethearts, married young, and stayed married. He respected that.

Becker heaped two quivering mounds of Jell-O onto his plates and pointed his body toward his wife, giving the feeling of protective hovering from across the room. "Look, Chacón's a good guy, he just has a habit of doing things that get him in trouble."

"What kind of trouble?"

"Administrative mostly. He does what he thinks is the right thing. That doesn't always agree with the big boys. This last stunt is probably going to buy him some freeway therapy."

Freeway therapy, St. John thought, *Admin.'s way of sticking it to you.* You took a wrong step and you found yourself working down at the harbor when you lived fifty miles away in Simi Valley, or pulling nothing but night shifts. Transfers like that seriously fucked up your quality of life. The brass justified such actions by saying that rotation kept a guy from getting too settled—read that complacent—in any one job. A cop had a right to his rank was the message, but not necessarily his duty assignment. And guess who had the biggest gun?

"Who'd he piss off?" St. John asked.

"Let's just say the boy has ideas how the job should be done and sometimes those ideas lead to not the best decisions. Your friend better keep her eyes open."

St. John nodded. This was advice he'd learned too late to give himself. Sometimes you see, but you don't see. You hear, but you don't hear. Love had a way of making a person squint away the rough edges, ignore the evidence. He looked at Caroline across the room. As much as he loved his wife, he would never be blind to the signs again. No way. Temptations were everywhere, but they didn't need to be indulged.

Kathy dabbed at Chacón's mouth with a napkin. Chacón looked annoyed, but accepted her kiss. *Guy must have a twenty-four-karat dick,* St. John thought.

I hope he gets transferred to Cucamonga.

Chapter 16

⟱

E arly Sunday morning, Rico called Munch. "Is today good?" he asked.

"For what?"

"Meeting my kid."

"Sure, except that Asia has a rehearsal in Santa Monica."

"She's in another play?"

"A musical, if you can believe it. *Peter Pan.* She's going to be Tinker Bell." Munch lowered her voice. "She was so thrilled to have a starring part, I don't think she's noticed yet that Tinker Bell never speaks or sings." Munch suspected that this was a huge factor in the casting director's decision.

"So can you get away?"

"Sure, I don't need to stay. She's more comfortable on a stage than in her bedroom, and she knows all the grown-ups at the theater." Munch had planned to hit an AA meeting while Asia learned her moves, but missing one wouldn't kill her. "What time do you want to go?"

"I'll pick you up at eleven. We'll all go out to breakfast."

She hung up the phone as Nathan walked into the kitchen yawning. "What are you doing today?" she asked.

He opened the refrigerator and studied its contents. "I thought I'd go see my grandma."

"Your grandma?" Deb's mama had died a few years ago. He had to be talking about Walter's mother. "Where does she live?"

"In Compton."

Munch suppressed a shudder, glad that he was planning on going in daylight.

Nathan pulled out the carton of milk with the photograph of a little girl on the side and the caption "Have you seen me?" Munch opened the cabinet where she kept the cereal and got him a bowl and a spoon. He selected the Cocoa Puffs and filled his bowl to the brim.

"That's great. Can I meet her too?"

"Why?"

"Because I'm interested in your life, your family." She had also made her own inquiries with the Social Security department, but before she discussed what she'd learned with Nathan, she hoped to enlist his grandma's support.

He grunted and filled his mouth with cereal. She wasn't sure if this meant sounds like a plan, no way, or we'll see.

"What's her name?"

"Doleen Franklin." Franklin was the last name Nathan used on the insurance forms and car registration. He said it came from his daddy's side.

She went back into her bedroom and opened her closet. Asia

was on Munch's bed watching cartoons, but swiveled around to watch her mother.

"What are you doing?" Asia asked.

"Trying to figure out what to wear."

Munch's choices were limited. Jeans, uniforms, and two dresses.

"What's wrong with what you have on?" Asia asked, coming to stand beside her.

"Rico's coming over and taking me out to breakfast."

Asia pulled on the hem of one of Munch's two dresses. "How about this one?"

The dress was one of Munch's not-so-subtle, going-to-get-laid-tonight numbers. A slinky wraparound with a hemline that barely covered her ass.

"I don't think so, honey. Not for a Sunday morning."

"It's not like you're going to church," Asia said, the slightest hint of reprimand in her voice. Asia was probably the only kid in the world who nagged her mother to attend Mass. Munch put her off, explaining that she didn't need a special day or place to talk to God. She used the same argument for New Year's resolutions or giving up something for Lent. If you needed to change something in your life, you didn't wait for some date on the calendar. People died waiting to change.

"Screw it," Munch said. "I'm good enough as I am."

"Of course you are," Asia said.

Munch looked at her and laughed. She hadn't meant to voice her thoughts out loud.

"Now," Asia said, "what should I wear?"

Munch dropped Asia at the theater, made sure another mother would keep an eye on her, and was standing in front of her small wooden house when Rico pulled up at five minutes to eleven. She was wondering how the house would look painted a light gray, with a dark gray trim. Her roses had put on buds and she was anticipating a bumper crop.

Rico was wearing his ever-present sunglasses and an open-collared white shirt that showed off the St. Christopher medal on his dark chest. His metallic green '66 Chevy Impala had a fresh coat of wax. He was very proud of his low rider with its custom coil springs, low-profile mags, and wide racing tires, which brought the car just inches from the ground. Munch secretly thought the look was ridiculous. Why screw up perfectly good suspension?

It was a measure of her love that she deigned to ride in the thing. The truth was, she had already bottomed out in the vehicle department. Her last boyfriend, Garret Dimond, had owned a Vespa, and she had straddled its seat a few times for local jaunts, hiding her face in Garret's back when a real motorcycle passed them. Garret had even worn a helmet. He'd embossed his blood type with a Labelmaker on red self-stick tape and stuck it on the oversized Plexiglas head bucket. *Oh, please.* As if he couldn't just stand up if he saw trouble coming and let the scooter proceed without him.

"Where are we going?" Munch asked as she settled into the tuck-and-roll upholstered bucket seat and reluctantly fastened her seat belt.

"Downtown. Angelica's mother had to work today and dropped her off at the restaurant."

"How old was she when you got divorced?"

"Eight. Sylvia got pregnant when we were in high school. My dad said I didn't have to deal with it, that I could go back to Mexico. We still have family there."

He pronounced it Meh-he-ko. His English was largely unaccented until he said a word with a Spanish origin. Sometimes she asked him to speak to her in his first language. She didn't understand the words but she loved the exotic roll of his consonants, the way his mouth moved to shape his vowels.

"I couldn't leave her like that," he said, "to go through it alone. I had to be responsible."

She loved that about him. His main parenting rule, he told her once, was never to make a promise he couldn't keep. It seemed to her that he also made that a life rule.

Rico's hand rested on the gear shift. She ran a finger over his knuckles. "Nathan is trying to be responsible. I wonder if he and Angelica would—"

"Don't even finish that sentence," Rico said, his mouth tightening in anger.

"Why? I was just saying—"

"This guy's already taking advantage of you, and now you want to sic him on my daughter. And you want to know what my problem is?"

"Nobody's taking advantage of me. I make my own decisions of what I'll put up with." She looked at him pointedly.

"You want me to turn around?"

For a second she was tempted to just say yes, to say something like, "You know what? Fuck this and fuck you. I didn't get sober to put up with this shit." But she waited, thinking the words over before she let them escape her mouth. Sure, it would make her feel good for the moment: powerful, righteous, and all that. But she'd learned long ago the difference between reacting and choosing her actions, and how consequences lingered long after the heat of the moment passed.

Her sponsor, Ruby, had also spoken the truth when she said

that Munch knew how to leave a relationship—to pack her shit and storm off in a huff. That was the easy thing to do. It was staying that was the challenge. And how do you know when it's worth the effort? she'd ask. Ruby said no one could answer that for anyone, you just had to wait and see.

They were quiet as they jumped on the Santa Monica Freeway eastbound. Munch turned on the radio and found a station that played rock 'n' roll. After a few minutes, Rico picked up her hand and kissed it. Goose bumps erupted down her left leg. She caught a whiff of his musky cologne.

"You look nice today," he said. "I like that color on you."

She made a mental note. Purple.

Rico had arranged for them to meet his daughter at a Mexican restaurant on Olvera Street, in the city's oldest district. Pueblo de la Reina de Los Angeles, every Southern Californian schoolkid learned, had been founded in 1781, and its oldest street had been converted into a Mexican marketplace in 1930.

Rico badged his way into a parking space at Parker Center. As they walked the two blocks down Los Angeles Street, he took her arm and positioned her to the inside lane of the sidewalk, taking the side exposed to traffic. The freeway bridge overlooked murals painted for last summer's '84 Olympics, depicting L.A.'s diverse culture. Munch happily noted that they were unmarred by graffiti. Musicians wearing large black sombreros, tuxedo pants, and bolero jackets were setting up in the gazebo as Munch and Rico cut across the Plaza.

"I came here when I was little once," Munch said, "with my mom."

"We should come back on Cinco de Mayo," he said. "It really jumps then."

Munch smiled so hard she had to keep her face averted from

him. May was three months down the road, and he was talking as if of course they would be together.

A large wooden cross, reminiscent of the early Mission days, marked the entrance to Olvera Street. Two-story buildings of whitewashed adobe and ancient red brick flanked the cobbled street. Vendors hawked their wares from freestanding palm-frond-thatched-roof wooden stalls. Everything from embroidered peasant blouses and square-hemmed guayabera shirts to dashboard saints and Aztec calendars was offered in a dizzy array of color and smells. Rico and Munch stopped at one of the crowded booths. Munch bought three delicate strings of beads for his daughter and had them gift-wrapped with colored tissue paper.

She didn't want to arrive empty-handed.

She also bought Asia a ceramic bull piggy bank covered with bright pink flocking. Using white glue, the vendor wrote Asia on the side in cursive and sprinkled the name with silver glitter. Rico dropped the first quarter into the slot on the bull's withers.

The restaurant where they were meeting Angelica was festooned with weathered Christmas garlands and Mexican flags. Piñatas and crossed wooden mariachi rattles, painted bright colors, hung from the ceiling. Bullfighting posters and multihued serape blankets covered the walls. A Mexican trumpeter blew sweet notes for the diners. The music made Munch think of grand outdoor parties and women in black lace shawls with high combs in their hair.

She spotted Rico's daughter immediately, seated at one of the rough-hewn tables near the indoor fountain. Angelica had his eyes and jawline—a nice-looking kid, not gorgeous. At fifteen, she was still growing into her looks, waiting for her complexion to clear, her hair to make up its mind. Her skin was the creamy café au lait color of a half-breed, a term Munch was trying to stop using out loud.

Angelica rose to greet them. She was stick thin and dressed in skintight jeans and a scoop-necked sweater. Rico hugged her and kissed her cheek. She pulled away and studied Munch.

Munch smiled and waited for Rico to make the introductions. She wanted to hear some glowing recommendation, some indication of their status, but Rico just said, "You want coffee?"

"Sure." Munch thrust her gift into Angelica's hands. "This is for you."

"Thank you." Angelica smiled politely and left it unopened in front of her. Asia would have torn the wrapping paper with her teeth. There was something sneaky about this kid, Munch felt. She was holding back her true feelings. *Give the kid a break,* Munch then thought, *she's only fifteen. She probably has hundreds of true feelings a day and they all slam into each other.*

Munch and the girl took chairs on opposite sides of the rectangular table. Rico hesitated a moment and then sat down beside Munch, facing his daughter. He slid the paper place mat toward himself and almost overturned his water. In reaching to catch the glass, he nearly knocked it down the other way.

Angelica arched a plucked eyebrow, but made no other comment.

"So," Munch said, hearing the word echo inanely in her head. She clenched her hands together under the table. "What grade are you in?"

Angelica laced her hands loosely on the tabletop, showed her perfect teeth, and said, "I'm a freshman."

Munch had to think a minute, she could never keep those grades straight. Freshman came before sophomore, she was pretty sure, but did it mean the first year of high school or second to last? She would have it all figured out by the time Asia came of age. Munch put her own arms on the table, rocking it with a clunk that rattled the flatware. She grabbed a napkin from one of the other tables, folded it, and leaned down to jam it between the gap of floor and table leg.

When she resurfaced, Angelica was staring at her.

"It was driving me crazy," Munch said, feeling she had failed somehow, wishing someone would compliment her.

The waitress arrived. Munch asked for a quesadilla, Rico ordered huevos rancheros, Angelica requested a salad with the dressing on the side, no avocado or cheese.

They made some small talk about the drive there and the weather. When Angelica spoke, she looked only at her father.

"I like your dad," Munch said, feeling the need to lob a grenade, to get the real conversation started.

"Really?" Angelica leaned over to Munch and looked her directly in the eye. "Let me ask you something. If your dad and my dad were both in a burning building, who would you save first?"

Rico said, "Angie."

Flower George in a burning building—now, there was an image. "You might want to pick a different scenario," Munch said. "My dad's dead already."

Angelica's eyes brightened and she finally dropped her fakey little smile. "I'm sorry," she said in a small voice.

Munch considered telling her the whole truth, that the death of her father had not been a bad thing. The day Munch saw Flower George off to hell was her liberation day and literally the first day of the rest of her life because it marked her first day of sobriety. For her own serenity, she had released her anger over him, and now eight years later, only thought of him once a week, usually following a dream where they still lived together. Sometimes she was sober in those dreams, sometimes she had gone back to the needle. She even had dreams that she had never really gotten sober at all. Ruby said that that was the part of her subconscious mind that couldn't believe it was true.

The food arrived. Angelica stirred her salad. Rico took a bite of his eggs and made an umm-good sound. He cut off a section of tortilla and egg, put it on his fork, and offered it to his daughter.

"No thanks."

"Just try it," he said, "it's good." He kept the food at her lips until she relented and accepted it.

For the next few minutes, they all ate—chewing long and silently. Finally, Rico broke the silence.

"Angie, wasn't there something else?"

The teenager slipped her aren't-I-cute mask in place. "My dad says you have a limo business?"

Munch took a sip of water. "That's right."

"A bunch of us are going in together to hire a limo for the Madonna concert?" It wasn't a question, just a young girl's inflection. "We want an eight-passenger, brand-new, nineteen eighty-five or -six, white stretch. But we just need it to take us to the concert and back again, so we don't want to pay for all the in-between time."

Munch wondered if this was all Rico had said about her, that she owned a limo business. "It doesn't work that way. The driver has to stay in the parking lot during the concert. If he left and tried to come back when the concert let out, he'd never make it in past the traffic. Besides, my car only seats six in the back."

"Two could ride up front, couldn't they?" Rico asked.

"I'm not sure anyone would like that arrangement," Munch said, annoyed at Rico for jumping in, knowing that chances were good that she would be the driver. She sure as hell didn't want to spend an hour up front with two snotty, complaining kids. She got enough of that at prom time. "Besides, my car is silver and she wants white."

"I'll have to check with my friends," Angelica said.

"The car's not brand new either," Munch said.

Rico looked at her sideways, then back at his daughter. "You ready?"

"I need to use the bathroom."

Rico half stood when his daughter got up and then nudged Munch, saying under his breath, "Go with her."

Munch stood, wondering if he thought they would bond in the ladies' room.

"Make sure she doesn't throw up."

Munch accompanied Angelica to the bathroom and went into the stall next to hers. Angelica's shoes pointed the correct direction the entire time.

When they got back to the table, the waitress brought the check and a take-out carton. Rico threw down a twenty and said, "Let's go."

Munch still had coffee left in her cup, but she didn't argue.

They had to walk single file through the marketplace crowds. Munch took the lead, with Angelica in the middle, and Rico bringing up the rear. They reached the Plaza, and Rico caught up to them. Wrought-iron benches, shaded by large trees, faced the raised stage of the Plaza's central gazebo.

"Did you know that Native Americans were sold as slaves here?" Angelica asked as they picked their way across the time-worn stones, her lips pursed in disgust at the couples taking advantage of the romantic setting.

"No, I didn't," Munch said.

"You don't hear about people having picnics at Auschwitz."

"*Viva la raza,*" Munch muttered under her breath.

Rico broke away from them and walked over to where a homeless man was sitting cross-legged on the sidewalk, his back against the brick wall of the old firehouse. He was staring at traffic, occasionally lifting a dirty index finger as if to address the cars passing him by.

Munch studied his clothes, dark with street grime and little more than rags. You could see bits of filthy feet through his disintegrating tennis shoes. He was the kind of guy emergency room nurses described as a DPOH: Disgusting Piece of Humanity. She was sorry he'd ended up this way but didn't want to get anywhere near him.

"Hey, *Mosca,*" Rico said, "gimme a dollar."

The homeless man looked shocked and then grinned. Rico handed him the carton of leftovers. "*La Mosca*" saluted a thanks.

When they got back to the car at Parker Center, Rico told his kid to climb in the backseat. Munch was relieved, having had an image, and then discarding it, of herself yelling, "Shotgun."

They drove several miles north on the Hollywood Freeway to Echo Park. The light poles of Dodger Stadium were visible on the right; the towering skyscrapers of downtown L.A. loomed in the yellow-gray sky to their left.

Echo Park was a hilly neighborhood of thirties-vintage wooden homes with covered porches and burglar bars on the windows. Rico pulled into the driveway of one of the few houses that was stuccoed. Some kind of tropical plant with leaves like elephant ears dominated the small front yard. Security floodlights were mounted on the roofline. The cement stairs leading to the front door were painted red and matched the trim.

Rico shut off the engine and they all got out.

Rico leaned into the backseat and pulled out a color television still in its carton. Angelica looked at the box and said, "Another one?"

"This one is better," he said, pointing to the printing on the box. "See? It's cable ready, gets fifty-two channels, and you can plug earphones into the side."

"Daaad," she said, rolling her eyes. "There aren't that many channels in the known universe."

Can't she see how pleased he is to be doing this for her? Munch thought. *How can she resist his little-boy enthusiasm?* Rico's countenance darkened; Angelica had ruined the moment for him.

"When I was your age, I didn't even have electricity," he said.

"I know, I know," Angelica said wearily. "Or running water or glass in your windows."

Munch looked at Rico. Even though this story was old hat to Angelica, it was the first Munch had heard it. It struck her how little she really knew about this man, how all her images of him were more visceral than visual.

Rico lifted the television easily.

"C'mon," he told Munch, and the three of them approached the house. Angelica went first with her key. Munch walked behind Rico, enjoying the way the muscles of his broad back shifted under his shirt. Angelica's room was at the end of the hallway, past a living room full of overstuffed furniture flanked by amphitheater-sized speakers. The couch faced a large console television with a VCR.

He brought the television into her room and set it down on a dresser in front of a wall covered with a collage of shirtless young men with guitars and pouty looks. Munch looked at the angst-ridden performers and wondered what it was about them that adolescents related to and how the kids could so neatly disregard the fact that most of these boy wonders were making big bucks and had nothing to cry about.

In her heart Munch knew that money wasn't everything, but it sure seemed to be everything else.

Shelves held an astounding array of stereo equipment. Angelica already had a television and Atari. Near her closet was a car stereo still in its box. The car stereo and TV carton were both stamped with the name PASCOE APPLIANCES. It occurred to Munch that Rico was overcompensating.

He slit the cellophane tape across the top of the carton.

Munch sneaked a look through Angelica's open bathroom door and was overwhelmed at the variety and number of beauty products amassed on the vanity. It was clear that they were well used. Half of the bottles were empty. Munch had yet to use up a bottle of nail polish or a can of hair spray, and only recently had she had to buy a new tube of lipstick.

"Look at this mess," Rico said, sweeping his hand to encompass it all. He stared in disgust at the hair in the sink, the spray of toothpaste on the mirror. "Just like her mother," he told Munch, not bothering to whisper.

Cheap shot, Munch thought, but she also knew something else in that instant. Sylvia, Angelica's mother, had been the one who wanted out of the marriage.

"You want any help setting this up?" she asked Angelica.

"No," the girl said. "Thank you." The smile was back in place.

"Don't put the box out at the curb," Munch said. "Either fold it up and stuff it in your trash can or throw it away in a Dumpster. Otherwise you're advertising that you have something brand new to steal."

Angelica nodded her head and looked at Munch with something dangerously akin to respect. "I never thought about that. Thanks."

As they drove away, Rico said, "I hate them living there."

"Their house seemed nice," she said.

"It would be nicer in Santa Monica or Palms."

"Would Sylvia move?"

"Her business is downtown, but I'm working on her."

Munch didn't like the sound of that. It took several minutes for her to get her jealousy under control. She couldn't worry about everyone he ever slept with. What if the reverse were true?

She turned to him. "You're sweet."

"What?"

"Giving the food to that bum guy."

"Actually," he said, checking the rearview mirror, "it's not as nice as it looks. When I was growing up, even though we lived in a house my mom built herself, a house with dirt floors and cardboard for wallpaper, we knew we were superior to those people who begged at the border. My mom made like a buck a day making tortillas, but she always had change for the beggars. So you see? Not so noble."

"Where was your dad?"

"He came to America"—he paused and looked at her before adding—"illegally."

Munch shrugged. He'd get no judgment from her.

"He was going to send for us when he got set up, but it took a while. I made money too. In Mexico, they have big dumps of trash. I used to go through them looking for copper, and then I'd haul it to this guy who paid me by the pound. That was hard work for a ten-year-old."

Munch nodded. She knew junkies who used to steal radiators and pipes from work sites and sell them for the copper. She always thought it was a lot of physical labor to go through to steal something.

"Did you go to school?"

"Oh, sure. There were two sessions, morning and afternoon. I went in the afternoon. I was too scared of my mother not to go, even though it cost. Nothing is free in Mexico." He switched lanes aggressively. "My dad used to deliver Sparklett's water before he went North. The cops there stopped him once, wanted their *mordida,* their bribe. My dad said, 'Look, I've got no money.' The cop said, 'Okay, I'll catch you tomorrow.' From then on, my dad had to hide from this guy. This cop got this attitude that my dad owed him."

"He felt entitled," Munch said, sitting up straighter. Entitlement was an interesting concept to her.

"Yeah, it's a mess down there. Fucking bandits. I wouldn't pay it either."

"When did you come North?"

"When I was twelve. My dad got an apartment and sent for all of us. I was blown away when I got here. I couldn't believe this place, the paved streets, the inside toilets. I'd never seen a park before. It was beautiful and free. You could play there all day if you wanted."

"How'd you get from there to being a cop?"

"I used to watch those shows, *Adam-12, Dragnet.* I thought cops were great."

"American cops," she added.

"Right. When I was in high school, I wasn't in a gang, but I used to dress the part." He paused, then chuckled. "One time I was standing there at the school yard with all my little girlfriends and I see these three blurry images across the street. I needed glasses, but I never wore them. Too uncool, you know?"

Munch looked at him in surprise. She was so used to seeing him in his Carerras, it never occurred to her that they were prescription.

"So anyhow, I'm staring and staring, and trying to see who it is. This is something you don't do with gangbangers. If you look at them hard, it's a challenge."

"Mad dogging," Munch said.

He nodded. "So these three guys walk over to me and say, 'Where you from?' Now I got to declare myself. There's three of them, but I'm on the other side of this big fence."

"Surrounded by all your girlfriends."

"Yeah, so I start talking trash, mothers are mentioned, but my machismo is intact. I'm still a big man on my side of the fence. Well, lo and behold, this fence I'm on the other side of has a gate, and this gate isn't locked. Those guys beat me bloody. The one was a big guy, a football player. He kept picking me up and throwing me on the concrete. Every time, these flashes of light would go off in my head and I would pass out, only to come to with them still beating me. I just wanted it to be over. I thought they were going to off me, and I'm looking this guy in the eyes, I can't even talk, but with my eyes I'm saying, 'You don't have to kill me.' "

Munch wondered what all his so-called girlfriends had been doing while this epic ass-kicking was going on.

"The first guy who punched me said, '*Setenta y ocho.*' Seventy-eight, which was his street corner. He was going to kill me for a street corner. About forty-five minutes into the beating, an L unit rolled up."

"What's an L unit?"

"A one-man patrol car. Just his presence made the *cholos* split. The cop didn't even have to get out. I knew then that's what I wanted to be. Plus I was laid up for two weeks recovering, so I had a lot of time to think. I stopped wearing gang attire, started taking school seriously—"

"Got some good glasses," Munch added.

Rico grinned. "You bet your sweet ass."

Munch smiled at the compliment, thinking how the puzzle of Rico was coming together. Now she understood his interest in boxing, why he had worked at it until he excelled.

"And then your girlfriend got pregnant."

He looked at her with an amused smile, perhaps flattered by her chauvinism toward him. "I had a little something to do with that, I think. Anyway, it all worked out. I love being a cop. I've never wanted to do anything else."

She wondered why he looked so sad as he said those words.

He lifted her hand to his lips and kissed it. For a moment she had the paranoid sensation that he was saying good-bye. She had to stop doing that. Hadn't he just taken her to meet his kid?

"Yeah," she said. "I love working on cars. Every day there's something different. There's also that instant gratification of making something broken work."

They got on the freeway. Rico floored the accelerator and the exhaust rumbled from the blown-out glass packs. *At least he had a good stereo system,* she thought, adjusting the volume on his Blaupunkt to override the freeway noise.

She also wished the car had a bench seat so she could snuggle into him. She reached across the console and rubbed the back of his neck. He rolled his head back and sighed with pleasure.

"I'm sorry about that thing with your dad," he said.

"Don't be, it wasn't a loss."

"But, still, she was a jerk to put you on the spot like that."

"She was just being protective, and she's fifteen."

"Tell me about it."

"You never brought me a television," she said playfully.

"There's a reason for that."

She stroked his ear.

"C'mon," she said. "From the look of your kid's room, you must own a share of an electronics store."

He looked at her warily and said, "You don't want to know where that stuff came from."

"Ask me no questions and I'll tell you no lies."

"It's not that."

"No, it's okay," she said. "I got it." Something warned her to say no more.

Chapter 17

⟹

Sunday afternoon, Munch emptied out the pockets of Nathan's jeans before she threw them in the wash. Three round seeds rolled out of the right-hand pocket. She also found the remnants of a joint, recognizing immediately the burnt yellowed paper and the familiar smell.

She wasn't surprised. Weed was widely smoked up there in Oregon, and although Deb made it a point to shield her son from her snorting of stronger stuff, or at least she had seven and a half years ago, Deb never hid her drinking or smoking from her son and neither did Munch. Looking back, it was a wonder they hadn't killed him—a little bit of Southern Comfort in his bottle when he was teething; the time they got him drunk on beer on his fourth birthday, drinking toasts to him until he got sick and passed out. They'd never heard of alcohol poisoning back then, and even if they had, they would never have understood the risk to themselves. They were going to live forever or to twenty-five, whichever came first.

She emptied the other pocket and found a disposable Bic lighter. She struck the flint and the flame shot out like a blowtorch. Nathan had the lighter cranked to its highest setting. She knew you didn't use a flame like that to smoke pot, but you did need a lot of heat to smoke crack or boil dope in a spoon.

Munch set the lighter on top of the washing machine. Part of her was afraid to touch it—as if contamination might spread with prolonged physical contact. She couldn't have someone doing drugs in her house, both for Asia's sake and her own. If she called Rico or St. John, they would confirm this immediately. Besides, Rico was already prejudiced against Nathan; this would only cement his opinion.

She went into the kitchen and called her sponsor. Ruby answered on the first ring.

"You've got to create a crisis, honey," Ruby finally said.

"How do I do that?"

"Make a scene, yell, throw things. Confront him. React. You want him to link using dope with trouble. Make it unpleasant as you can for him. Can you do that?"

"Yeah," she said. "I can do disagreeable."

Nathan arrived home twenty minutes later. Munch was waiting for him, sitting in the armchair opposite the front door. Asia was in her room. Munch warned her there was going to be yelling. She'd cleared the coffee table of magazines and put the lighter there instead, plainly visible.

After a brief glance around the room, Nathan froze. "What's up?"

"I found this in your pocket."

"Yeah, so?" His expression hovered on the verge of outraged protest.

Munch flicked the lighter on and a six-inch tongue of flame whooshed out. She lifted her finger off the butane lever. The flame died. She threw the lighter against the wall, chipping the paint above the wall socket.

"Hey," Nathan said, more out of surprise than anything else.

"Do you want to go to prison?"

He visibly blanched. "What are you—"

Munch didn't let him finish. "You want to die? Go crazy? What the fuck's the matter with you?" She kicked the table. It overturned with a cracking noise. She stood with her fists clenched.

Nathan stared back, openmouthed, obviously unsure how to handle an angry woman who was a foot shorter but didn't seem to care.

"Are you going to hit me?" he asked, his voice sounding unusually calm. The coldness in it or rather the lack of emotion made her pause.

"I'm so pissed at you, I might. I thought you wanted to build a life for yourself."

"You're not my mother. You've got no right—"

"The fuck I don't," she screamed. "I care, and you're hurting yourself and that hurts me."

"How am I hurting you?" he screamed back, forgetting to lower his voice.

She grabbed his left hand and scooted his sleeve up. His arms were cut and scarred, but there were no telltale puncture wounds over his veins. He didn't pull away.

"I'm not a hype," he said.

"Not yet."

"Not ever."

She looked down at his forearm. He had a homemade tattoo there, the name Walter. His daddy. Deb had one just like it on her shoulder. A deep scratch obscured the letter "t."

"Your mom mentioned you'd had some trouble. Was it drugs?"

"Nah. It wasn't about dope. I got in a fight with this guy. Cops called it mayhem at first. I was just taking care of business. Some chump didn't know who he was messing with." Nathan pulled his arm back and scooted his sleeve back down.

"Mayhem?"

"They switched it to aggravated assault."

Munch wondered about the distinction. Wasn't assault always a result of aggravation? "So you have a juvenile record?"

"They ended up dropping all the charges. My mom talked to the DA, got it all cleared up."

Munch had a quick picture of what Deb must have done for the DA, who was obviously a man.

"So now what?" Nathan wiped his eyes fiercely with the sleeve of his Pendleton. "Do you want me to leave?"

"No," she said, "I want you to live." Tears filled her eyes and she willed them to flow freely. "I want to save you from my mistakes." She raised her voice. "Both of you."

Nathan stood his ground uncertainly for a moment and then in a gesture reminiscent of his childhood, he hugged his side with one hand and buried his face in the other. His shoulders heaved as he rocked his head side to side. "It's just so hard," he said between sobs. "So hard."

Munch put her arms around him while he cried. She knew it was difficult to be so young and on your own. Asia peeked her head out her door, her eyes wide. Munch gave her a nod of reassurance. Asia ran into the room. Now she cried too as she joined their embrace.

Munch pulled her in, stroking her soft curls as she spoke to the top of Nathan's bowed head. "You didn't choose this, but this is your life. You've got to be your own parent. Your mom is an alcoholic. She always has been. Your daddy . . ."

"He's dead."

"I know and I'm sorry. I lost my mom young too and that's just the way it is. Don't you think he would want you happy and alive?"

Nathan sniffed wetly and straightened his back. "I'm not a crackhead. I don't even smoke cigarettes. I used the lighter for something at work."

"I hope that's true."

"It is."

Asia had stuck her thumb in her mouth, something Munch hadn't seen her do in years. She lifted the little girl up and held her in her arms. Asia wrapped her legs around Munch's waist and Munch felt a sudden pang of sadness. Soon Asia would be too big to carry.

"I want to go see your grandma, Nathan."

"Why?"

"I'm helping your mom get you Social Security benefits. They'll keep paying if you go back to school. I know you don't think more school is for you, but that option is open. You don't have to decide this minute or this day, just don't be quick to say no to a possible good thing."

"I told my grandma you wanted to meet her."

"What did she say?"

He shrugged. "She said, 'Sure, why not?' "

Munch set Asia on her feet and brushed a stray curl behind the little girl's ear. Nathan righted the overturned table and picked up his lighter. A quarter fell from his pocket. Asia picked it up.

"You keep it," he said. "Put it in your piggy bank."

Munch smiled at her daughter's retreating back. "That was nice of you."

"No biggie."

Later that afternoon, Munch gathered the Sunday newspaper to take it out to the recycling box in the garage. In all the day's drama she hadn't had a chance to look through it. As she stood now in the kitchen doorway, a headline jumped out at her.

MURDERERS GO TO PRISON. There was a picture of a young Asian man in a prison jumpsuit, shackles around his ankles and wrists. Lately, she'd been reading every article about murder and/or robbery. The suspects were always young, eighteen to twenty on average. This one was no different. He was holding a packet of paperwork—his useless defense, no doubt. "Killer sentenced to 25 years to life" was the caption. She scanned the article for the circumstances of the crime. The young man had stabbed a woman with a ten-inch kitchen knife and stolen her purse. Two men were arrested for the homicide. The second, described by police as the lookout, also was convicted of murder. Under California's "felony murder rule," the article stated, if the murder occurred during the commission of a felony—in this case an armed robbery—everyone involved in the felony was culpable for the murder. The lookout guy was to be sentenced the following month.

"I'm screwed," she said, horror drying her throat.

Tortilla Flats, 1975

Munch checks the rearview mirror for the thousandth time. She is hunched down in the seat of Thor's Chrysler and parked in front of a project apartment building on Vernon. Sleaze, Thor, and New York Jane have been gone forever and she feels like a target.

Three black kids on bicycles ride by and hoot at her through the window. They circle the car like little hungry crows.

"Junkie bitch," they taunt, pegging her right. She sinks lower, checks the doors to make sure they're locked. She wants to start the engine, but the gas gauge is already on empty, and no telling how much longer they'll be.

She feels the dampness on her face and back, an oily sweat that only has one cure. "C'mon," she hums under her breath, her foot tapping uselessly on the brake pedal. She watches the doorway where the three of them disappeared minutes ago, maybe twenty. An eternity for a dopesick white girl in the wrong part of town. At least she hasn't seen a cop car. Just the kids on their rusty Schwinns, who have correctly assessed her mission in their world.

Thor promised they wouldn't come back empty-handed. They all went together. Trust goes as far as the door in their world. You save yourself first and make up excuses later. The last time Thor had gone to cop dope by himself, he returned an hour later, scratching his nose and saying he had no choice but to swallow the dope, the pigs were on him, and he had to get rid of the stash.

This is the first time Munch has gotten strung out. She's played with dope for months, and now she's gotten serious. In a perverse way, being strung out has made the dope much better. The difference of feelings between being dope-sick and being loaded has increased and this contrast has improved the high.

They were short on the money, but Thor promised. He said he knew this guy was holding. It is Munch's special day. She's turning nineteen and wants to get loaded.

The thick steel security gate at the bottom of the stairwell is open.

Some of the other buildings hire a guard to stand there, but not this one. Here the lowlifes are welcome.

She sees a movement. "Please, let it be them," she says. She doesn't ask God. He's not a part of this equation. There is just the need and the dope, only one altar to worship at.

Sleaze appears first. His head is down. Munch leans across the seat and unlocks the door. He's not smiling, she realizes, heart sinking. They didn't get it. Thor said they wouldn't come back without it, but Sleaze won't even look at her.

Jane is next. Thor holds her arm and hustles her in front of him. The three of them get in the car.

"Drive," he orders.

"Did you get it?" Munch asks as she pulls away.

Thor stares at her hard, his expression angry, even accusatory.

Sleaze slumps in the backseat and moans. It doesn't sound like him. She looks back once and sees a smear of something dark on the brown cloth of the seat, bright red drops on the vinyl door panel. Jane is humming.

"Shut up," Thor yells.

"Did you get it?" Munch asks again. It's all she can think to say. Thor has blood on his Army jacket. Jane is rocking now, but the humming has stopped.

When she stops at the traffic light, Thor puts a knife to her throat. The blade feels warm. "Did you say something?" he asks. His eyes are alert. He wants her to argue, she senses. He wants a reason.

"No," Munch mumbles, hating herself for cowering, for being a chump. She lives in a world where how bad you are, how crazy you are, defines who you are, but she is no match for Thor.

He sticks his knife back in its scabbard.

She drives them all back to the Flats. Tortilla Flats is a loose compound of apartments on Rose Avenue, where the barrio meets the ghetto—a land of No-tell Motels, Mexican mercados, *Laundromats, and liquor stores. Even though it is late in the afternoon, the smell of baking bread rises from the Pioneer Bakery factory.*

They park on the dirt lot off the alley and file through the hole in the oleander hedge. Munch goes first. The other three follow in the same order they used to exit the apartment building in Ghost Town.

Munch unlocks the door and they all head for the kitchen. Sleaze goes to the sink and throws up. He runs the water, then fills a glass and brings it to the kitchen table.

The spoons are already there. Jane sits, her mouth is open, her expression blank.

"You going to be useless all day?" Thor asks.

"What do you want me to do?"

"Get a bag, one of those big plastic garbage bags, and a magazine."

Jane walks over to the pantry and tears off a bag from the roll on the shelf and shakes it open. Thor reaches into the pocket of his Army jacket and pulls out a quart-size Baggie. It's filled with glittery white powder. He tosses it to the center of the table and it lands with a thunk.

"Happy Birthday," he says, looking only at Munch.

She has never seen so much coke in one lump. She's seen mounds of brown heroin, but coke is more of a rich man's drug.

Thor reaches behind him; his long arms find the radio on the windowsill. He switches it on and tunes it to an A.M. *station. Traffic and news, updates every fifteen minutes. He opens the bag of coke. The air fills with a bleachy smell. Thor dips the corner of a playing card into the bag. It's a three of hearts, not that it matters to him. He is not a superstitious man.*

He dips the corner of the card into the white powder and dumps it into the waiting spoon.

First things first.

There is only one outfit, so they take their turns. Thor goes first, then

Jane, then Sleaze. Munch ties off while Thor sheds his clothes and throws them in the garbage bag. He tells Jane to do the same. Sleaze doesn't have to be asked.

Jane goes into the bedroom and gets them other clothes.

"News on the hour," the radio says. They stop and stare at the radio speaker. The announcer's voice is tinny, there is a sound like typing in the background. "Here are the headlines making the news: American troops evacuating Saigon as North Vietnamese swarm in, President Ford declares that the war in Indochina is over as far as America is concerned, American and Soviet astronauts dock in space."

Thor, dressed only in jeans and socks, starts tearing pages from the magazine.

"And locally—"

All activity in the kitchen hangs suspended.

"Chief Davis says that Jim Hardy, general manager of the Sports Arena, is 'sort of a baby.' Hardy has accused the Los Angeles Police Department of using excessive force during the five-night performance of the English rock group Pink Floyd. Police arrested five hundred and eleven persons on charges ranging from possession of marijuana to assault with a deadly weapon, sex perversion, disturbing the peace, and ticket scalping. Stay tuned for traffic and weather."

Thor stops working and stands. Jane rubs cocaine on her gums.

The two men pace, working their dry mouths and not looking at each other, but not leaving each other's sight. Jane renders herself catatonic with the coke, slamming hit after hit.

"Watch it," Munch says. "You're going to have a heart attack."

Jane draws up more water with the syringe, shakes more coke into the spoon, barely waits for it to dissolve before she sucks it back into the works. The needle glistens with body fluids and narcotics. She doesn't bother to mop the drops of her own blood rolling down her wrist.

"This is getting sickening," Munch says. "You're just wasting it."

Thor is quiet as he spoons quarter teaspoons of the cocaine onto squares of glossy magazine paper. They don't own a scale, so he estimates. Sleaze folds the squares into bindles.

They don't leave the Flats for two days, except for one beer run when they buy a newspaper.

Munch doesn't ask any other questions, not even when Sleaze reads the newspaper cover to cover. She looks up her horoscope. "Taurus: Study new ideas, but wait for a better day before putting them in operation."

She doesn't ask about the one-half-column report in the Metro section of a triple homicide in the Oakwood Projects section of Venice Beach. She doesn't want to know any more details about the three men found with their throats slashed at the house where she had parked, and served as the "wheelman."

Chapter 18

⟹

Monday morning, St. John checked in at work, picked up his copies of Cyrill McCarthy's court transcripts, and then headed over to meet with Art Becker at the Pacific station.

Becker greeted St. John in the lobby. "You should be talking to Chacón."

"Oh?"

"He's fresher on the facts."

"I'd like to just start with the evidence," St. John said. "No offense to your boy, but the last thing I want to hear are theories from some wannabe Dick Tracy."

"This guy kick one of your dogs or something?" Becker asked.

"No, I just have my own way of doing things."

Becker brought St. John over to his desk, which was crowded with framed photographs. St. John sat down in the wooden chair beside the desk and the two men exchanged reading material.

The murder book was a large, blue three-ring binder. It began with the initial incident report recorded by patrol cops, followed by the homicide investigator's narrative. St. John scrolled down to the name of the lead detective: Chris Yanney—a notorious rummy who had been a dinosaur when St. John was a rookie. Yanney had died two months after retiring.

As yet there were no addendums from Chacón.

St. John turned the page and studied the forensics reports, autopsy findings, and witness statements, leaving the photographs of the death scene for last.

The bodies of three black men were sprawled throughout the shotgun flat. There was one victim in the kitchen, and one in the bedroom, where—judging by the blood on the carpet and walls—most of the killing had occurred. The third victim was in the hallway, which was also thinly carpeted. The dying man had apparently crawled across the length of the narrow egress, his path traced clearly in blood and tissue. Judging from the condition of his clothes and the positioning of his limbs, he hadn't been dragged.

The Scientific Investigation Division had recovered many fingerprints from the crime scene, and most of those fingerprints could be matched to individuals with criminal records. None of those individuals questioned knew anything about the murders, of course. Most of them denied ever having been in the house on Vernon.

The criminalists focused their attention on latent impressions created with blood, particularly footprints left on the hall carpet. St. John found several photographs showing the variety of shoe sizes, ranging from a man's size twelve to one that was much smaller.

At autopsy, all three bodies were discovered to have V's

carved into their chests—*V-13* had been written on the walls in blood.

Given the atmosphere of the time, the police would have assumed that the murderers were gangbangers, but there were a few problems with that theory. Why come into the middle of the Oakwood Projects to establish turf? And why sign a murder scene? It didn't make sense unless the purpose was to mislead investigators. Or could V stand for Viking? Was McCarthy that fucking ballsy?

One of the few witnesses who came forth was a ten-year-old girl named Donzetta Williams. Donzetta told police that she saw a big black car parked in front of the building at the time of the murders. She also saw three white people come out of the building and get in that car. Two white "hippie dudes," according to her statement, and a "white chick."

When investigators tried to reach her again, they were told by her mother that Donzetta had nothing more to say and did not have her permission to get involved. Now that ten years had passed, Donzetta would be a young woman. Parental consent was no longer needed.

"Can I use your phone?" St. John asked.

"Help yourself."

St. John called the phone number listed for Donzetta and got a recording that the number was no longer in service.

Becker watched him hang up the phone. "Like I said, you should get with Chacón."

"Where is he?"

"He had some personal business to take care of. He'll be in."

St. John went over to Chacón's work space. He grabbed a pen from the mug on the corner and bent over to write a note. Chacón's desktop had the look of a working detective's. There were stacks of files, some of them dated, newspaper clippings turned brown with age, black-and-white mug shots. On a telephone message pad, the name D. Williams was written in pencil followed by two phone numbers with local prefixes. One of the numbers was denoted G, the other W.

St. John called the W number and found it connected him to B&B Hardware. He asked how late they stayed open and then hung up. Next he called the G number. A woman answered the phone.

"Is Donzetta Williams there?"

"No. What you want with her?"

"Are you a relative?"

"Maybe. Who's this?"

"I'm a detective with the Los Angeles Police Department."

"Another one?"

"Yeah, but I'm better-looking."

Becker glanced up in surprise. The woman on the phone responded with a throaty laugh. "Then she's gonna want to see you, baby."

"Is she home now? I can be there in fifteen minutes."

"You know where B&B Hardware is?"

"On Washington?"

"Yeah, she's over there. She works in the tool section."

St. John thanked the woman and hung up.

Becker held up Stacy Lansford's letter. "Pretty thin. We haven't even been able to contact this woman for verification."

"I'm working on it, though I'm sure she lacks faith in the system."

"Assuming she's still alive."

"Right, assuming that."

"Have you located Cyrill McCarthy?" Becker asked.

"Not yet. I've put out a want on him, and searched custody records, but nothing so far."

"I'll give this to Chacón and tell him you want to talk to him."

St. John left the Pacific station and drove the few long blocks on surface streets to B&B Hardware. He parked in the lot in the back, pushed through the turnstiles by the cash register, and followed the overhead signs to the tool section.

A dark-skinned young black woman in a red shirt was extolling the numerous features of a cordless drill that was on sale to an enthralled thirty-something white guy in a polo shirt. St. John stepped close enough to glance at the woman's name tag and confirm her identity. He waited until the sale was complete before introducing himself.

Her smile was warm and open even after she learned he was a cop. He found that refreshing.

"What can I do for you?"

"I'm looking into the triple homicide that happened ten years ago, in April of 1975. You made a statement to officers that you noticed a carful of individuals that seemed out of place?"

"Yeah, they was white," Donzetta said with a laugh. The plain gold crucifix resting on her throat took a few bounces. "That's why I noticed them in the first place; then I heard about those murders, and I thought it might mean something. I called the police myself. My mama like to have a fit."

"Why?"

"She said good riddance to them people, they was dope dealers. My mama said their kind ruined the neighborhood, made the people slaves."

"Do you think they got what they deserved?"

"I don't know about that."

"Can you give me a more detailed description of the people you saw?"

"It's been a long time, but I still remember. Like I told the other detective, one was a big white man with reddish-blond hair, the other might have been a Mexican; he had long hair too, a goatee, looked like the devil or a pirate or somethin'."

"Anything unusual about the woman with them?"

"She had what my grandmama would call a hitch in her get along."

"You mean like a limp? Can you show me?"

Donzetta took a few steps across the floor. As she moved she went down on one side and swung the other leg to catch up.

"You know," she said, "that's how those Crips took their name; they used to walk like that, all tilted, swinging their arms wide like they were some kind of cool."

"So Crips came from Cripples?"

"Yeah, ain't that the most ridiculous thing you ever heard?"

"Comes close," St. John admitted. "Was that your mother I spoke to at the eight-eight-oh-one number?"

"No, sir, that was my grandmama. My mama passed."

"I'm sorry."

"Cancer," Donzetta added, her hand going to her crucifix.

"Your grandmama said you had another detective speak to you recently?"

"Detective Chacón. Mexican guy."

"Yeah, I know him." St. John wondered when Chacón was going to get around to adding his notes to the report.

"Is he, uh, you know, like, married?"

St. John stared at her a moment, but Donzetta didn't back down.

"I'm going to put together some pictures I'd like you to look at. I'll bring them by this afternoon if that's all right."

"More pictures?" She chuckled. "Sure, why not? I'm not going anywhere."

St. John returned to the police station to assemble a six-pack. Two, actually. One of Jane Ferrar and five additional women, the other would be of old mug shots of Cyrill McCarthy and five different similar-looking white guys. If Donzetta could pick Cyrill McCarthy and Jane Ferrar out of those two photo lineups, he was well on his way to establishing motive for Jane's murder, not to mention solving the triple.

He didn't know yet which event triggered which. Did the reopening of the investigation of the old homicide prompt Jane's murder or was it the other way around?

The last block manufacturing company on Cassiletti's list was the Cascade Block Company. It was located in Santa Fe Springs in between a junkyard specializing in Cadillacs and a piano manufacturer. He parked beside a pink mock piano tagged with black spray paint. Its condition advertised more than the company probably meant to reveal.

Cassiletti removed a large white handkerchief from his pocket and draped it loosely over his left hand. Keys in his right hand, he opened the trunk of his Oldsmobile and removed the block with his protected left. He had repeated this gesture fifteen times already since last Monday. Lifting the thirty-two-pound block in and out of his trunk had given him new respect for construction workers. But he was no nearer to finding the block's source.

His left eye watered, as it always did when he came to the eastern industrial section of Los Angeles. The sky overhead had the consistency of dishwater. Grit darkened the green leaves of the dandelions growing between the chain-link fences and turned the normally bright yellow flowers a poisonous shade of mustard.

He entered the yard. Beige dust covered everything, including a seemingly deaf rottweiler that trotted across the open ground. Steel racks held rows of drying brick. A large water hose was tapped into a fire hydrant. Mexicans wearing red ear plugs and working the silos and stamping equipment eyed him warily. He heard the word *"migra"* spread across the work platform.

The trailer office was next to a pair of Porta Potties and a dust-covered Coca-Cola vending machine that was out of all six choices. He tried the dark screen door at the top of the corrugated steel stairs but found it locked. There was no bell to ring.

"Hello?" Cassiletti called out. He checked his notes. "Fred Wood?"

"That's me." A squat man with a cigar clamped between his teeth emerged from the trailer and blocked the doorway.

Cassiletti handed the man one of his coveted business cards. Wood looked at the card and yelled over Cassiletti's shoulder, "He's all right. Get back to work." He extended a stubby hand to Cassiletti. "Call me Woody."

Cassiletti had to duck his head as he entered the small trailer. The cigar smoke made him long for smog.

"Let's see what you got. Set her up here."

Cassiletti lifted the block to the top of Fred Wood's desk next to the photograph of two big-toothed blond children. The drawers were open and sagging with the weight of invoices. Woody peered at the block under his desk lamp.

"Yep, that's one of mine."

"Are you sure?"

"Yeah, custom job, had to mix the color special. They were getting the block from a company in Yuma, but the company folded and the contractor needed a match."

"Can you give me the name of the contractor?"

"Sure, I even have the address of the job site."

"That would be even better, Woody."

The address for Cascade Block had a Brentwood zip code. The street was called Pinehurst. Cassiletti had to get out a *Thomas Guide* map to find it. It was only a block long and off Mandeville Canyon.

He contacted dispatch and asked them to locate St. John.

Cassiletti drove, while St. John wrote his notes about the Donzetta Williams interview. They shot across Sepulveda to Sunset, and then turned toward Brentwood. Both men craned their necks as they passed Munch's gas station. If she was there, she wasn't in sight.

The large home on Pinehurst was getting a new swimming pool and cabana. A backhoe had turned the backyard into a crater. Pallets stamped CASCADE BLOCK were piled high with distinctively hued concrete blocks. Next to the pallets were piles of rebar, sacks of concrete protected by blue tarp, and white PVC pipe.

They parked behind a white Ford truck with a utility bed. There was an overturned wheelbarrow in the back, loose shovels lying beside it, and a stack of two-by-fours. Ladders were tied to the top rack. A bumper sticker read HIGHER POWERED.

Cassiletti hung back to study the white rope binding the ladders to the steel hooks welded to the bed, while St. John looked for the foreman.

A crew of five men was laying rebar in the pit. Tattoos rippled on straining biceps. Another four men, with tool belts strapped to their waists, were assembling the framing of the pool house. St. John studied the faces, then the arms, looking for Viking horns.

A white guy in a hard hat approached St. John. "Can I help you?"

"Are you the boss?"

"I'm the contractor." He extended a hand. "Mike Peyovich, Big Mike."

St. John shook hands. "Detective St. John, and this is my partner, Detective Cassiletti. We're investigating the homicide of a woman whose body was found about a mile from here."

"I think I read about that. In the storm drain?"

"Yes, sir."

"That was wrong."

"Yes, sir," St. John said, having nothing to add to that brilliant assessment. "Her body was weighted with a concrete block. We believe it came from this site."

"No."

"No, it didn't?"

"Huh?" Big Mike looked at St. John. "No, I mean no as in 'you don't say.' "

"Have these blocks been sitting here all week?" Cassiletti asked.

"Yeah, they were delivered on the tenth."

"Do you have any security on the site?" St. John asked.

"You mean like a guard?"

St. John blinked but kept his face calm. It was obvious that he needed to keep his wording simple and precise with Big Mike.

A black kid with a T-shirt wrapped around his head interrupted. "Mike? We're done with the south wall."

"All right, I want to take a look before the inspector comes."

Big Mike turned back to St. John and Cassiletti. "Anything else you need from me?"

"A list of your employees and their shifts for the last two weeks," St. John said.

"You got a warrant?"

"Do I need one?" This guy really was a Class-A idiot.

"Only if you expect access to my records. I don't mean to be a hard-ass here, but I have to look after my crew."

St. John spread his hands in a let's-be-reasonable gesture and relaxed his face into a grin. "You're going to make us drive all the way back to the courthouse and bother some judge?"

The contractor looked at his watch. "We're wrapping up here in another hour. So it looks like you're out of luck today."

St. John took a step closer, planting himself in Big Mike's path. Now he was going to have to be a prick. "A lot of things can hold up a job like this. Additional inspections, license checking. I'll start by running warrant checks on all your workers, then we'll make traffic stops on deliveries. That should cut into your deadlines, kill any bonuses."

"And if we did need to go get a warrant," Cassiletti added, "we'd be well within our powers to put a freeze on this work site until we return. It's called probable cause."

"Jesus, what the fuck do you want from me?"

"Just your cooperation. I believe I asked nicely the first time."

"All right. Let's go into my office."

The detectives left fifteen minutes later with a list of employees and, at Cassiletti's request, a sample of the rope from the work trucks.

When Cassiletti got behind the wheel of their Buick, he said, "There's one thing I don't understand."

"What's that?"

"The killer marked the body, right?"

"Yeah. There was a V scratched into her torso, postmortem."

"But then he went to some lengths to conceal the body. So who did he mark the body for?"

"I've always said it was personal."

Chapter 19

⟱

Munch hit the Monday night meeting at the clubhouse on Ohio Street. Nathan had offered to stay in with Asia.

The first speaker was a middle-aged woman who talked about living in New York and drinking all the time. She took a business trip to California, rented a car, drank through her business meeting, and then flew home. A month later the bill came for the rental car that she had forgotten to return. She had left it parked on the street and the rental company had charged thirty days of rental against her credit card. Munch knew people forgot all kinds of things when they were on a binge: the job they were supposed to be at, the husband at home, the kid in the car.

Years ago, her friend Ellen once went to Tijuana as some rich guy's date, failing to remember that she was on probation and not supposed to leave the state, never mind the country. It always seemed to slip Deb's mind that she was in love with somebody else when she was out drinking. Munch tended to forget she wasn't six feet tall after three shots of Jack Daniel's.

There were all sorts of cute sayings about substance abusers and the murky swamps of their judgment facilities. *"Last to remember and first to forget,"* was one of Munch's favorites. It also helped to have scars, lingering medical conditions, and unadjudicated felonies to keep a person humble and on course.

Before the coffee break, birthday cakes and plastic chips for varying lengths of sobriety were handed out, beginning with the people who had reached the milestone of thirty days without a drink or a drug.

A guy who seemed vaguely familiar stepped up to the podium. Munch often had feelings of recognition at these meetings. Cons tended to carry themselves in a way that was universally identifiable. When they walked, their arms rolled forward from their shoulders, held akimbo by muscle mass forged in prison. There was the way they held their heads, their chins slightly up, mouths slack, dead eyes that expected nothing—not fairness, nor forgiveness, nor brand-new worlds. Their hands tended to cross over their genitals when they stood. Cops, she noticed, did that too.

This guy at the podium was nothing new. He was about six feet tall, his hair was cut short, and he was clean-shaven, though his face seemed to beg for a stubble to fill in the mottle caused by years of self-induced, slow-acting poison and repeated contact with hard surfaces. He would never be mistaken for a white-collar worker or a well-toned Yuppie, not with a mug like that.

Yuppies also didn't have spiderwebs tattooed on their elbows, or walk around at night with speckles of dried house paint still clinging to their hair.

"My name's Cyrill," the guy said, accepting the white poker chip with **30 Days** drawn in gold script across the face, "and I'm a grateful drunk."

Now the voice was familiar too. Munch leaned forward for a closer look at his arms. She saw the Viking horns tattooed on his biceps, but they only confirmed what she knew as soon as she heard him speak. It was Thor, sans the ZZ Top beard and older, especially in the eyes.

Her heart seemed to freeze within her chest. She couldn't hear what he said. The words were lost below the roar in her ears. Someone sitting behind her had to nudge her when her own name was called to take a cake for eight years of sobriety.

Thor's eyes widened when Munch stood and never left her as she blew out the candles.

"I'm a miracle," she said. "Nine years ago in 1976 I hadn't been arrested enough." This announcement was greeted with appreciative chuckles. "My last year of using was the worse. I hit bottom and just kept on going." Out of the corner of her eye she saw Thor nodding.

"The ninth step has been coming up a lot lately in my life. For all you newcomers, that's the one where we make direct amends to all the people we have harmed." She noticed now that Thor was sitting very still and listening intently.

"I've been given the opportunity to make amends to the kid of another alcoholic who I used to drink with. I can't undo the bad years, but I can set an example.

"Today I am blessed. My life changed completely once I surrendered to the disease and turned my will and my life over to God. A little over eight years ago, I was arrested for that final time." She knocked on the wood podium and the audience laughed. "When I was in jail, God sent me an Eskimo. You know the joke, right? Guy's sitting in a bar in Alaska. He tells the man sitting next to him how it's a miracle he's there.

" 'Why?' the first man asks.

" 'Well,' the guy says, 'I was out there in this godforsaken country, I'd lost my sled dogs, my bearings, and I'm in the middle of a terrible storm when the iceberg I'm on starts to break loose. I knew I was gonna die, so I pray to God to save me.'

" 'He obviously answered your prayer,' the second man says, 'because here you are—sitting in this bar, safe and sound.'

" 'Oh, it wasn't God,' the first guy says. 'A goddamned Eskimo came out of nowhere, over the iceberg, in the middle of the storm, and took me back to his filthy igloo.' "

Munch waited for the laughter to subside, then continued.

"I was a bad-ass biker chick eight years ago. I hated cops, I hated women, and I wasn't overly fond of black people. So you know who God sent me, don't you?" Munch nodded. "That's right. A black female police officer. She listened to me, heard that I had really surrendered, and brought me a piece of scripture that got me through many long nights: 'When God is with me, who can be against me?' On that note, I'll shut up and sit down."

Thor applauded with everyone else. Munch was aware that she hadn't mentioned Asia in her litany of what she had to be grateful for. Common street sense warned her to keep the existence of that which was most precious to her hidden.

The leader of the meeting announced the coffee break. Thor was waiting for her as she stepped down from the podium.

"Eight years," he said. "That's fucking amazing."

"No more than thirty days," she said, taking a step back so she wouldn't have to crane her neck so far to look at his face.

He nodded in understanding.

"Why haven't I seen you before this?" she asked. "At a meeting, I mean."

"We've been hitting mostly men's stags in the Valley."

"We?"

"I'm in a halfway house. New Start. It's in Sun Valley."

"Is Danny T. still the director?"

"Yeah, he's here tonight. We drove over in his car."

She scanned the crowd, finding Danny near the literature in earnest discussion with a teenage boy. Hispanic and not tall, Danny T. was a charismatic speaker with his Fu Manchu mustache, collar-length black hair, and multiple tattoos. He could easily work as a stand-up comedian. He had a hilarious story about stealing power lawn mowers when he was a junkie. In fact, hearing him speak at one of her first meetings had made her feel as if Narcotics Anonymous was a cool enough place for her.

She also saw a group of six cons holding up the back wall whom she immediately pegged as New Start residents. They were predominantly Chicano and dressed in dazzling white T-shirts and crisply pressed khaki pants. Their faces bore I'm-here-but-that's-all-I'm-copping-to expressions, barely flickering to life even for the brazenly dressed newcomer women who swished past them on their way for coffee and cake.

She knew the type well, in trouble since they were juvies and well on their way to being permanently institutionalized. Letting that bullshit pride thing get in the way of anything good or new in their lives. Hip, slick, and terminal. Even now, they were in doing-time mode. They weren't in prison, but they weren't on the street either. One in thirty might eventually be able to see that he was his own worst enemy.

"How long have you been there?" she asked.

"Thirty days," Thor said, holding up his chip.

"Of course."

"You still working on those cars?"

"Sure am." She held up a hand so he could see the grease stains. "You painting?"

He reared back slightly, his chest expanded, and his hands rose waist-high. If he were a dog, the hair along his back would be bristling.

"How'd you know that?" he asked, eyes dark.

For an instant she saw the old Thor and had to remind herself that he couldn't hurt her here and now. *When God is with me . . .* "The paint on your arm was a big clue."

He smiled and shook his head. "Of course."

"Nice to wear short sleeves again, huh?"

"Nice to be doing a lot of things again," he said. He took a step closer so that his chest was in her face. "You seeing anyone?"

"Yeah, I am." She heard her apologetic tone and wondered if part of her would always be emotionally stuck at fourteen, when—in a pathetic bid to be wanted and needed and accepted—she would screw anyone who asked her. Or maybe it was the glimmer of hope she saw on Thor's face that she responded to, his glimpse of possible redemption and a life free from crime and punishment, violence and jail. At thirty days—had he been drug-free for thirty days?—he had no business thinking about dating. It was much too soon.

"Can I have your number?" he asked.

"You got it already. It's eight."

"And your sign is stop, right?"

She smiled in spite of herself, still trying to come to grips with seeing him again, and at her home meeting of all places.

"I heard about Sleaze," Thor said. "There but for the grace of God, huh?"

She wanted to laugh out loud, hearing those words from his lips. Life was too bizarre.

"And now New York Jane," she said.

"Oh yeah? When?"

"A week and a half ago."

A woman in a see-through top walked by and Thor was momentarily distracted. He turned to watch her with his whole body. When she disappeared out the back door for some of that "parking lot sobriety," Thor brought his eyes back to Munch. "She OD?"

"Yeah, on a tire iron."

His expression was genuinely puzzled. "What do you mean?"

"You don't read the papers?"

"No." He paused then, and looked at her with deeper understanding. "I didn't have anything to do with it. I haven't seen Jane in years. Whose kid?"

"What?"

"You said you were helping someone's kid from the old days. Anyone I know?"

"Deb's kid. Boogie."

"The nig— Uh, the little black kid?"

"Not so little anymore."

"That's real nice of you to be helping him out and all."

She considered telling him that the cops were looking for him and had some questions, but then he would want to know how she knew what the cops wanted or what they knew.

"Hey, Munch, the past is past, right?"

"You'll have to figure that out for yourself."

"Nothing to figure out," he said. "Unless someone after all this time gets in a confessing mood."

"Who would that be?"

"Alls I'm saying is a person worried about their soul only need tell the parts about themselves."

"I believe that's how it works unless it looks like someone else is going to get hurt."

"As long as we understand each other."

More than you know.

The break was over. Munch walked over to where Danny T. was refilling his coffee. She picked up an empty cup and got in line behind him. "Can I talk to you a minute? Outside?"

She went out to the parking lot. A moment later Danny emerged with a quizzical expression on his face. "What's up?"

"There's a curfew at your house, right?"

"Eleven o'clock. Unless a resident is at a meeting with his sponsor or on an approved pass."

"Is that for everyone?"

"Well, they're only eligible for passes after the first thirty days."

"That's what I thought."

"What's this about?"

"I thought I might have seen that guy Cyrill out late the weekend before last, but no way was that possible."

"No, especially not that weekend. The whole house was locked down. Nobody went anywhere."

Right, Munch thought, *and a lifelong con would never dream of breaking curfew.*

Rico Chacón finally called St. John on Tuesday morning.

"Nice of you to get back with me," St. John said.

"Oh yeah and guess what?" Chacón said. "You weren't the only person on my list."

"I've heard you have friends all over."

"What did you want?"

"You get a chance in your busy schedule to read the document I left?"

"Stacy Lansford's statement? I saw it."

"I've got an appointment with Donzetta Williams. I thought you might want to be there when I show her some six-packs."

"Yeah, all right. She still working at B&B?"

"How long ago did you interview her?"

"Last month. I'll meet you there. Is two good?"

St. John arrived at the hardware store just as Chacón pulled up. He checked his watch. It was only half past one.

They parked three spaces apart, each man pulled on his coat, aware of the other but not exchanging greetings. St. John carried a manila envelope. Chacón's arms swung free.

They approached the store together but entered through separate turnstiles.

Donzetta was sorting individually packaged drill bits and hanging them on hooks near the counter. She smiled at the two cops, revealing a wide gap between her teeth.

"We've got to stop meeting like this," she said.

St. John smiled. "How you doin' today?"

"Like Grandmama always says, I woke up."

Chacón smiled but said nothing.

"I hate to keep bothering you at work, Donzetta," St. John said.

"I'm just not sure how much help I can be after all this time." She turned to Chacón as she spoke and smiled prettily. "But I'll do my best."

Everybody was smiling. It was starting to hurt.

St. John opened his packet of paperwork and extracted a Traffic Collision report form. "When we talked before, you said you got a pretty good look at the three people you saw leaving the apartment building on Vernon. Where were you standing?"

"I was across the street, in my yard, waiting on the mailman."

The TC form had a basic diagram of parallel and perpendicular lines depicting streets and intersections. He asked her to fill in the appropriate street names and landmarks. She wrote in Lincoln Boulevard, Vernon Avenue, and Main Street. Then she drew a square on one side of Vernon and labeled it her house, and a larger rectangle across the street that she identified as the apartment building where the three murder victims were found.

"And where was the car they drove away in?" St. John asked.

Donzetta drew in the car and showed it pointing westbound.

"So the Mexican guy, where was he?" St. John asked.

"He came out first and got in the backseat. Then the woman with the limp and the big guy with the red hair came out. He was helping her walk, like, holding her by the arm."

"And then she got in the car?"

"Yeah, into the back with the other guy."

"And then the redhead came around to the front to the driver's side?"

Donzetta scrunched her nose and looked skyward. "No, he got in the passenger side."

"So who drove?" St. John asked.

Donzetta looked at Chacón before answering. "The other girl was driving. I didn't see much of her at all."

So there were four of them. St. John showed her the pictures he had assembled.

Donzetta picked out Jane Ferrar from the first set and Cyrill "Thor" McCarthy from the second. St. John thanked her for her help and walked back out to the parking lot with Chacón following.

St. John opened his car door and threw his paperwork on the front seat. "So how much has Munch told you?"

"About what?"

"Jane Ferrar."

"She hasn't said a thing to me."

"She didn't tell you I had come to see her about the murder?"

"Which murder?"

St. John held his mouth open in exaggerated shock. "Jane Ferrar, Munch's old running partner. Her body was found in the storm drain near Riviera last week."

"I know of the case," Rico said carefully, "but Munch didn't say anything to me about it."

"I guess it's not like you to tell her everything."

"That's none of your business."

"Is that right?" St. John slammed his door shut and planted himself in Chacón's path. "I'm making it my business. She's a friend, a good friend, and I don't like seeing her dicked around."

Rico raised his palm chest-high. It was a cop interrogation tool (or trick, depending on your perspective). Human nature was to stop talking when a hand was lifted thus.

"Don't pull that shit on me," St. John said.

"You don't know everything. I'm telling you for your own good to just leave it alone."

They were chest to chest now. Chacón had St. John by six inches and fifteen years, but St. John didn't give a fuck. Chacón might kick his ass, and that was in no way a given, but St. John could hurt him too. Maybe he'd get lucky with a punch or a knee in the balls before Mr. Readycock saw it coming.

"The last thing I want to do is hurt her," Chacón said.

St. John breathed hard through his nose, feeling his heart go boom, boom, boom. He got pissed off all over again. "I'm not going to get myself upset over this. You heard what I said. You fuck with her and you fuck with me."

"Fair enough. Now, are we going to box or are we going to work?"

Chacón seemed happy to follow whatever lead St. John cared to take, and St. John felt a grudging respect for the guy. He wasn't a sissy anyway.

"All right, here's the deal. I'm going to help you with your case and you're going to help me with mine." St. John held up four fingers. "We got four assholes at the scene of a murder." He folded two fingers. "Two of them are ID'd as Cyrill McCarthy and my victim, Jane Ferrar." He added a finger. "You've got three dead dope dealers with V's carved in their chests. I'm putting my victim at your scene. Jane Ferrar suffered from polio as a child. Her right foot is a size four. We've got small bloody footprints in the carpet, a V carved in her chest, and a well-documented history with Cyrill 'Thor' McCarthy."

"And we've got Stacy Lansford's letter," Rico said, "about McCarthy's involvement in a multiple murder that substantiates years of rumors from other sources."

"I want the second guy and the driver." St. John opened his car door and started to lower himself into the driver's seat. "I'm going back over old FI cards for known associates and see what I come up with."

Chacón held St. John's door open. His sunglasses were dark in the bright afternoon sun. He held his mouth as if he were in pain. "You're going to find Munch's name."

"I know that. I'm interested in the second man."

"So was I." Rico produced a photograph of a laughing Hispanic man. The guy was holding a brown quart bottle of Budweiser in one hand and flashing the peace symbol with the other.

His black goatee was trimmed so that it formed a point beneath his chin. All that was missing were the horns, tail, and red suit.

St. John stared at the picture, a sick, bleak feeling beginning deep in his stomach. "Isn't this Asia's dad?"

Rico nodded. "Jonathan Garillo aka Sleaze John."

"Oh boy," St. John said. He rubbed a hand over his mouth and exhaled loudly through his nose.

Chacón returned the photograph to his pocket. For a long moment, neither man spoke.

St. John shook his head as if to negate the words he spoke next. "One of us needs to ask her."

Rico raised his sunglasses and stared into St. John's eyes.

"What?" St. John squinted back. "You think it should be you?"

"There is a third option."

"You want to bury it? Is that what you're saying?"

"I didn't say anything and you don't have to do anything. You've got your own case. But ask yourself, how is justice best served here?"

"You think that's our choice?" St. John asked.

"Who better?"

Chapter 20

⸺

Munch took a break midmorning, telling Lou she had some personal business, and went to the law office of Jim McManis. McManis was an attorney who specialized in criminal law, and Munch had hooked him up with her crazy friend Ellen, who had recently needed his help.

He ushered her into his private office and took a seat behind his big desk. She sat opposite him. A big picture window offered a view of West Los Angeles all the way to the ocean. She watched a plane fly north and wondered how long it took to get a passport.

McManis asked her if she wanted coffee, but she declined. These guys charged by the minute.

"I need to ask you something, about a point of law."

"All right." He moved aside a file on his desk, clasped his hands in front of him, and gave her his full attention.

"Say there was a murder committed, a dope rip-off gone wrong, and the dope dealers were killed."

"More than one?"

"Yeah."

"Definitely a one eighty-seven. First-degree murder and probably special circumstances because the murder was committed in the commission of a robbery and there were multiple victims. So the DA could ask for the death penalty. Wait a minute and I'll look it up."

Munch waited while he grabbed a book off the shelf behind him. Her heart was beating so hard that it hurt her throat. She pressed a hand against her chest and took deep breaths.

"Who's this for?" McManis asked. "I can ask the prosecutor in the case."

"There is no prosecutor."

"Charges haven't been filed?"

"No. I don't want to get too specific. Don't ask me to name names."

"I won't."

"It's for a friend of a friend. And I don't know the last name. And this friend wasn't one of the killers, they were in the car, waiting outside." *Shut up now.*

"Killers plural?"

Munch wished she had never come. "Yeah."

"Was the friend the driver?"

She hesitated for a second, then answered reluctantly, "Yeah, the friend was the driver."

"Okay, here it is." He adjusted his bifocals. " 'Anyone with knowledge of unlawful purpose is considered equally culpable.' So your driver of the getaway car is responsible for the full crime. It goes to natural and probable consequence of the crime.

Is murder a natural and probable consequence of armed robbery? Certainly. Did the driver know the perps were armed?"

Thor was always armed, Munch thought, then realized that McManis was waiting for an out-loud answer. "Is there any way I can get a copy of what you're reading from?"

"Sure. It's from a book of jury instructions—what the judge reads when he instructs the jury. I refer to this all the time when I want a succinct statement of law without all the doublespeak. I'll have my secretary make a copy for you." He pressed a button on his phone.

Eighty bucks later, Munch returned to her car. Even behind the familiar steering wheel, she felt no control. Every short-haired man around her looked like a cop. She wondered for a moment if Thor was in on the conspiracy. Maybe he'd come to the meeting as a plant and was wearing a wire, hoping to draw her into an admission. It was crazy thinking and didn't pan out for a variety of reasons. Shit, he had done much worse. He was up there in the apartment. It was his knife, probably his idea. But what if he told his version first, made some kind of deal with the cops? Did they believe the first witness who came forth? Had she already lost the race she didn't have enough sense to enter?

Back at work, the phone seemed to ring at twice its normal volume. She prayed it wouldn't be Rico. She needed to come clean with him or break it off. She practiced the scene in her head. She pictured them sitting in a room, maybe her kitchen.

"I need to tell you about some things," she would say. "I want to lay it all out for you. So you'll understand about me, the things I know, the things I've seen and heard and done."

She'd never told anyone the whole story beginning to end. There had always been parts she'd kept to herself.

Even now, even in this fantasy version, she knew she'd put a slant on it all. It was not just the winners who wrote the history books, it was the survivors.

She'd explain to him how then, in 1975, the going slang for heroin was boy, cocaine was referred to as girl. Thor gave Munch a share of the coke and she made a trade with a dealer in Inglewood, the girl for the boy. She returned to Venice. Possessed of more dope than she could use in a week, she drove to Main Street. She was not by nature a hoarder; hoarding would indicate an expectation of a future.

She found two hookers working, her friend Roxanne and a black woman named Evie.

"Take a break," she told them. "I've brought a gift."

They spent a quarter to use the bathroom in the Laundromat. The three whores huddled around the fixture so often called the porcelain altar. It was fitting, as they were on their knees in fervent adulation. The sink was broken, so they used the water from the toilet tank to mix their dope. They planned to boil it before they injected it into their bloodstream, so what was the big deal? They giggled as they went through the preparation ritual, giddy with anticipation.

Evie lifted her blouse and showed them her distended belly, hitting it with her fist in frustration.

"I don't know what's the matter with me," she said. "I've always had a flat stomach, and now this lump is hard as a rock."

Munch glanced up briefly, pretending to care, then went back to preparing the dope.

Days later, the dope was all gone. She didn't look for more. Instead, she drank. The whiskey gave her sharp pains in her stomach, but those stopped after a week. It was like smoking.

Sometimes the only thing that cured a cough was lighting another cigarette.

She decided she needed time to think this through, time out from dope and crazy violence. She was a legal adult, had been for a year, and if she kept going along with Thor and them, it was going to get worse. She wasn't afraid of dying, but she was afraid of life in prison.

She left the Flats. There were no dramatic good-byes. She just walked out the door one day and didn't come back. She heard that Sleaze went to Texas for a while. Thor got busted for shoplifting steak; the cow blood seeped through his white T-shirt and gave him away. Jane went back to New York because her father died.

And much more happened.

Bikers were killed in late-night crashes. Babies drowned in bathtubs, while others were born missing fingers. Munch moved in with some biker chicks who had a small wooden bungalow on one of the canal streets. The house burned down while she wasn't home, destroying all her worldly possessions. Deb and Boogie moved to Oregon—took their dream of going to the country and made good on it. Or so it seemed. Roxanne headed up to Alaska, where they were building a pipeline, lured by the promise of adventure and easy cash.

At some point Sleaze returned to L.A. He straightened up long enough to get a job driving for Sunshine Yellow Cab and began hanging out with some square broad named Karen, who worked for the phone company.

He's only with her to scam her, Munch told herself.

She doesn't remember who called who first. There was always a magnetism between the two of them, an attraction of like molecules. What began as a morning fix turned into a weeklong binge. And then she and Sleaze were at it again, playing every-one around them, including Karen, who Sleaze went to see on her lunch breaks, wheedling twenties out of her while Munch waited in the front seat of his cab, parked around the corner with the meter off.

But then Sleaze made a big mistake. He started giving Karen tastes of dope. He had to, he said, or she'd cut him off.

It didn't take long before she was through at the phone com-pany, standing on street corners, still looking like someone's sec-retary. But she'd learned the look. That bold stare at the single men cruising Main Street. Karen, with her college education and orthodontic-straightened teeth, was getting in those cars, talking the talk, doing the deed, bringing the money back to share with Sleaze. And then Sleaze told Munch they couldn't hang out together anymore.

Munch said, I was about to tell you the same thing.

For some reason that she didn't understand, she made one more attempt to find another way to live. She started spending time with a mechanic named Al at Venice Cab Company, fixing the high-mileage sedans in the small hours of the night. She wasn't screw-ing Al. He seemed to like her for some other reason.

Around that time, Al moved in with his girlfriend. The land-lord of his single apartment on Paloma Canal wouldn't give Al his first month's rent back so Al told Munch she could stay there for that month since it was already paid for. She stocked the small refrigerator and got a glimpse of what life could be like. She found peace hanging brake shoes, working until her knees felt locked open, and she was too tired to do more than bathe and collapse into bed with her hair still wet.

Wizard, who owned Venice Cab, gave her a three-nights-a-week job and a little room at the back of the garage when the month ran out on the single apartment.

The space Wizard let her use was once part of the garage. It had a concrete floor, cinder-block walls, and a small window that looked out to his vegetable garden. He had built an interior wall with plywood to make this little harbor. The bed was a mattress on a wooden workbench built from two-by-fours, four feet off the ground. There was plenty of room for storage underneath. She didn't come close to filling it. The bathroom was at the other end of the shop, a toilet and a sink, and she made do.

She loved the night shift, loved it when the world slowed down to a trickle of the infrequent lone driver. Bars were closed, drunks passed out, druggies stayed indoors. At four in the morning, an occasional trucker lumbered down Main Street. Delivery trucks came with dawn.

She started collecting wrenches and sockets, soon outgrowing the lunch-box-size tackle box Wizard had given her. At his encouragement, she saved her money and bought a five-drawer Craftsman toolbox new at Sears. It was red with gray handles. She engraved her name on the top and kept the key to the lock in her pocket.

She was really getting a handle on things, not drinking until the end of the shift, and then just to take the edge off the bennies.

Then, one day, she got that little urge, triggered by any number of things. The smell of burning sulfur was enough to do it, to give her that feeling in the back of her throat, to start the clatter of demons in her head. She remembered thinking she'd get a taste—just a taste—to fix a particularly nasty hangover. Once the idea entered her brain, she could think of nothing else. Maybe she could handle it this time, shoot a little smack without getting all strung out again. Dope fiends even had a name for it: chipping. Meaning occasional use. A now-and-then thing. If it had a name, it must be possible, right? She didn't know then that one time was already too many and a thousand was never enough.

She was out of touch with the life and had to search all the old haunts until she found a dealer. By then her nose was wide open. There was no question but that she would find it.

It was a dangerous combination: money in her pocket and knowing who had the bag. Soon she was camping out in the alley outside Donna Dumbcunt's little basement apartment, waiting for the bitch to get back and open for business.

Munch didn't forget exactly, she was just too busy chasing the bag to go back to work. She let Wizard down one time too many. And then she was right back at it with one more sorrow to drown.

Too sick to turn tricks, she dragged herself back to Flower George, telling herself that staying with her father was only going to be a temporary arrangement. She would get out, she would make it to the country, and she would have that little house that was all her own, her own kitchen to stock, a little plot of ground where she'd grow vegetables, maybe even have some chickens, yeah, and a milk cow.

Flower George took her to the Mexicans, living five, six, ten to a flat, and waited outside smoking cigarettes while she serviced the masses. Even then, at ten bucks a pop, there were those who refused her. Somehow this hurt her feelings. What did it take, she wondered, until nothing was left?

The Mexicans had pickup trucks and wore black cowboy hats. There were decals of brown horse heads on the rear windows of their pickup trucks. Their jeans and boots smelled of manure.

She saw her face in the mirror, saw the dark black sacks

beneath her eyes, and realized to her horror that she'd done it again, she'd gotten all strung out. She didn't want to be a slave to grains of powder, to sloppy middle-aged fat men who tried to put their mouth on hers no matter how many times she told them, "No kissing."

She wanted a new town where nobody knew her, a job fixing cars, maybe even a motorcycle if that wasn't too much to dream.

And then the cops were on her again. She totaled two cars while driving a borrowed truck and tried to flee the scene. They found her syringes. They couldn't keep the revulsion from their faces.

"You use these?" they asked.

In the cold harsh light of the booking room, she saw how disgusting her works had to look to these people. The cotton thread she'd used to tie the rubber to the plunger. The bent needle. The old blackened spoon, licked clean too many times.

She went to jail, but only for a month.

Flower George wasn't waiting in the parking lot for her when she got released.

She had to hitchhike back to Venice. Sleaze was back in town, she heard. She didn't have the energy left to find him.

She never asked, but once someone mentioned that Thor was in the joint. She waited for them to say for what, but the specifics didn't come up, and she let the news wash past her.

She meant to get a place, but got no farther than the mattress on the floor at Flower George's. One of the Mexicans gave her a card to the free clinic after they'd had sex. Only half sex really because the sores on his dick made it too painful to continue. The card was written in both Spanish and English.

It read: *You may have been infected.*

She threw it away. There were some things she didn't want to know, but mostly she didn't care. What comes around, goes around.

She saw Evie again. Evie, the hooker with the knot in her belly.

Evie said, "Guess what? You're never going to believe it. You remember how big my stomach was getting? Turns out I was pregnant. I didn't even know until I went to jail. How about that?"

Munch acted mildly amused, imagining Evie's surprise. She didn't think that would ever happen to her—the not knowing part. She'd only been pregnant once, when she was seventeen. The pregnancy was over before it barely begin, yet she knew the whole time. Felt an excited flutter at the thought of a new life inside her, started collecting baby stuff, had a crib and everything. It was Sleaze John's baby, she was sure of that. She couldn't believe how much a miscarriage hurt. The hospital shot her up with Demerol and after that she was on her own.

And then it was February 12, 1977, and she was on a bar stool at the Venture Inn and some sad-eyed man was buying her drinks. The man was Mace St. John and he was there to arrest her for the murder of Flower George. By the grace of God and the programs of Alcoholics Anonymous and Narcotics Anonymous, she hadn't had a drink or a hit of dope since, and all it took was complete abstinence and changing everything about herself. Simple. Not the same thing as easy.

Sometimes she wondered if Sleaze had to die so she could live. If he hadn't died, would he have eventually drawn her back into the life? Did God toss a coin to make the choice? No, that wasn't right. God didn't test people. He didn't have to. Life tested people. Every day in a person's life, every action taken or not taken went against his or her final grade.

With all these images from her past raging in her head, Munch arrived back at work. Safe, comfortable work, where all her customers knew her as the lady mechanic—the woman they could count on to fix their problems and give them a fair deal. The guys she worked with knew she had some problems in her past, but they didn't talk about them. It wasn't relevant.

God, please, let me keep my life. Don't let this end.

Chapter 21

M unch looked up as a pickup truck outfitted for construction work pulled up to the self-service pumps. She saw the HIGHER POWERED bumper sticker and watched to see who got out. The driver looked familiar. He was big, well over six feet, and about forty judging by the gray in his hair and the seasoned look to the muscles in his arms.

She walked out to greet him. "You a friend of Bill W.?" This was program code. Bill Wilson was one of the founders of AA.

The guy grinned. "Sure am."

They exchanged names and lengths of sobriety. He was Mike, he told her, Big Mike.

"Yeah," she said, "I've seen you around. What do you run in this thing?"

"Regular," he said, "especially at these prices."

Munch made no apology. The station was in Brentwood. Everything cost more, including the rent. She handed him the pump nozzle and flipped the cradle up. "Do you have a job around here?"

"Mandeville Canyon."

"There's been some trouble up there lately."

"The cops came by yesterday. They wanted to look at my employee manifest."

"Did they say why?"

"They were investigating a murder. Some woman was found down by the junior high school."

Munch held her reaction in check. "In the storm drain. I've been following it in the newspaper. What did it have to do with your job site?"

"I don't know. They wouldn't say. Maybe they go after all the working stiffs. All I know is I got a lot of guys working for me who are trying to get their lives together. Guys with records. I know these guys. They're sober. They're trying. How would it be if they knew I gave them up to the cops?"

"You got a guy named Cyrill painting for you? He's on the Program."

"We're not far enough along in the project for finish work." The gas pump clicked off at $19.85. Big Mike removed the nozzle from his gas tank and replaced his gas cap. He handed Munch a twenty before she could explain that she wasn't a pump attendant. She went to get his change, but when she looked up from the cash register, he was already driving away.

She went into Lou's office and sat behind his desk. He had been calling junkyards earlier, looking for a steering column for a Ford Econoline van, and the phone book was still lying on top of his desk.

She was thinking about all those TV and VCR boxes Rico had

that were stamped PASCOE APPLIANCES. She didn't want him to be crooked, necessarily, but it would level the playing field between them if he was.

She turned to the Yellow Pages and looked up Pascoe Appliances. They had a quarter-page ad that claimed they were a family-owned business established in 1952. The phone number was in bold red ink.

A man's voice answered the phone. "Pascoe. How can I help you?"

"I know this is going to sound strange, but have you been robbed lately?"

"Personally?"

"The store, I mean."

"No, and nobody better mess with me either. My daughter is engaged to a cop."

"Would that be Kathy?"

"You know her?"

"I know the name. I hadn't heard about the engagement."

"We just found out ourselves. We couldn't be happier. And who are you?"

She mumbled that she had to go and hung up just as Lou walked into the office.

"I'm not feeling too good," she said.

"I can see that. You want to take off early?"

"Yeah, I won't be any good to you here." They talked a few minutes about the jobs in progress and what she expected to come in.

"You think this bug is going to last?" he asked.

"Too soon to tell."

"Go now if you want."

"Thanks, I just have a few more calls to make."

He held her gaze for a minute. "You need anything else, ask. What about Asia?"

"She's got rehearsals after school. I don't need to pick her up until six."

"Good, good. Well, then. I'll, uh, be outside."

"Thanks."

She didn't know where she wanted to go, she just knew it needed to be somewhere where no one would know to look for her. She reached into her purse and pulled out Roxanne's phone bill, then she turned to the front of the phone book. This time she looked up prefixes, checking them against the Los Angeles phone numbers Nathan had called from Roxanne's. She found two calls to the same number in Compton, several more to three different numbers on the Westside, and one to a Valley exchange.

Deb kept up connections, it seemed. Were any of these dope connections? Is that where Nathan had gotten his drugs?

She called the Compton number. "Is this Mrs. Franklin? Doleen Franklin?"

"Yes it is."

"You don't know me. My name is Munch Mancini."

"You the girl Nathan's been staying with."

"Yes, ma'am. Do you think I could come visit you? I want to discuss something that involves your grandson."

"What's he done?"

"Nothing too terrible. I was hoping to keep it like that."

Munch wrote down the address and told the woman she'd be there as soon as traffic permitted.

Doleen Franklin had a small wooden clapboard house with a cactus garden. The spiniest species grew beneath the windows. Munch knew this was no accident. All the windows on the block were protected by burglar bars. Likenesses of big-jowled dogs and the business ends of large-caliber revolvers hung on chain-link gates. Red-and-white signs read BEWARE OF DOG and BEWARE OF OWNER.

Munch parked on the street. The front door opened; an older black woman emerged and lifted a hand in greeting.

"Mrs. Franklin?"

"Call me Doleen. That or Mama D. The onlyest people ever call me Mrs. Franklin want my money or come to tell me bad news."

"I'm here for neither."

She chuckled and held the door open. "Come on in. I made us some lemonade."

The house smelled of fried food. Doleen was a big woman with fleshy arms and wide hips. Her fingernails were trimmed short. Her mostly gray hair was permed in tight curls and held flat against her head with a hair net. She was wearing a flowered housedress, cotton hose, and sensible shoes—black and rubber-soled. She wore thick-lensed eyeglasses with dark, no-nonsense frames. Munch sat on the living room couch on cushions wrapped in knitted blankets. The chairs on either side of the coffee table were upholstered in fabric from different decades, but coordinated with lace doilies on the backs and arms.

Religious statues adorned the bookshelves. The television was on and tuned to the soap opera *All My Children*.

Doleen shuffled into the room with a lacquered tea tray. Munch stood and took it from her.

"Bless your heart. You want some cookies? I got some HoHos up in the freezer."

"No, I'm fine. Please sit. I don't mean for you to go to any trouble."

Doleen sat next to Munch and fixed her attention on the television, where skinny white women plotted against each other. She chuckled at their antics, shaking her head and murmuring, "Don't that beat all?"

Munch watched the soap people confront each other on the fuzzy black-and-white screen. Years ago, she and Deb had followed this same show, and when Munch went to jail that month, she learned that prisoners male and female followed the series with religious fervor. Susan Lucci's Erica was as conniving as ever and still beautiful. It wasn't difficult to pick up the story line. Erica was scheming to break up yet another happy couple.

Munch waited until the show broke for commercial to broach the subject of her visit. "Nathan's a great kid."

Doleen's eyes loomed large behind her thick lenses. "Um hmm." She said it as if she were waiting for the "but."

"He's working hard. Got himself a job as soon as he got to town."

"Bless his little heart. You see what he gave me for my birfday?" She got up before Munch could stop her and lumbered off to the bathroom. She returned moments later holding a glass swan hand-towel holder.

"When was your birthday?"

"January."

Munch turned the swan over in her hands. She would treasure such a gift. "I never met Walter, but I knew Deb pretty well."

The older woman closed her eyes as if in prayer and said, "Deborah."

Doleen limped stiff-legged down her hallway, telling Munch over her shoulder, "Wait here." When she returned from the back of the house, she had a photograph album. She set it on the coffee table, moving aside the bowls of waxed fruit and peppermint candy. She opened the thick cardboard cover and showed Munch pictures of smiling black people.

"This is my Walter," she said. Walter was sitting in what appeared to be a living room, looking up and smiling at the camera. His arms were skinny, but knotted with muscles. He was wearing a white sleeveless T-shirt, a thick gold chain, and a big smile. His hair was styled in a big Afro and he was no-lie gorgeous.

"Walter was one fine-looking man," Munch said.

Doleen smiled fondly and traced his picture with weathered fingers. "He was beautiful just like his daddy."

"Was he always into music?"

"Um hmm." Now her voice was deep and melodious. It often seemed to Munch that black people had a way of tapping into a rhythm of a world that she had no access to, some undercurrent of beat that connected them all. Infinitely hip, dangerously seductive. She heard tantalizing wisps of that cadence in every "uh-huh" and "That's right" uttered by people of colors mysterious to her. Her old boss Wizard was suffused with it. She used to time herself to the rhythm of his nodding head, falling easily into the beat of it when she was standing next to him, as if she were listening to a song with a contagious pulse. It was a wondrous thing about him—perhaps born of a heritage of pain—its root in exotic lands rich with color and texture. Nathan didn't have it, she realized suddenly. Another thing they'd stamped out of him.

"Black is beautiful" wasn't a sentiment expressed much up there in redneck land.

"Walter played the piano over at the church when he was li'l. Such beautiful hands." Doleen kissed her fingers and touched them gently to the photograph.

"Deb said he worked three jobs at once?"

"Oh, child, yes. That boy was going places. Alls he ever wanted was to make his music. The ladies loved him too. Yes they did."

Doleen turned the page to a picture of young Nathan dressed in his Sunday best—a powder-blue suit that Deb had sewn herself.

"I remember when Deb had these taken," Munch said. "We got these coupons from someone who came to the door."

"She was always good about pictures, bless her heart," Doleen said, then added, "Yes she was," under her breath, talking more to the past than to Munch. She turned the page to show Munch a group of four more photographs, this time of Nathan and Walter side by side on the Venice boardwalk. Munch wondered if the Social Security people would accept pictures as proof. Nathan was wearing his little Levi's coat, the one with the Harley wings patch sewn on the back and treble clefs embroidered on the collar. Their little Boogieman. Walter wore a leather vest with nothing underneath and was making a peace symbol with his right hand. Nathan squinted into the sun, his Kodak slung around his neck.

"Do you have any of Nathan's work?"

"I do indeed." Mrs. Franklin cast a longing look at the images in her scrapbook and then pulled herself to her feet. "Come on this away."

Munch followed the older woman down the hallway, matching her pace to Nathan's grandmother's lumbering gait. They stopped at a room at the end of the hallway. The smell of candle wax filled the air. There was a single bed in the corner covered with another knit Afghan. On the dresser beside the bed, a Christmas card stood propped atop a lace doily. The front was a blue angel. "Holiday Blessings" was the printed inscription. Someone had added a handwritten note. "I haven't forgotten you."

Doleen's hand made a sweep in the direction of the card. "Sends me one every year. She shore does."

A dozen black-and-white photographs hung on the walls. They were blown to eight by ten and mounted in cheap dime-store frames that did nothing to diminish their simple power.

Munch felt the summertime joy of the stick-thin kids running through sprinklers. A seagull perched on a lamppost looked regal. She stopped before an interesting shot of traffic moving in a blur down Lincoln Boulevard and recognized the old Fox Theater marquee.

"That's an indoor swap meet now," she said. "I have one he took on Market Street, in front of that mural."

"The one wif all'n his cousins?"

"I didn't know they were his cousins. I never even knew he had all this other family."

"Yes, ma'am, he's got cousins and uncles and aunties. He never did get to knowing them like he might've."

"Because he and Deb moved to Oregon?"

"Broke my heart to send him off."

"Deb always dreamed of living in the country."

"It was safer there," Doleen said.

Munch figured the difference between safety in L.A. and Oregon was about a draw. Doleen obviously didn't know about the crowd Deb ran with.

They returned to the living room. The photo album was still lying on the coffee table. Munch flipped the page to another picture of Walter. This time it was he who was decked out in his Sunday best—a dark suit jacket with the folded triangle of a white handkerchief showing at the top of the breast pocket, starched white shirt, black tie. His head rested against the satin pillow of his open coffin. He looked asleep and not much older than he had in previous pictures. Munch had to wonder who brought a camera to a funeral.

"Such a sweet, sweet child," Doleen said. Her smile was filled with ancient and perpetual pain, but her eyes were dry, as if all her tears had been shed.

"Losing a child must be one of those things you never get over."

"No, you never ever do. That's for shore."

"Do you believe it's up to God? Do you think He chooses who dies young?"

"Some say it's always the good ones."

"I don't buy that."

"Neither me." Doleen looked long and hard at Munch as if to gauge her qualifications to receive the benefit of an old woman's wisdom. Whatever she saw seemed to satisfy her. "I think the good Lord gives us all our chances, and some just uses all theirs up'n early."

"If that's true, I'm sure on my last."

"Bless your heart."

"The reason I'm here"—*one of the reasons*—"is about Nathan's Social Security survivor benefits. Deb told me you helped with the paperwork. I called Social Security and found out they'll not only pay retroactively from the date of his father's death, but they'll keep giving Nathan a check as long as he's in high school."

"What do I have to do?"

"You need to sign a statement saying that you believe Walter is

Nathan's father. Better yet, if you have anything in Walter's handwriting acknowledging paternity ..."

"I don' know if I have anything like that. I'd have to look up in my closets."

"Thanks to you, Deb already put together most of the other stuff she needed—Walter's Social Security number, his, um, death certificate, and his tax returns. She's out of the country now, so she can't follow through, but you could." Munch reached in her pocket. "I have the number of the Social Security office in West L.A. I'll call and make an appointment."

Doleen sat down. "I don't know. I don't get around so good no more."

"I can give you a ride. This is money your son paid into a fund coming back to him through his son. It's owed to him. Actually, it would probably come to you since Nathan is a minor. I wouldn't want him getting a big lump of money right now anyway."

"Why's that?" There was a challenge in her voice.

"I'd just hate to see him blow it all. You know how kids are."

"You think he's messin' with drugs?"

"A little bit of weed. He says he's staying away from the stronger stuff, but you never know."

"Oh, Lord, not again."

"Again?"

The old woman wasn't listening. She was staring at her ceiling, a weathered hand on her ample hip. "Yeah, them things might even be up in the attic. It'll take me some time to go through them."

"Can I help?"

"Don't you have to go back to work, child?"

"Not today." She didn't mention that she was lying low.

Doleen directed Munch to the garage to fetch a ladder. The garage was a small wooden structure standing alone on the far side of the yard. Doleen had a garden of greens and sunflowers. An assortment of white cleaning rags that smelled strongly of bleach hung from the clothesline. The garage resembled a small barn with its peaked roof. Double wooden doors on ancient hinges opened to the dirt-paved alley. The garage was full of old coffee tables, lamps, boxes of odd pots and pans, and souvenir ashtrays. There was a sheet of plywood with the words GARAGE SALE TODAY painted in red block letters.

Munch used a broom to clean the rungs of cobwebs and dust and then brought the ladder into the house. The attic was actually a small crawl space in the rafters. Access was gained through a panel in the hallway. She had to go back out to her car to fetch a flashlight from her trunk before she went up.

There were several boxes stashed beneath the eaves and taped shut, which slowed her search for the artifacts of Walter Franklin's brief life.

"How you doin' up there?"

"Good, just give me a second." It was hot, the air stale and smelling of insecticide and camphor. Doleen's voice reached her as if through wads of cotton. She thought of those three men who died all those years ago in Oakwood. Did they have family who still mourned them? Was she cheating them out of a final justice? She thought of Walter's smiling face in the family album. He seemed more real to her now. Would she feel different about the Ghost Town murder victims if they had been white men? Probably not, and it still wouldn't change her actions now. The dead were dead, and ten years dead was ancient history. Like Doleen said, some people used up all their chances quick in this life.

Some kept getting new ones. For whatever reason, she had been blessed with chances. Maybe Thor was on the right path too. Who was she to bring him down?

"Wait a minute," she said, "before you break into a chorus of 'Amazing Grace.' We're talking about Thor."

"You say somethin'?" Doleen called up.

"No. I was just thinking out loud." *What about Jane's path? That should count for something. And what about the other victims? Did they have parents who mourned them? Children? Brothers and sisters?*

Ruby told her once that if she had a difficult decision she should toss a coin and then pay attention to which side she hoped would come up. That worked great on either/or situations, but was no help with matters of ethics.

She found the box marked *Walter* and dragged it over to the crawl space opening. Doleen waited below and took it from Munch as she climbed down the ladder.

Doleen limped over to her coffee table and set the box down.

"I need to go," Munch told her.

"You comin' back?"

"Yes." *I hope so.* "I have to go do something. Something I've put off for too long." Munch put the ladder away and headed for the place, the person, she should have gone to first. Mace St. John.

She drove to the police station, not knowing if he was there or what she would say to him, but feeling the need to place her life in his hands one more time.

She parked on the street and went inside the bunker-like building that housed the small West Los Angeles police force. The cop working the desk greeted her with a smile. That always took her aback, how she could go into places like this and not immediately arouse their suspicion. She had to look in a mirror to remember that what they saw now, in 1985, was not who she had been.

The cop wrote down her name and called upstairs. A few minutes later Mace St. John walked out into the anteroom. She smiled at him, feeling her lips quiver at the corners.

"What's wrong?" he asked.

"I want to help you."

"Good."

"What do you need me to do?"

"Come upstairs."

He sat her down next to his desk and started handing her photographs. "Tell me if anything jumps out at you." They were of Jane, the dump site, the stables, the autopsy, the doll she was clutching.

"How about the shelter?" she asked. "Did you find out anything there?"

"They had nothing to tell me. They don't trust the LAPD."

"I've heard that."

He started to thumb through his paperwork, stopped, looked at her. "I ran into Rico the other day."

"Yeah?"

"He's working a cold case from ten years ago."

Munch felt as if her blood had stopped circulating. She was still holding a picture of Jane and now stared at it hard, not trusting herself to speak.

"A homicide in Venice, in Oakwood. A triple homicide."

She licked her lips, not able to prevent herself from making such a telltale gesture, hoping he hadn't noticed.

"Evidence recovered at the murder scene suggests that Jane Ferrar might have been involved." He showed her the picture taken at autopsy of the slashed V on Jane's midsection. "Have you ever seen anything like this before?"

She looked him in the eye, relieved to the point of tears that he had asked her a question she could answer truthfully. "No, never. What does it mean?"

"The three victims of the Oakwood homicides had similar markings left on their torsos."

She wondered if he would make her look at pictures of those too. She had a fairly good idea of what the apartment must have looked like afterward, but she had no images of the faces. Sleaze told her once about the guy who crawled with the slit throat. He was trying to say something, Sleaze said. The dying man's lips moved, but the only sound he made came out of the gaping wound in his throat. She imagined that he must have left a thick trail of blood. She saw how it had splashed to the tops of Sleaze's, Thor's, and Jane's shoes.

"What are you thinking about?" St. John asked.

"What's fair?"

"What do you mean?"

"Say a person does things when they're young."

"Like murder?"

"Yeah, just like murder. Jane was young. She was on dope. Maybe she got caught up in a bad situation and then later turned her life around. Should she still have to pay?"

"I know people do some dumb things when they're teenagers. But three men were killed. Marks scratched into their chests, throats cut to their spines. Anyone who went up to that apartment that day and participated in that carnage crossed the line. And statistics show that anyone who participates in mass murder, multiple murder, will do it again. I couldn't let something like that go."

"Even if they were no longer a threat?"

"Even if that were true, that's not the point."

"So even if a person got into rehab, found God, and rejoined society . . ."

"Are you asking me if that could be done?"

"Yeah."

"It's done. If the killer had no conscience. If he could live with himself. If nobody rolled over on him."

"That's a lot of ifs."

"There always are."

"And they never go away."

"I don't think so," he said quietly.

She looked at her watch. "I've got to go. I've got to pick up Asia from school."

"Are you coming back?"

"Give me a few hours."

"I'll be home all night."

Chapter 22

⸺

I t was dusk. Through the front window, St. John watched Munch's car pull up to his curb. Overhead, the last birds were flying home. A duck quacked in the canal. St. John waited while Munch exited her vehicle, her feet dragging as if she barely had the energy to lift them. She walked around to the passenger door and helped Asia out of her seat belt.

He opened the door before she had a chance to knock. She had already started to turn away. The dogs piled out around him and surrounded Munch and Asia. Asia sank to her knees and let the animals lavish her face with wet licks.

"Come in," he said. "Where else would you go?"

"You're having dinner."

"It can wait."

Caroline came in from the kitchen, a dish towel in her hand. She started to ask, "Who is it?" but got no further than "Who is . . ." and then just stood there, framed by the light.

"You got a minute?" Munch asked.

Caroline pulled her in without asking what or why and hugged her. "Come inside." She led Munch into the living room and turned off the television. Mace handed Asia a tennis ball and told her to throw it for the dogs in the backyard.

Munch sat on the couch with Caroline beside her.

"Tell me," Mace said.

"I've spent all day bringing myself to think of what's happened, what it all means, what everybody wants."

"Is it all that complicated?"

"Not really. Thor wants to live on, somehow to get out from under what he's done, as if turning over a new leaf could wipe out the past. That's what I want to believe about myself. The only thing different about the two of us is degree. Like with Deb. I criticize her for being a shitty mother, and the only thing that stopped me from having some poor baby when I was using was the damage I'd done to my body. I would have had Sleaze's baby when I was seventeen, and would have dragged the poor kid from bar to bar while I searched for Prince Charming on his white Harley come to rescue me from myself." She paused to look him full in the face, her eyes large, guileless. "I never dreamed that my knight would come to me dressed in blue."

St. John wanted to take her in his arms, but he needed to hear what she had to say. Besides, she probably wasn't talking about him anyway, not anymore.

"Now I criticize Ruby for enabling her son, yet when the moment arrives, I do the same with Nathan, driven by my guilt, my contribution to his lousy childhood. I was quick to spank the kid, quick to ditch him when he wasn't convenient or interfered with my partying."

St. John didn't know who Nathan was, but didn't interrupt.

"And I condemn Jane for being in imperfect relationships, subjugating herself, taking the backseat. And here I've done it myself, gotten involved with a man who already has a woman. Pinning my hopes to the motherfucker only to find out he's marrying another woman and I was just an easy lay along the way. How do men do that? How do they disconnect their feelings from what their body does? How could he kiss me so deeply and not think of a life with me, a future with me? How could I not notice that it was only physical?"

"You're wrong about that," St. John said, drawing a surprised look from both women.

"I don't think so."

"I know so. He's looking out for you."

"He's marrying someone else. How is that looking out for me?"

"Oh, honey," Caroline said.

St. John glanced at his wife, then back at Munch. "Maybe it's a bigger favor than you know. Tell me about Thor."

"I saw him at a meeting. He's living in a halfway house here in L.A. It's in the Valley. I know the director. Thor just took a chip for thirty days and he's talking about God like he means it."

"I just want to talk to him."

"I know. You think maybe he killed Jane."

"To keep her quiet." St. John caught Caroline's eye and motioned with his head toward the back door.

She looked at him quizzically, but then said, "Asia and I are going to take the dogs for a walk."

"That would be great."

He loved her for not needing an explanation. It was time to

give Munch the old "come-to-Jesus" speech, time for him to be an asshole. It was a side of him he didn't want Caroline to see any more than she had to.

"Who wants to go for a walk?" Caroline called out the back door, the leashes already in her hand. She had a chain with a coupler that they used for the big dogs, Sam and Nicky. The new dog, Brownie, had a thinner lead made of woven fabric. Caroline handed the smaller leash to Asia.

"If you want her to come, call her. She's very good about that."

"Not like Sam," Asia said, well acquainted with the black lab's stubborn ways.

They had all migrated to the kitchen.

"Listen to Caroline, honey. Give her a chance before you yank her chain." Munch was speaking to her daughter, but she could just as easily have been directing her comment to him. He'd already given her her chance. She had to know that.

They watched Caroline, Asia, and the three dogs head off down the sidewalk. Munch licked her lips and took a breath. St. John lifted his hand before she buried herself in any lie she couldn't dig out of. Whatever she thought of herself, she wasn't a very good liar.

He shut the door, leaving just the two of them standing in the kitchen. He pointed to one of the chairs pulled out from the table and seated himself in the other. "I need you to make a choice and you need to make it now. You can be a crook or you can be a witness."

"I can't pick 'none of the above'?"

He waited.

She shook her head, an almost bemused expression on her face. "Jane's been quiet for years. I don't know what he thought he had to worry about. She would have never turned on him."

"Quiet about what?" He needed her to say it.

"The murders. The ones in Ghost Town in April of '75."

The silence between them stretched to three minutes. He realized she was crying. He waited for that to finish too. Then she told him everything.

He listened to her story with stoic patience, not letting his pleasure show. With the information she provided, and her willing testimony, he was looking at closing Jane's homicide and the triple.

"You know," he finally said, "you should have come to me sooner."

"I went to see a lawyer and he said under the felony murder law I was just as guilty."

"You went to go see a lawyer instead of talking to me?"

"Well, yeah. I didn't want to put you in a bad position. You know, of having to bust me or not."

"But if you came to me to help with the case, why would I bust you?"

She looked down at her hands, picked at the grease in her cuticles.

"What?" he asked.

"I wasn't sure about helping you."

"Why not?"

"I've given that a lot of thought in the last few days."

"You've helped the police before."

"I know. But never as a coconspirator."

"And that makes a difference?"

"Felt like it. I've never bought my way out of trouble at the expense of someone else."

"Look"—he took her hands in his—"the way it sounds to me, you didn't know they were going up into that apartment to kill anyone, you didn't know they were going up there to do anything but get high."

"I didn't."

"I'll talk to the DA myself. With your cooperation helping us close these cases, I don't see that you'll have any charges leveled against you."

"Thank you."

"Now, is there anything else I should know about?"

"No, that's it."

She answered way too quickly for his liking.

"We're not quite done."

"I know," she said. "You need me to finger him."

"Finger him? What kind of talk is that? You think you're doing something wrong? Breaking the code? You want to be an asshole? You want to be a homegirl?"

"No."

"What the fuck's the matter with you? This guy is a murderer. A multiple murderer. He needs to pay for what he's done."

"I know, I know. I want to help. I want to be one of the good guys."

"And how are you going to do that?"

"I'll go see Thor and I'll wear a wire."

"You sure?"

"I need to do it."

"It could be dangerous."

"You'll be nearby."

He felt the weight of her utter trust and knew he would never abuse it.

Chapter 23

Munch called New Start halfway house. Danny T. answered the phone.

"I need to talk to Cyrill," she told Danny after identifying herself.

"I'll go get him."

"No, it has to be in person." The cops wanted the meet somewhere alone and in the open.

"He isn't allowed to leave the premises, but you can come here."

"All right, I'll do that."

She hung up and turned to the representatives of law enforcement surrounding her. They were at the West Los Angeles police station, upstairs in the detective bullpen. Rico was there, though, as if by some prearranged agreement, made no effort to speak to her privately. Cassiletti and St. John took the chairs on either side of her. Three other men were new to her. They had been introduced as Josh Greenberg, an assistant DA, Sergeant Flutie, the watch commander, and a slight, bearded guy named Tam Spiva, who was in charge of the audio equipment.

Spiva handed her a small black microphone attached to an alligator clip and instructed her to snake it up under her shirt and clip it to her bra.

"Give me a sound check," he said.

"Our Father who art in heaven—"

"That's good."

"I wasn't done."

He patted her shoulder. "You'll be fine. Just try not to sweat."

She smiled at that.

"You think of a word yet?" Rico asked.

"For what?"

Rico looked at St. John, something like surprise on his face. "If something feels wrong, you say the code word and we'll move in."

Spiva chuckled. "Last month, I wired this feeb for a solicitation sting. The plan was, when the hooker took off her clothes, he was supposed to say, 'Looks like Christmas.' "

"What went wrong?" Munch asked.

"The woman was so ugly that when she took off her clothes he said, 'Looks like Halloween.' "

"Help me," she said, adjusting the clip so that it didn't jab her breast.

Spiva moved to assist her but she waved him off. "No, I mean I'll say 'Heaven help me' if I think it's going bad."

"That'll work." Spiva patted her arm. "Don't worry. We'll be listening."

"I know. The force is with me."

* * *

The halfway house was in Sun Valley near the intersection of Tuxford and Lankershim. Sun Valley sounded like it should be a happy place, and maybe it was for some people. To her, it was an ugly town, defined by sweatshop factories, junkyards, and railroad tracks. Most of the billboards were in Spanish and offered services such as legal assistance and family planning. Compared to someplace like Tijuana, it was probably a slice of heaven.

Rico wore a blue beanie cap pulled down to his eyebrows and a hooded sweatshirt. St. John had a five o'clock shadow to go with his stained tan windbreaker. Cassiletti, in a black cable-knit sweater, sat slumped in the backseat tapping his foot nervously against the hump in the carpet until St. John growled at him to stop.

The halfway house was in a converted motel complex and enclosed in ten-foot-high chain link. She signed in at the front desk, leaving St. John, Cassiletti, and Rico parked halfway down the block with earphones.

The guy at the desk, a wizened little dark-skinned black man who made her think of a homeless version of Sammy Davis, Jr., led her across a hard-packed dirt courtyard to a building in the back. Thor was already inside sweeping the linoleum floor.

"Your visitor's here," Sammy's double said.

Thor gave his push broom one last thrust and then leaned it against the wall. He was dressed in jeans, work boots, and a T-shirt that read PARKER CARPET and below that the helpful motto THE FUZZY SIDE GOES UP.

"Aren't you cold?" Munch asked, pulling her coat tighter around her.

Long tables were pushed against the wall. Collapsed metal

folding chairs stood next to them on a wheeled gurney. AA banners hung on the wall with the usual proclamations: WE CARE, LET GO AND LET GOD. Each of the twelve steps and twelve traditions were spelled out on individual placards. In English.

Thor lifted two chairs easily from the rack, opened them, and invited her to sit. "I'm used to it. Did you come here to get warmed up?"

She thought about how those words would sound to her lover's ear and sent a nervous look over her shoulder out toward the street. "I'm not here for me."

"Oh yeah?"

"We need to talk."

"About?"

"The cops came to see me. About Jane." She opened her coat, lessening the layers between his mouth and the microphone.

"Yeah." His tone was completely neutral. She'd have to do better than that.

She leaned closer to him. "They know."

"What do they know?"

"They know she was at the Ghost Town thing in '75. They know all about Sleaze and Jane and you. They have evidence you were there."

"They don't have shit. They never have. They're playing you."

"Nobody's playing me. They might have played Jane, but she was never that bright."

"She wasn't that dumb either."

"How's that?"

"She would never go against me."

"Maybe she wasn't as scared of you as you'd like to think."

The clip digging into the soft flesh of her chest began to burn.

She longed to itch the spot. She squeezed her arms at her sides, pushing her breasts together to relieve the pressure.

The movement brought his focus to her cleavage, but his expression was dark.

"What are you saying?" he asked.

She followed his gaze and saw the slight square protrusion in her blouse. "If they talk to you, what will you say?"

"I won't say shit. I wasn't there."

"Someone must have seen you guys in the hallway or leaving the building."

"Who?"

"They didn't tell me."

"They didn't tell you because there isn't anyone. It's bullshit."

The clip on her bra made a slight click as it disengaged.

Thor reached out to her with surprising speed and clamped a hand over her mouth. His other hand went to the back of her head and he lifted her like that, right off the chair. She kicked at it, hoping to make a racket. Her heel only glanced off the seat. It scooted back a few inches, but remained upright.

She ripped at his hands, trying to pry them loose. He was covering her nose too and she couldn't get any air. He dragged her to a side door, pushing it open with his hip, and then they were outside next to the halfway house's small fleet of vans. Her feet made periodic skips on the dirt seeking leverage, but he was too strong. Her vision grew dark and her fingers tingled as the lack of oxygen shut down her body. Thor spun her so that the back of her head was in his chest, which freed his hand to rip open her shirt.

She flailed at his eyes, but he seemed impervious to her attack. The wire separated easily from the microphone in his big hand.

He slid the van door open, lifted her head by the hair. She only had time to draw one breath before his fist slammed into the bridge of her nose and sent her spiraling to the back of the van.

"Something's wrong," Rico said.

St. John felt it too. "We've lost the feed."

"Let's go in."

They opened their doors and stepped out just as a white van burst through the chain-link gate.

Munch felt the thickening flesh between her eyes. She wasn't out, not completely, but it was a moment before she could collect her thoughts.

"Is this your doing too?" Thor snarled as he waved a blue greeting card envelope over his head. "Every fucking year? You and that cunt fucking with my head?"

She buried her face in her knees, fighting to return to full consciousness.

Get it together.

The van shook as it rumbled over unpaved ground. She heard a train's air horn from a distance. A crate full of plumbing fixtures slid out from beneath the front seat and came to rest by her foot. There were no good-size lengths of pipes, none suitable as a club, mostly elbows and threaded brass tees.

She heard sirens and hoped they were coming for her, hoped they wouldn't be too late. She stood, grasping at steel reinforcement beams on the van's walls. The back door was blocked by gallon cans of paint, thick canvas tarps, and wooden ladders. There was no handle on the inside of the side door and she would never make it to the front passenger door without him grabbing her and stopping her. The sound of the train grew louder. Now she heard the ding, ding, ding of the railroad crossing gate.

She grabbed a plumbing fixture from the box and threw it at his head. It missed him but hit the windshield, cracking it. He pitched the steering wheel hard to the right and she went down again. The box of plumbing parts spilled out and rolled with her on the van's dirty uncarpeted floor. She picked up whatever was loose and threw the various pieces of copper and steel at him, aiming at his head, all the while screaming at him in her rage. The van rocked as the steering wheel jerked from side to side in his hands. She knew that the chances were good they'd roll, but in her fury she didn't care. She wanted him hurt and she wanted him stopped. At any cost.

There was a sound of cracking wood as the van burst through the red wooden arm of the semaphore signal pole. She heard the hiss and scream of the train's air brakes, the blare of its warning horn. The rear of the van cleared the tracks. Almost. There was a sickening, ugly crunch as metal tore into metal, then mated in a deadly embrace. The van was blown along as if in a hurricane. She braced herself for impact. The scream of steel on steel filled her head. Different-colored lights flashed through the windows. She threw an arm across her eyes and knew she was going to die. The forward momentum stopped, shifting suddenly and violently to a sideways roll as the van broke loose from the train. She rolled with the inside of the van, losing sense of up and down, night and day. At last it came to a creaking halt upright.

Some time must have passed because she realized she was waking up. The roof was dented in. The shattered glass of the windshield held together by its lamination folded inward, leaving the windshield wipers sticking, incongruously unbent, into midair.

She realized something else. She was alone.

Carefully and slowly she moved her limbs. Everything seemed to work. There was a sharp stabbing pain in her right ankle and when she pulled her pant leg up she discovered she'd lost some flesh on her shin. Floodlights from overhead filled the van. A voice on a megaphone warned her to come out slowly with her hands in the air.

Fuck 'em, she thought. They could come to her. Then she had an unpleasant notion involving tear gas and stun grenades and decided that she'd better do as they asked.

She limped to the front seat of the van, climbing over the engine cover to get there. Broken glass littered the seat. The engine had stalled. She reached over and shut off the key while yelling, "I'm coming out. Alone."

The train had come to a stop and the night was filled with urgent sirens. St. John, Rico, and Cassiletti arrived in their undercover car. Their badges were now displayed prominently on their chests. Rico had lost the beanie. He got to her first.

"Are you all right?"

"Just a few bumps."

He had her face between his hands and was examining her nose. "I don't think it's broken but you're going to have a couple shiners."

"Did you get him?"

"Not yet. Was he hurt?"

"Not enough apparently."

"That's my girl."

"Am I?"

St. John reached them. "Did you see what direction he went?"

"No, sorry."

"Don't be sorry. Shit, I'm the one who's sorry." He spit. "Let's get an ambulance over here. Move it."

"I'm fine."

St. John put an arm around her and squeezed. She heard something go crack in the joints of her back, but tried not to wince.

He glared at the damaged van. "What a fuckup." He squeezed her again, drawing her into his reassuring warmth. "You sure you're okay?" Before she had a chance to answer he said, "Let's get you checked out. Son of a bitch."

"I'll take her," Rico said.

"No," she said. "I just want to go home."

"First we have to go back to the station," St. John said. "I'll call Caroline and tell her what's going on. We better get some ice on that nose."

"I was going to say that," Rico said.

St. John looked at him coldly. "Yeah, you were going to say a lot of things, weren't you?"

"Oh for crying out loud," Munch said.

Chapter 24

M unch accompanied St. John, Rico, and Cassiletti back to the station in West Los Angeles, where Munch was ensconced in the victims' room. It was the size of a cell, but decorated like a drawing room with comfortable armchairs, a table lamp, and pictures on the walls, which were painted a soothing shade of tangerine. The walls were thick enough to keep out the sounds of the police station, but there was nothing to be done for the voices shouting in her head.

Cassiletti brought her ice wrapped in a short white gym towel and helped her clean out the wound on her leg, apply salve, and wrap it with a bandage.

Rico stood by until Cassiletti announced, "That should do it."

Munch stood and tested her ankle. It took her weight, but just to make sure she bounced on it a few times.

"Go easy," Cassiletti warned.

Rico handed him two dollars. "Would you mind getting us a couple sodas?"

Cassiletti took the bills and the hint.

When they were alone, Munch spoke first. "I know about you and Kathy."

"What do you know?"

"Her dad says she's engaged to a cop. Has to be you. Tell me I'm wrong."

"You're not wrong."

She let the towel full of ice slip to the floor. "So that's it?"

"No, there's more."

She breathed through her mouth shallowly, trying to lessen the pain around her heart. "What more can there be?"

"All I've ever wanted is to be a cop. I love my job. I've told you that."

"You've told me a lot of things."

"I've always tried to do the right thing. It's not always the easy choice, but for me it's always been the only one. Until now. I've been going back and forth, asking God for a sign."

"Couldn't you have waited one more day?"

"Kathy's pregnant."

Munch sat down heavily, not expecting this additional wound. "How long?"

"A few months."

Munch nodded dumbly, the math was simple. Their relationship was doomed before it had ever begun.

"She's Catholic," he said. "So am I, supposedly."

Her stomach cramped with the onset of diarrhea. He reached for her hand, but she pulled away.

He nodded as if he understood. "The brass has been scrutinizing me pretty heavy this last month."

"Why?" She managed to ask the word, but couldn't summon the energy to care.

"Politics. It's never-ending. They want to see some clearances. I've been accused of sitting on a case. Here were my choices." He pulled out a heavy three-ring binder and flipped it open. "Solve it or pass it on. But before I passed it on, I needed to write a thirty-day report on what I'd discovered."

"And what had you discovered?"

Rico lined up three photographs side by side. They were mug shots of Jane and Thor, and another picture of Sleaze John. The photograph of Sleaze was one she recognized from Asia's collection.

"You took this from my house?"

"I found a witness who put them all at the scene. She said there was a driver. I knew it had to be you. I'm recusing myself from the case and I'm marrying Kathy. Neither thing is absolutely perfect, but our options are what they are. You've done the right thing coming forward. And when this is over, you still have your life to live. We're all going to have to live with our choices, our past deeds."

"That isn't exactly a news flash."

"What are we going to do with you now?"

"What makes you think you're involved with that decision?"

"Cyrill McCarthy. Witnesses against him have a habit of getting lost."

"He won't come after me. I've got friends in high places. Thor only goes after the ones who don't have a chance."

"You want me to drive you home?"

"I want you to leave me alone. I want to never have to see you again. I wish I had never met you."

"I don't."

"Don't you have a rosary to go say or something?"

He left. Munch buried her face in her hands, wishing she could cry. Time passed. She stared at the wall, too busy with her own thoughts to need a magazine or a television or another person's company. There was a small knock at the door and then it opened.

"You ready?" St. John asked.

"Any word?"

"Not yet. We're broadcasting a bulletin on the eleven o'clock news and his picture will run in tomorrow's paper. We'll get him."

She almost felt sorry for Thor, then caught herself. He didn't deserve her sympathy. What a chump she was. No wonder Rico didn't love her.

"Say something," St. John said.

"Like what?"

"I don't know. Call me an idiot."

"I'm the idiot."

He sighed deeply and sat down next to her. "You see but you don't see, you hear but you don't hear." He placed a small porcelain pig in a blue police uniform on the table in front of her. "See that? This could be the most important thing in your life right now. Six months from now"—he moved the prop for his metaphor away, out of her sight—"it won't mean shit. Something else will be there. My dad taught me that."

She looked at him. Her eyes felt like they would never blink again. "Six months?"

"Sometimes a year."

"I can do that standing on my head."

"That's the spirit. C'mon, let's blow this joint."

She followed him out to his car. It was a clear night. The moon was a thumbnail in the western sky.

St. John toggled the automatic lock switch. She waited for the click and then opened her door. He started the engine. "How's the investigation going otherwise?" she asked.

He cracked a smile.

"I know you talked to a contractor guy."

"We've talked to a lot of people."

"You wouldn't forget Big Mike."

"What about him?"

"He said you were asking questions the other day, wanted him to give up all his workers."

"We have a piece of evidence connected to Jane's murder that we've linked back to one of his work sites."

"Was Thor working there?"

"Not according to the manifest, but that doesn't mean a whole lot. I doubt he knows the true names of half his workers. Guys who work construction are a transient bunch. Lots of cash paid under the table."

"Especially to the lower-skilled guys doing the grunt work."

"Exactly." St. John adjusted the heater controls. "Were you planning on going to work tomorrow?"

"I hadn't thought that far ahead. I guess I'll see how I feel in the morning."

"You won't be alone. Bring an extra uniform to work. We'll send in a policewoman to take your place and put a trap on your phone line in case he tries to contact you."

She looked out the window. "What do you think he's doing right now?"

"Probably curled up in a hole somewhere. You were talking about McCarthy, right?"

"Yeah." She searched the night sky for constellations she recognized. "Do you think he's thinking about me too?"

"I'm sure of it." He pulled on the headlights.

She poked at the swelling around her nose, wincing as she explored the extent of the damage. "What else do you have?"

"You know I can't really discuss the details of an ongoing investigation."

"I'm not going to tell anyone. Besides, I'm part of the team now, right? Just tell me if you have anything else that ties Jane's murder to Thor."

"There was skin under her fingernails that we believe she scraped off her assailant. The lab says it had tattoo ink in it and we've got a blood type."

"I'm glad she got a piece of him."

"I'll be gladder when we have all of him."

Chapter 25

M unch called home from the St. Johns'. The answering
machine clicked on and she spoke to the recorder,
telling Nathan to pick up.

He sounded groggy.

"You okay?" she asked.

"Yeah, I just fell asleep in front of the TV. What's going on?"

"You need to go over to your grandma's house."

"You want me out?"

"It may not be safe. Remember I told you about New York
Jane getting killed?"

"Yeah."

"I think Thor did it and he might be after me."

"Shit."

"Yeah, exactly. We won't be coming home tonight and I don't
want you there by yourself."

"Does he know where you live?"

"He could look it up in the phone book."

"Let him come. I'm not afraid of that motherfucker."

"This isn't about being afraid. The police have offered to come over and escort you."

"Don't set the pigs on me."

"Nathan, I'm not going to argue with you. I'm telling you to get out of my house and go to your grandma's. I'll call you tomorrow."

Munch and Asia spent the night at the St. Johns'. The next morning, Caroline took Asia to school. Munch drove alone to her house to change and to pick up an extra uniform. Cassiletti followed her at a discreet distance in an unmarked police car. Nathan had taken his duffel bag with him and that saddened her. He probably felt abandoned one more time. When this was over, she was going to have a whole new list of people to whom she owed amends.

St. John told her to carry on at work as if it were a normal day. *Yeah, right.*

She parked her car near the bathrooms. The uniform she'd brought for the policewoman decoy was tucked under her arm. She'd folded it carefully and packed it in a brown supermarket bag. Now she carried it in what she hoped was a casual manner as she walked into Lou's office. The first thing she did every morning was go over the repair orders that had been paid the day before and make sure each mechanic was properly credited for his or her work. She and Lou also used this time to drink their morning coffee together and make small talk before the day began.

Lou was bent over his desk, going over the gas books. The guys at night read the meters on the pumps before closing. Lou double-checked the numbers in the morning, making sure that no gas "evaporated" overnight.

"Good morning," she said, then noticed the chinless woman with blue eyeliner and light brown hair standing in the corner. She directed a nod her way.

"You must be Miranda," the woman said. "I'm Officer Halliwell."

Munch handed her the uniform, noting their six-inch height difference. "Call me Munch. The pants might be a little short on you."

"I got your coffee here," Lou said, turning in his chair. "Holy shit, what happened to you?"

"Looks worse than it is," she assured him.

She grabbed her coffee and a stack of work orders. Lou returned to his computations with a scowl on his face.

"I'm going to stick the tanks," he said. "Stay here. Jesus. I can't believe this."

"Business as usual," Munch said.

Lou left the office muttering obscenities. Munch watched him lift the small manhole covers that protected the underground tank caps and insert one of two long wooden dowels he used like a dipstick. The longer stick was notched to measure up to ten thousand gallons and was used for the three tanks that held the grades of gasoline. The smaller stick was for the five-thousand-gallon diesel depository. It was a primitive but effective method to determine how much gas they had remaining underground.

"He's cool," she told the cop. "And he'll be nicer after his third cup of coffee."

Halliwell just nodded and continued standing there as if she were on full military parade. Munch wondered if one of the gas-level measuring tools or something like it had found its way up one of the woman's orifices.

Lou returned to the office. Gas orders were placed forty-eight hours in advance, and though normally the calculations involved to figure the order weren't exactly rocket science, this morning Lou seemed to be using the eraser more than the lead of his pencil.

"Just forget I'm here," Officer Halliwell said.

Munch sat at the corner counter that served as her desk. "Is that Chevy van on the corner part of the operation?"

"Don't draw attention to it."

"We're not idiots," Lou said.

"I wasn't suggesting that you were, sir."

Munch punched some numbers into the calculator. "Kids, don't make me stop this car."

Halliwell cracked a grin and Munch felt like she'd made progress. "Seriously, I appreciate that you're here. I'm still not sure it's necessary, but I know you're willing to risk personal danger."

"Where can I change?"

"Use the storage room to your right. The light switch is by the door."

Halliwell was just barely out of earshot when Lou muttered, "So where was she last night?"

"I was the only one who could go in and talk to Thor. It wasn't anybody's fault that it went bad. Thor is an animal."

"Exactly my point. What was your boyfriend thinking?"

"It was my decision. I'd do it again."

"If that guy shows up here, we'll take care of him." Lou opened the bottom drawer of his file cabinet and pulled out a sawed-off baseball bat. "He'll rue the day he was born."

"Rue the day?"

"You heard me."

"Drink your coffee, you big lug."

She finished her paperwork and went out to the repair bay.

The police audio tech, Tam Spiva, was wearing a telephone repairman uniform and stationed in the supply room next to the telephone junction box.

Opening her toolbox, she spoke to him, feeling as if she were in some James Bond flick. "Do I need to keep him talking for any length of time?"

"Depends how far away he's calling from and how many switching stations are involved."

"In the movies they always need like three minutes."

"That's the movies. If he's local, five seconds will do it."

At nine, Munch was deeply involved in the wiring of a Corvette's steering column when she was paged for a call. She was glad for the break. The car's steering wheel telescoped as well as tilted and was fighting her all the way. Carlos handed her the phone, so she double-checked that he had put the call on hold and that she still wasn't on loudspeaker. She and Carlos had pulled that prank on each other in the past. When the unsuspecting victim said "Hello" into the phone, the voice was broadcast across the shop. The amplified words that followed were invariably, "Oh, shit."

Carlos walked away disappointed when Munch pushed the button to open the line, but she heard only a dial tone when she put the phone to her ear.

"Who was it?"

Carlos shrugged. "I don' know. Some guy."

The phone rang again. She gave Spiva the high sign and he acknowledged that he was ready. She picked up the receiver.

"Bel Air Texaco, this is Munch."

"How could you do this to me?"

Her pulse accelerated, but not so much as to cloud her mind. She lifted a thumb in the air. Spiva activated his gear.

"You see yourself as the victim here?" she asked.

"You've ruined my life."

"*I* ruined *your* life?"

"Are they listening now?"

"What do you think?"

"I think you're a bitch. You're only so holy rolly cuz you went to the cops first. That doesn't make you clean. We've all done shit in our past."

"I'm not talking about ripping off hippies for their weed money or rolling drunks. Shit in our past? What are you talking past? Jane died last week."

"Is that what they told you? That I had something to do with that? I was locked down. Ask Danny T. I've been with someone from New Start every minute of every day for the last month. When would I have had time to hurt Jane?"

"So turn yourself in."

"Yeah, right. You fucked that up for me." He wheezed into the phone.

"Are you hurt?"

"I can get around. You'll see me again. Bet on it." He hung up.

She turned to Spiva. "Did you get it?"

He was already on his radio. "Yes. You did great." He toggled off and clipped his Handie-Talkie to his tool belt. "We've got the number he was calling from. Now all we need to do is look it up in a reverse directory. If the number he called from is listed, we'll have him."

"It's not brain surgery, right?"

"What do you think brain surgeons say in these situations?"

"It's not auto mechanics."

"You might be right."

Before he could ask about anything else she said, "We get lots of doctors in here."

"Not surprising."

"Yeah," she said, "they come in two forms: the cheap ones who question everything, especially the bill, and the nice ones who give you the green light, pay any price, just as long as it's fixed."

"How are cops?"

"As customers?"

Spiva nodded.

"I don't get many as customers in Brentwood."

"Yeah, I guess you wouldn't."

"What's your take about what Thor said about having an alibi for Jane's murder?"

"I don't know that much about the case. You think he was telling the truth?"

"Felt like it. What do you think?"

Spiva unrolled some wire from a cardboard spool and cut off a foot of it. "Hard to say. It might be true or he might have talked himself into believing it was true. It's not for me to sort out."

She watched him strip an inch of insulation from one end of the wire. "You gonna stick around?"

"Until I get orders otherwise."

"Is Mace St. John coming by later? Did he say?"

"You want me to call him?"

"No, don't bother him. I'm sure he's busy catching bad guys."

Spiva's handset rang and he lifted it to his mouth. "Go ahead." He listened for a moment and then said, "Good. Ten four."

"What?" she asked.

"We got it."

"Where is he?"

"Santa Monica."

"Where in Santa Monica?" She didn't need him to answer. She knew the words that were coming and recited the address.

He looked at her surprised more than suspicious. "How did you know?"

"That's my house."

St. John was not at the police station. Early that morning he had gotten a call from Janet Moriarity, the director of Shelter from the Storm.

"I've heard from Stacy," she said, "and she's agreed to speak to you."

He almost fell off his chair. "When? Where?"

"She's in my office now."

"I'm on my way."

Twenty minutes later he was introduced to a tall blonde with a slightly crooked nose and a gentle smile. When it was clear that Ms. Moriarity had no intention of leaving the room, he began his interview.

"Miss Lansford, I read the letter that you wrote to Judge Helmer about Cyrill McCarthy."

"Detective Yanney asked me to do that. I was angry at Thor then."

"Yes, it was a good letter. We're very close to indicting Mr. McCarthy for murder. Would you be willing to testify?"

"Do you really need me?" She looked at Janet Moriarity for support.

"It would help put him away," the older woman said. "Isn't that what we want?"

"I know he did some bad things, but that was a long time ago. I don't want him to go to jail forever. He might, right?" This time she looked at St. John.

"The man is a felon. He's hurt a lot of people."

"He is the father of my child. I mean, I don't hate the guy."

St. John looked down at his notebook and wondered what Ms. Moriarity thought of this. He clicked his pen open. "Who's your dentist?"

"Dr. Wassenmiller."

"And you had some surgery as I remember. How many scars do you have?"

She lifted her chin. "I have two on my stomach."

"Birthmarks, tattoos?"

"Why are you asking me all this?"

"In case we need to identify your body sometime. If we don't find it right away and decomposition has set in, it makes our job just that much more difficult."

Stacy Lansford's mouth opened in shock, but when he risked a glance at Janet Moriarity, damned if she wasn't wearing the ghost of a smile.

A knock on the door interrupted the moment.

"Mace?" Cassiletti said. "We need to go." His eyes strayed to Stacy Lansford and he blinked as if struck by something. "I'm sorry to interrupt."

Stacy stared back. "You're just doing your job, I'm sure."

Janet Moriarity walked St. John to his car.

"I'll work on her. You did good."

He felt better than he had in the last twelve hours.

"That was Stacy Lansford?" Cassiletti asked once they were in the car. "I didn't expect her to be so beautiful."

"I didn't see a wedding ring," St. John said.

"Neither did I," Cassiletti said without blushing.

St. John smiled. Maybe they'd hook Cassiletti up yet.

Chapter 26

‗‗‗

T he Chevy van Munch had noticed earlier pulled up in front of the office. Spiva and Officer Halliwell, who was now wearing Munch's blue Texaco uniform, climbed inside. The driver said, "St. John is meeting us there."

"What do you want me to do?" Munch asked.

"We'll keep a unit here," Halliwell said. "Just sit tight."

Munch returned to the Corvette. She tried to lose herself in the job, but her thoughts were in turmoil. She went back to her tool-box for a pair of vise grips. The ratty purse she carried to work gaped open and she saw Roxanne's folded phone bill. She pulled it free and went to the phone.

Doleen Franklin, Nathan's grandma, answered on the third ring.

"Hi. It's Munch. Is Nathan there or has he gone to work?"

"He said he had some stuff to do and he'd be to work later."

"I was really hoping to talk to him. I didn't want him to think I was kicking him out."

"He said you had yo'self some trouble."

"Did he seem upset?"

"No, he's fine. We called his mama. She's over there in the Neverlands."

Munch smiled to herself. Close enough. "Yeah, I know. Nathan thinks she might send for him."

"That's what they talked about. In fact, she already sent him a ticket. Bless her heart. It's comin' in the mail."

"To my house?" Munch asked.

"I expect so. That's where she thought he would be."

"I hope he wasn't planning on going over there today."

"I know the boy's anxious to see his mama. He got him his passport and everythin'."

"If you hear from him again, please tell him to stay away from my house. The police are on their way there now."

"Oh Lord, what'd you do?"

"They're not after me. Some guy broke into my house. A really bad guy."

"A white man?"

"Yeah."

"The police know that? They know they looking for a white man?"

"They know." *Some of them know,* she thought. "I'll go over there and make sure."

"You do that. You go there right now. I don't want my boy to be no accident."

"I'll call you later."

Munch locked her toolbox.

"What's going on?" Lou asked, coming up behind her.

"I'm going home. Thor's there now and Nathan might be on the way."

"I'm coming with you."

She saw he was resolute and she didn't feel in a position to be turning down any help.

St. John deployed patrolmen throughout the neighborhood. He distributed pictures of Cyrill McCarthy and the warning that the man was armed and dangerous. As they were setting up, a white Honda Civic pulled in front of Munch's house. St. John ran the plates. Santa Monica was a long way from Sun Valley. If McCarthy was mobile, then he probably had wheels. He only had time to steal or borrow. The Honda had not been reported stolen. It was registered to one Nathan Franklin.

"Nathan Franklin," he said to Cassiletti. "Ring any bells for you?"

"No, but somebody's getting out," Cassiletti said, seeing a light-skinned black teenager exit the Honda and approach Munch's door.

"She said something about a kid named Nathan," St. John remembered. "This must be him."

"He has to know she's at work."

They watched Nathan reach into the porch light and extract a key. He was calm, acting as if he belonged there.

"Shit," St. John said, seeing Nathan slip the key into the lock. The kid's back was to them. St. John got on his radio and alerted the backup teams that an unidentified individual who was not their suspect was entering the premises. St. John got out of his car and approached the house, his eyes on the front windows, watching for movement in the blinds. "Hold on there, partner," he said.

Nathan jumped at the sound of St. John's voice.

St. John had his badge out. "Step away from the door."

"I live here," Nathan said, his voice cracking.

"I know. I just need you to back up a few steps."

The front door crashed open and a wild-eyed Cyrill McCarthy stood there. Still-wet blood glistened on his shirtfront.

Cassiletti got on his megaphone. "Hands up, McCarthy. Do it now!" Gone were his usual nervous affectations. Nathan feinted quickly, jabbing a fist into McCarthy's solar plexus. McCarthy doubled over and then lunged or fell into Nathan, sending them both rolling backward down the concrete step and onto the lawn. Sirens whooped loudly over the still morning.

St. John pulled his revolver and yelled, "Halt, motherfucker."

McCarthy was big, but the kid was young and strong and uninjured. They wrestled on the grass, grunting in mortal combat. Nathan wrapped his hands around McCarthy's neck and pressed his thumbs into the man's Adam's apple. McCarthy flailed at the teenager's face, connecting with the kid's nose and mouth until blood flowed. St. John holstered his gun and grabbed Nathan from behind. Cassiletti joined them, grabbing at shirt backs and hair. Two other uniformed cops drew their batons. Nathan took a crack to the head.

"No, not him," a woman's voice screamed. "Get the white guy."

St. John looked over and saw it was Munch. Lou held her back as she screamed, "Stop it, you're hurting him."

Nathan's eyes rolled back as he loosened his grip on McCarthy's throat. Tears streamed down his face, mingling with the blood. St. John grabbed the kid in a bear hug and rolled with him, carrying him away from the fighting, away from danger.

McCarthy was exposed now and the remaining cops descended

on him with force. Moments later, McCarthy was handcuffed and his ankles bound with plastic restraints.

"Somebody help me get this scumbag to the car," Cassiletti said.

McCarthy moaned as he was dragged.

St. John loosened his hold on Nathan. They were both panting. "You okay?" he asked the kid.

Nathan put a hand to the side of his head and then looked at it. "I'm bleeding."

"We'll get you to a doctor. Just sit tight for a minute."

St. John struggled to his feet, checking for pains in his chest, but as far as he could tell he was only winded.

"Sergeant?" one of the uniforms said. "You better look at this."

The uniform was pointing to the glistening stream of blood trailing McCarthy's body.

"Hold up," St. John told Cassiletti.

McCarthy coughed, spraying blood, lots of blood. St. John lifted McCarthy's shirt. McCarthy's chest was crushed. A circular gash between his nipples exposed ribs. He coughed again, spewing another pint of blood. "Shit, call an ambulance."

He pressed a hand to the open wound. McCarthy's flesh was cold already. St. John didn't think Stacy Lansford was going to need to testify after all. He'd let Cassiletti deliver the news.

Munch stared at him. He shook his head to indicate that it was over.

Nathan sat on the edge of the lawn, his expression relaxed. One arm looped around his knee, his other hand cupped his head wound. St. John felt a twinge of recognition, but was distracted from the thought with the arrival of the paramedics. He motioned for the cops guarding the perimeter to let Munch pass. "It's okay," he told them. "She's with us."

Chapter 27

⇒

Thor was taken to the hospital. His prognosis was not good. Something had ruptured deep in his body. The medics had had trouble starting an IV, partly because of his almost non-existent pulse, and partly because of the excessive scarring over his most commonly used arm veins.

At the house, a second ambulance arrived.

"Check out the kid," St. John told them.

Nathan sat on the hood of his Honda. The medic had Nathan track his finger and asked him if he was dizzy.

"I'm fine," Nathan said, holding an ice pack to the side of his head.

"Does he have a concussion?" Munch asked.

"I don't think so. But just to be safe you should watch him for the next twelve hours. Make sure he wakes up easily."

"I'll go over to my grandma's," Nathan said. "She'll take care of me."

"You can't drive," Munch said. "It's not safe."

Nathan eyed the police around him. "I just came here to check the mail."

"Yeah, and I warned you not to. Next time maybe you'll listen to me," Munch said. "Stay here a minute." Several of her neighbors had gathered on the sidewalk. They were going to have to wait for their explanations.

Munch was allowed into her house. Lou helped her repair the damage to her doorjamb enough so that the lock would hold. Accompanied by St. John, she did a walk-through. There was some blood in the bathroom where Thor had apparently dressed his wounds. She wasn't allowed to clean it up until the criminalists processed the scene. They did allow her to retrieve her mail. She was happily surprised for Nathan's sake to find a thick envelope addressed to him with a European postmark. She brought it out to him, glad to see that Deb had come through on at least one of her promises.

"The police will take you to your grandma's."

"I can't do that," he said. "What are her neighbors going to think?"

"Oh for crying out loud," she said, wishing he wouldn't fight her on everything. "I'll get Lou to take you over there and I'll call you later."

"All right," he said, his voice sounding more adult than it had that morning. She hugged him until he pulled away, uncomfortable with her show of affection, his feet pointing away from her. She hoped Asia would never go through this stage, but it was probably inevitable.

Rico had arrived and joined the ring of cops on her driveway. He was exchanging words with Mace St. John. She wished she didn't have to see him anymore but knew that it couldn't be avoided. At least until all the shouting died down and the DA declared the case closed.

"We all need to go to the station," St. John said. "We're going to need Munch's full statement. I'm sorry, but it's better to do it while all the events are still fresh."

"I'm practically still bleeding," she said, directing her venom at the lover who'd ripped her heart out.

Rico stared at his feet.

"You can ride with us," St. John said.

"You want me to follow?" Lou asked, joining them in time to hear this.

"No." Munch put a hand on his arm and squeezed it gently, trying to convey to him that he was still connected but needed elsewhere. "I was hoping you would take Nathan home to his grandmother's. He seems pretty anxious to get out of here."

"Can't say that I blame him."

She glanced at the fresh blood on the sidewalk and wondered if the cops would hose it down or if that was something she would have to do later. "And then you should get back to work. Someone has to mind the store."

Lou grimaced.

"I'll be fine," she told him. "One of these guys will bring me back."

Lou gestured for Nathan to get in his car. She waved as they drove away, watching the car until it turned the corner.

Cassiletti touched her elbow. "You want to sit in front?"

"No, I'm okay in the back. Let's just get this over with."

Cassiletti drove. St. John rode shotgun. Munch sat in the center of the backseat so she could be part of their conversation. Cassiletti was going on about some knot.

"It's called a timber hitch," he said. "Lumberjacks use it when they need to drag logs."

"So you think he dragged the, uh, package before he dumped it?" St. John asked.

Munch leaned forward. She was pretty sure "package" was a euphemism for something far more sinister.

"Most likely it was a knot he was familiar with and just tied it out of habit," Cassiletti said. "Even with the block, the, uh, package wasn't that heavy, not for a big guy like him."

"Something to think about," St. John said.

Munch slumped back in the seat, crossing her arms over her chest in frustration.

"What?" St. John asked.

"You need to brush up on your code work," Munch said. "Package would be the body, right? Jane's body? The killer used a rope to tie something to her before he dumped her body. I'm thinking that would be the block. The block came from Big Mike's construction site. The knot was unusual and could be important. How am I doing so far?"

St. John grinned. "Pretty good."

"Elementary, my dear Holmes."

"By the way," Cassiletti added, "we didn't get a match on the rope from the samplings we took at the construction site."

"We probably have enough without it," St. John said, but he didn't look happy.

"I hate loose ends too," Munch said.

"Chacón is going to be at the station," St. John said. "He'll need to be there when the DA debriefs you."

"Whatever we need to do to end this thing."

"We're almost there."

It took hours to go through her statement. She described one more time the events surrounding the murders of the three suspected drug dealers in 1975. Rico had several questions for her and kept referring to a large three-ring binder.

"Is that the murder book?" she asked.

"Yes."

She held out her hands. "Can I?"

"You sure you want to?"

"They can't be any worse than what I've carried in my imagination all these years."

"Don't be so sure. Besides, I don't want your recollection of the events tainted if you're called to testify."

"Everybody's gone now, remember?" Thor had never regained consciousness. He had died at the hospital from what surgeons discovered to be a rupture in his aorta. The lethal injury was the result of the van's steering wheel compressing his chest during the accident, but it took a day and the extra tumble with the cops and Nathan for the tear to fully dissect. "Who would I testify against?"

Rico spun the loose-leaf binder so that it faced her. She flipped to the plastic pages that held the photographs. The dead were sprawled throughout the flat, mouths slack, eyes staring, throats opened savagely. She saw the pictures of the bloody footprints and then noticed something Rico might have missed. It was a child's Levi's jacket. One with Harley-Davidson wings on the back and treble clefs embroidered on the collar.

"Oh no," she said. "Oh God, no wonder."

She found the news clipping from 1975. The dead men were

identified. She had never read the whole article, hadn't wanted to. She read it now, stopping when she came to the name of one of the deceased. Walter Franklin, twenty-five. A musician from Compton, survived by his mother: Doleen Franklin.

And a son, Munch realized. A son who had not forgotten nor forgiven. Nathan said he had come to town with a list of people to contact. Now she was thinking he had arrived with two lists.

Rico took the book back and studied the same page. Realization darkened his eyes. "It was the kid, wasn't it? He was there."

"No, this can't be right," she said.

"It doesn't look good."

"Let me make some phone calls."

"Why?"

"I can prove it wasn't him."

Rico hesitated.

"Just give me that much." Did he want her to beg? She let her voice soften. "Please."

She pulled Roxanne's Pacific Bell bill from her purse and reached for Rico's telephone.

He didn't try to stop her.

One by one Munch called the L.A. numbers highlighted on Roxanne's statement, signifying the numbers she didn't recognize and the calls she hadn't made. Munch was connected first to the pay phone at Shelter from the Storm, then the offices of New Start in Sun Valley, and finally the answering machine for Mike Peyovich Construction. She hung up on the machine without waiting for the beep.

Rico's face was a mask of sympathy. She imagined it was the same expression he wore when his job required him to deliver news no one wanted to hear.

Fuck him and his bad news, she thought.

He reached for the phone bill, but she wasn't ready to relinquish it. Not yet and not to him anyway.

"Wait," she said, not begging anymore. She dialed Roxanne in Sacramento. When Roxanne answered, Munch plunged into her questions without bothering to identify herself.

"Last month, did Deb send you a package of stuff to mail out?"

"I know what you're thinking. It wasn't dope."

"How do you know?"

"They were just letters."

"Letters to whom?"

"I don't know, greeting cards, like. Thank-you notes or late Christmas cards. No packages, just a handful of blue envelopes. I don't know what the big deal was."

"When did Nathan leave you?"

"The first week of February."

"Are you sure?"

"Yeah, I'm sure. Why?"

"He didn't get to me until after Valentine's Day. I had assumed he came straight to me from you."

"Not unless he walked."

"I've gotta go." Munch gathered up the murder book and pushed past Rico, feeling nothing as their bodies collided.

Still clutching the murder book, she stood before St. John's desk. He was in the middle of typing something and stopped, looking at her with a question on his face. "In the van last night, Thor had a greeting card. It was in a blue envelope. Did you find it in the wreckage?"

"I'd have to check," he said. "Why?"

"I just saw it for a second, but I realized I'd seen one exactly like it in the last few days. The note inside read: 'I haven't forgotten you.' "

"I found a card like that at Jane Ferrar's apartment. What are you on to?"

"Thor told me he gets them every year." Now she knew what the V scratched on Jane's chest stood for. It was vengeance.

Rico joined them then. "It was the kid."

"What kid?" St. John asked.

Rico pried the murder book from Munch's unwilling fingers and pointed to the small footprints cast in blood and then the newspaper clipping. "Jane Ferrar, Cyrill McCarthy, and Jonathan Garillo murdered Nathan Franklin's father, Walter Franklin. Nathan must have been in the apartment when it happened. He might have watched it all."

"He had to be, what, six?" St. John asked.

Munch sat down woodenly. "After the murder, his grandma sent him and his mom to live up in Oregon. His mom always kept track of everyone from the old days. She's out of the country—"

"And Nathan came down here to carry out his paybacks," Rico finished for her.

"The kid who was at your house?" St. John asked.

Munch nodded.

"I thought he seemed familiar. We saw him working at Big Mike's construction site." St. John turned to Cassiletti. "The kid with the shirt around his head. Remember?"

Cassiletti nodded. "He might have learned the knot in Oregon, maybe working in a logging camp. And a kid from Oregon wouldn't realize how quickly rainwater in L.A. subsides."

St. John took out his car keys. "I guess we need to go to the grandmother's house." He pointed to the victim profile report. "Is she still at this same address in Compton?"

"Yes," Munch said. "Let me come with you. I'll make sure he cooperates." While the men notified their chain of command, Munch eased into an empty office and made two other calls. The first was to hire the attorney Jim McManis.

They all drove to Doleen Franklin's house. Half of Munch hoped Nathan was gone already on some big silver bird headed for the "Neverlands."

It was not to be.

St. John started to walk to the front door while Cassiletti went around to the back.

"Can I talk to him first?" Munch asked.

Before St. John could say no she added, "He's not going to get away. Please, I need to do this."

"Five minutes," St. John said.

Doleen answered the door.

"We've come for Nathan," Munch said.

"That the poh-lice?" Doleen asked, looking very old, very weary.

"Yeah. They're friends of mine. They won't hurt him."

"C'mon, boy," Doleen called to the back of the house. "C'mon out here and le's get this out in the open."

Nathan emerged from the back bedroom. His face looked like he'd been in a car accident. The tears on his cheeks were fresh. "What's going to happen now?" he asked.

"You were there, weren't you?" Munch said. "You were in the house when they killed your daddy."

Nathan looked at his grandma, then down at his boots.

"And Jane?" Munch's grief was for all of them.

His jaw dropped open, quivering with emotion. It was several seconds before he could speak. "My daddy begged her to stop. He called her by name. That's when she cut his throat. When she was done with that, she carved a V on his chest. He was still alive when she did that. Did you know that? It took him a long time to die."

Doleen let out a keening wail and sank into the couch.

Nathan pulled up his shirt to wipe his face. "Those V's in the bodies were her idea. To make the cops think the 'niggers were offing each other.' She said that."

Munch shot a worried look at Doleen. The older woman's eyes were closed, her face seemed folded in on itself, but she was still breathing.

"Did you come here to kill us all?" Munch asked.

"I never meant to kill anyone. I just wanted . . ." He looked lost and very young. "I don't know what I wanted. I called her a few weeks ago, told her I had some pictures of her she might not want anyone else to see."

"And you knew where to find her because your mom kept tabs on everyone."

"My mom made sure it never went away for them. Every year on my dad's birthday she sent out those I-haven't-forgot-you cards. That's all she did," he added bitterly. "Just so they'd know somebody remembered."

"What pictures?" Munch asked.

"I didn't really have any. But I figured it would freak them out a lot more if they thought I had, you know, proof."

Munch spoke slowly and carefully, unconsciously mimicking Jim McManis's tone and cadence. "So you contacted Jane to confront her, to make her apologize, to face you."

"Lissen what she's saying, boy," Doleen said.

"The truth is you weren't really sure what you needed from her," Munch said.

Nathan nodded, tears flowing freely now. "She agreed to meet me at the job site where I went for an interview. She was drunk when she got there. Kept me waiting an hour. Everyone else had gone home for the day cuz it started to rain."

"It was also Valentine's Day," Munch said.

"She never said she was sorry. I told her what I saw her do. She was holding a baby. The rain started coming down real hard. She said, 'Let me get my baby out of this weather.' I told her I felt sorry for any kid of hers and she hit me with it."

"It was a doll," Munch said.

"I didn't know that. I thought she was swinging a real baby at me. I just snapped then," he said. "I went off on her and by the time I stopped swinging"—he paused to stanch the flow of watery mucus dripping from his nose—"it was too late. She was dead."

Doleen shook her head slowly and she said, "Jesus help us."

Munch considered the irony of Jane's demise, wondering if this was the first time Jane had fought back, and if that had cost her her life. Maybe in some sick, sad way that had been her hope all along. Suicide by instigation.

"Can't I just go?" Nathan asked. "I could leave the country and never come back."

"It's not up to me. The police are here. They're going to arrest you."

"But I—"

Munch held up a hand to silence him. "I'm not going to abandon you. When the cops read you your rights, you tell them you have a lawyer and don't want to speak to them without him. Here's his name and number." She handed him Jim McManis's business card.

"You think we can beat the charges?" he asked. The look on his face shattered her heart into another thirty pieces. He was five again and wanting to know if Santa would still come even if they didn't have a tree.

"No, honey," she said. "They have too much on you. The lawyer is so you don't have to spend the rest of your life in jail or be tried as an adult."

He looked at Doleen. "Do you think it would be all right if my grandmother kept the Honda?"

"I think that would be very nice."

St. John knocked at the door. Panic crossed Nathan's face.

Munch wanted to hold him, to comfort him, but the time for that had passed. If his father hadn't been murdered. If Deb had called the police ten years ago, instead of fleeing the state. If she hadn't taken her black-skinned baby to be raised among people who would revile him without mercy. If Munch could have been mother and father to him, stolen him away from Deb, and raised him herself. Things might have turned out differently. And if any of them had been different people, they would have had different lives.

The reality was that Deb was an outlaw and would never dream of calling the police for justice. She had raised her son to believe the same. Munch couldn't save anyone else until she'd found a way to save herself. And that had come too late for Nathan.

St. John entered Doleen's tidy little house. His manner was respectful, almost reluctant.

St. John asked Nathan to take off his jacket. Munch watched St. John examine the scratch on Nathan's arm that had torn through the tattoo of his father's name. There would be a match with the ink found under Jane's fingernails. Then St. John brought out his handcuffs. Nathan consented without protest. His shoulders relaxed with resignation, but also relief.

This was truly the only way to save him.

Love didn't get any tougher. He'd almost gotten away with it. But the truth was no one gets away with murder. Better he take his punishment now.

McManis had thought—although he wasn't promising anything—that the courts would take into account Nathan's age, the trauma of watching his father butchered. If Nathan came clean with everything, expressed remorse, and was willing to cop a plea and save the county the expense and hassle of trial, the cops and the DA would deal. One day, not too many years from now, Nathan would be able to face the world a free man. Munch vowed to do what she could for him to keep him on the right path.

Epilogue

$$=\!\!\!=$$

Munch sat next to the St. Johns. It was the eighteenth of March. The auditorium was filled to capacity with the relatives and friends of cast members. Tinker Bell was saving Peter Pan by drinking the poison Captain Hook intended for the hero of Never-Never Land. Tinker Bell, played by the ever-smiling and overenthusiastic Asia, was at a distinct disadvantage being that she couldn't speak and warn Peter Pan.

Throughout the play, Asia had done much with her part, especially showing her jealousy toward Wendy, but for the big death scene she was outdoing herself.

She downed the poison and then went into her death throes. First she clutched her throat and pirouetted. Then she staggered, an outstretched hand clutching in what was supposed to be a pitiful gesture, but lost some in the translation due to her wide smile and twinkling eyes. The child playing Peter Pan waited patiently to deliver his line, but Asia/Tinker Bell took her time to gasp her last breath.

A collective giggle started in the audience, flashbulbs went off. This brought another inappropriate grin from Asia, aimed at her adoring fans. She swooned to the floor, her legs kicking and arms flopping. Finally she lay still.

Peter Pan discovered the flask of poison and realized what had happened. The script called for Peter to appeal to the audience. If they believed in fairies, then the power of their belief (shown by applause) could bring the fallen Tinker Bell back to life.

The audience was apparently possessed of huge magic that day because no sooner had Peter Pan made his plea than Tinker Bell was back on her feet, bouncing across the stage with an ebullience reserved for the resurrected.

"Can't keep a good fairy down," St. John quipped.

Munch laughed in delight. Rico was gone, yet she didn't feel alone. Life was good and full of endless possibilities.

She had another reason to feel lighthearted.

The DA had allowed Nathan to plead to second-degree murder. He had also offered Nathan a deal whereby he would serve his time at the California Youth Authority. If he behaved himself there, he would avoid one of the tougher, so-called "gladiator school" prisons. There was a good chance he'd be out in time for his twenty-fifth birthday, which probably sounded like forever to a young kid, but, given the alternatives, it was the best anyone could have hoped for.

He'd have to do his penance one day at a time and cling to the belief that he'd be free while he was still young enough to make something of himself. He had avoided a more severe charge of first-degree murder. The police didn't have enough evidence to support premeditation or lying-in-wait.

The second call Munch had made from the police station was to Nathan's grandmother. She told Doleen to gather up all the clothesline at her house and put it somewhere where it would never be found. Doleen had not asked questions, which was telling in itself. The police never came up with a match or source of the rope that bound the cement block and doll to Jane's body. If Nathan had brought the rope with him to Jane's murder scene, the DA would certainly have argued premeditation and Nathan would have not seen the light of day again until he was an old man.

St. John, if he were ever to learn of Munch's choice, might not agree with it. But she remembered the little boy who was, and she had faith in the man he could still become.

Doleen and Munch had their little secret and each would take it to her grave.

Acknowledgments

Many good people helped with the composition and research for this book. I'd like to thank Marilyn Hudson for sparking the idea years ago when she asked me "Whatever happened to Boogie?" after she reviewed *No Offense Intended*. Terry Baker of Murder Ink in Venice Beach told me she'd like to see a prequel to *No Human Involved* that showed the events leading to Munch sitting on that bar stool. And Bay Area bookseller Sandy Graves told me the story of her little sister who, like me, ran away from home at age fourteen. Instead of going to the Haight Ashbury, the sister went to Spahn Ranch and lived with the Manson Family. She left two weeks before the Tate–La Bianca murders. This got me thinking about twists of fates and how lucky some of us were.

I also gained valuable insights and information from my friends Riverside County Sheriff's Investigator Carl Carter and his wife, Deputy District Attorney Dianna Carter—what a dynamic duo they are. Patty and Charles Hathaway for the info about the Riviera Country Club. Phyllis Spiva for her in-depth research on "The Eskimo Story." Scott of Valley Block for the clue about the pigment. Janet Newcomb for her explanations of the battered wife syndrome. My author friends Robin Burcell for police procedure and Sinclair Browning for the horse stuff. Barry Fisher for forensics information. LAPD Narcotics officer Joe Flores for helping me understand where Rico grew up. My Coachella Valley critique group, Poison Pen's Patrick Millikin, and the Fictionaires of Orange County for valuable feedback (with special mention to Patricia McFall and Gary Bale). And always my A-Team: Sandy Dijkstra and staff; Susanne Kirk, Sarah Knight, Laura Wise, Emily Remes, and all the wonderful, gifted people at Simon & Schuster; my publicists Jackie Green and Jim Schneeweis.

My husband, Ron, for making it all possible.

Con mucho gusto.

About the Author

BARBARA SERANELLA was born in Santa Monica and grew up in Pacific Palisades. After running away from home at fourteen, joining a hippie commune in the Haight, and riding with outlaw motorcycle clubs, she decided to do something normal, so she became a mechanic.

Her critically acclaimed and nationally best-selling Munch Mancini novels are *No Man Standing, Unfinished Business,* a *Los Angeles Times* "Best Book of 2001," *Unwanted Company, No Offense Intended,* and *No Human Involved.* She and her husband, Ron, and their dogs divide their time between Laguna Beach and La Quinta, California. Her Web site is *www.barbaraseranella.com.*